BLOOD

AND

BRIDGES

A NOVEL BY

Table of Contents

Chapter 1 – Just a Small Town Girl   1

Chapter 2 – TAG Team   13

Chapter 3 – Surprises   23

Chapter 4 – The Kids are All Right   33

Chapter 5 – Big Changes   49

Chapter 6 – Murphy's Law   69

Chapter 7 – Pandora's Box   87

Chapter 8 – Aftermath   108

Chapter 9 – Difficult Decisions   127

Chapter 10 – The Nest Empties   146

Chapter 11 – Back Again?   169

Chapter 12 – New Normal   188

Chapter 13 – Yates & Yachts   202

Chapter 14 – Best Intentions   225

Chapter 15 – Future Days   248

~ *Chapter 1* ~

Just a Small Town Girl

I'm Tabitha, and I have an important decision to make. When I was bitterly betrayed, I burned that bridge to ashes and walked away. After nearly three decades of bad blood, should forgiveness even be an option?

Allow me to explain.

Life was pretty average for my middle-class, Midwest, Catholic family of five in the midst of farmland. As the eldest Wilder and only girl, my two younger brothers, Leonard (Leo) and Micah, got away with a lot more than I did. Equality was not a priority in my childhood home.

Our father was a selfish individual who didn't listen to the rest of us. My resentment toward his disregard of my thoughts and feelings caused our relationship to plummet when I became a teenager. All three of us rebelled at some point against the unfairness of our father's ever-changing rules. Memories of my adolescence are filled with the angry sounds of people yelling and doors slamming.

My mom got caught in the middle on a regular basis, which was hard on her. She's a kind-hearted person who had a tough job of keeping peace in a house full of differing personalities. There was considerable tension that often felt suffocating. It could have been worse, but still I looked forward to the time I could put it in my rearview mirror.

Average also described me in school. I was smart, but not exactly brilliant; not ugly, but certainly not homecoming queen; a tomboy but still wanted to be noticed by boys; I played sports from fifth through eighth grade but sat the bench most of the time. I was halfway decent at volleyball but threw out my shoulder trying to land a killer spike and was done. I was one of the better players at rec league softball until I reached the age limit at sixteen.

Stacey Hanover was my best friend starting in third grade. Our similar dispositions meant we were ordinarily goofing off and laughing. She had a strict upbringing as well, and we made a concerted effort to help each other have fun any chance we had. We spent quite a few weekends together flying kites and riding bicycles down the paved roads near her house. Any time I convinced my mom to take me to the roller rink, I asked her to stop and pick up Stacey on the way.

During the 1980s and early 1990s, cell phone videos and social media did not exist. Instead, news circulated via the local grapevine. Small town gossip was a currency and took no prisoners.

Most everyone's parents were at least aware of each other if they weren't already friends or relatives. Kids who did things they shouldn't had very low probability of getting away with much. Someone who knew about it giddily told several others, the rumors spread further, and so on.

My mom was able to keep a close eye on us no matter what we did. She was with us every weekend as a Sunday school teacher AND she saw what I did and who I interacted with in class from being a substitute teacher. If I stepped out of line anywhere else, someone in the ruthless grapevine was highly likely to tell her about it. The kicker was when my friends would frequently tell me how awesome it was to have her as an instructor.

In the slang of my generation, gag me with a spoon.

Don't get me wrong, my mom's a marvelous person and I loved her dearly. But having no time away from her and continually trying to be "a good girl" was not ideal as a kid and young teen. Because everyone else thought she was amazing, I always had to be on guard and keep the majority of my thoughts and opinions to myself. I had no one to complain to except my brothers; it was torture!

Being a foreign exchange student overseas was a life-changing experience the summer before my freshman year of high school. My first trip on an airplane took me halfway around the world and opened my eyes to the beauty of travel. I marveled at all the cultural and historical differences and met tons of new people from various places. I came home bursting with excitement about everything I saw and learned!

Disappointment swiftly killed my enthusiasm when almost none of my friends wanted to hear about it. I endured several instances of being dismissed or outright ignored when I attempted to share stories of my adventures.

The group of popular girls I'd been closest to when I left didn't write me letters when I was overseas and didn't even seem to have noticed my absence. There were multiple sleepovers and parties I wasn't invited to after I returned, which compounded my desolation. More than a few times I saw them together in the hall and ran to the nearest bathroom to cry while my teenage mind swirled with sorrow and self-doubt.

I thought we were friends, why didn't they miss me?

Did I mean so little to them that eight weeks apart would cause them to forget about me?

What did I do to push them away?

I'm still the same person I was when I left, so what's wrong with me now?

Being ostracized by those girls showed me I couldn't always trust the ones who meant a lot to me. That harsh lesson became a cautionary tale for me to be slow to let people close for many years.

Due to their abandonment, I began widening my network. I started talking to people from various groups and grades but primarily associated with other – you guessed it – average kids, in band and drama club and the National Honor Society.

I was still cautious about trusting people, with the exception of Stacey. Her continued friendship was a saving grace for my depleted self-esteem, and I'm happy to say our bond has lasted a lifetime.

Lockers were assigned alphabetically every year. With a relatively small class and minimal newcomers, Allison (Allie) Vandenberg, Seth Watkins, me, and Alex Yates were always the last four, typically at the end of a hallway or stuffed in a corner. We jokingly called ourselves 'The Class Caboose.'

Over the months of school daily life, I got to know the moods of my fellow caboose-mates and could tell when they were having good or bad days.

Allie and I had a lot of classes together, plus we went to the same church, so we were extremely familiar with each other. At our lockers, we would chat briefly about assignments and teachers and complain about homework when we had it. If there was juicy gossip from church, we would spend a little time on those details.

Seth was a nice enough guy once you adjusted to the fact that he was loud and vocal about what was going on in his life. He was fiercely passionate about who had pissed him off most recently, with a lot of expletives for color. He wasn't part of my usual crowd, so I heard quite a bit about people I wouldn't normally meet!

Alex was the opposite – the more intense his emotions, the quieter he became. There were times when a sharp comment meant we should leave him alone completely. Other days he chiefly communicated in grunts and shrugs, but I was used to that with two brothers at home. I would sometimes try to lighten his attitude with a funny or sarcastic remark, which was hit-or-miss on whether it worked or not.

Alex usually had to explain to teachers at the beginning of each year he was **not** Alexander, just Alex. He was smart, hilarious, an athletic star at tennis meets, and moderately handsome. When he was teasing someone or in an excellent mood, his smile was half-smirk with a dimple. It was a unique feature I thought of as his smirk-smile. The combination of those traits made him part of the popular group.

When he was his normal self and not moody, Alex was fun to talk to. He didn't have girlfriends or dates very often. He didn't take local girls out more than one or two times, and we didn't hear about him being involved with anyone from nearby schools either. He focused on hanging out with his friends and was generally the life of the party when he did choose to socialize.

My parents didn't allow me to go to school dances in junior high, and I had to beg and plead to be able to attend the Homecoming one my freshman year. Once I got to go, I wasn't going to waste the opportunity.

I'd been warned that the dances were dangerous if you weren't already in a couple. When everyone knew everyone, how did you force yourself to risk potential humiliation by asking someone to dance? If they said no, you'd be mocked to the end of your days. If they said yes, the rumors began before the music even stopped.

On a dare, I worked up the courage to walk up to Alex. He was kidding around with his friends, and I knew he was a decent person less inclined to laugh at me.

"Hey, Alex. Um, will you dance with me?" I timidly asked in a shaky voice. My hands were trembling and every nerve in my body was buzzing anxiously.

"Sure, why not," he answered with a shrug and a shy smile. Thank goodness I wouldn't have to spend the rest of the evening in mortal shame!

We awkwardly slow-danced at arms-length for what felt like months. I'd never thought about how much taller he was until I had to crane my neck to see his face. I had a momentary thrill being so close to him and feeling his hands holding mine and touching my back, but I chastised myself for over glorifying the circumstances. It was one dance and there's no way it meant anything more to him.

We made it all the way through the song and returned to our respective groups of friends. I had bragging rights for not chickening out, and I ensured my first school dance was worthwhile.

A few of my friends (including Stacey) and I had been in our school plays since we were freshmen. To our surprise, Alex auditioned during our senior year, and he was talented! He landed a decent role, and it was great to see him enjoying acting as much as we did.

Mere minutes before the curtain opened on our inaugural performance, one of the yearbook photographers showed up backstage to take some cast pictures. Several of us girls hammed it up by depicting our strait-laced and elitist roles in the play. Then Alex did a ridiculous pose to make us laugh and break character! It ended up as a half-page shot in our senior yearbook, which was a fitting homage to our drama club's fun time together.

Later in senior year, our Social Studies class qualified for a competition with an overnight stay in a big city. It was exciting for the twenty of us to get away from our parents and feel like we were so grown up by staying in our shared hotel rooms.

As seventeen- and eighteen-year-olds, we predictably stayed up way too late. We did not go quietly in the night to find the people we wanted to be with. Our group eventually got in trouble for loudly traipsing through the hallways to each other's rooms in the wee hours of the morning.

At one point, I was alone in the slow, creaky hotel elevator with Alex. We had chitchatted during the bus ride and in passing earlier. Now he was looking at me strangely and kept moving closer to me. The more we talked, the more he appeared to be hitting on me… *Was I imagining things?*

My heart began to beat faster as the elevator reached our floor. He lightly put his hand on my back as we exited into the corridor, and shivers went up my spine at the warmth of his touch.

As we strolled toward one of the rooms, he halted unexpectedly and turned to me. As I peered up at him, my cheeks flushed with anticipation, he leaned down, smiling. His hand was on my waist and pulling me gently closer until our faces were almost touching, reminiscent of our slow dance in the dimly lit school gym freshman year. When I didn't resist any of those moves and continued gazing into his eyes, we kissed.

Right there in the hotel hallway for no apparent reason, popular Alex Yates kissed **me**, average old Tabitha Wilder.

I didn't have much to compare it to, but the soft pressure of his lips to mine was more thrilling than expected. It was conservative and short-lived, but my heart raced faster and my skin tingled from head to toe, so I knew it was a good kiss. I wasn't ready for it to end when he started to pull away from me.

We paused with our faces close as our breathing slowed and the heat left my face. After a moment of relishing the connection, we slowly turned and resumed the walk to our destination. His fingers intentionally brushed mine before we opened the door, and again my body quivered in response. I inhaled more sharply than usual, and he gave me a smirk-smile of satisfaction at my reaction.

There were no indications whatsoever as to what prompted it, what it meant, or if anything more would occur. We went in with our other friends, my head spinning with questions. We laughed with our classmates and acted as if nothing happened. There were a few secretive glances and smiles at each other, but nothing more.

We managed to be alone again for a short period later, with a small amount of making out until we had to go to our rooms for the night. I wanted more time with him, but I was exhausted. Before falling asleep, I lay in bed remembering his touch and feeling grateful for whatever possessed him to make his move.

Our poor chaperones had to deal with a grumpy group of sleep-deprived teenagers in the morning. The rest of the trip progressed with a discouraging stint in the competition and a boring visit to the state Capitol followed by a long ride back. Most of us slept in our seats on the bus. Alex and I did not have any more interactions, physical or otherwise, prior to everyone either getting picked up or driving home that night.

Tragedy struck our community the very next day.

One of Leo's friends died by suicide. It was devastating whether people knew him well or not. Our family did; Curtis had been at our house regularly. For a week, the school was a disaster zone of somber, crying, distraught students.

My brother was despondent and worried my parents, particularly when he wouldn't talk for two straight days. I burst into tears erratically with no warning. My thoughts incessantly returned to our inside jokes and the last thing I said to Curtis — it was so stupid. Sarcasm has always been my native language, but I understood it had the ability to wound. I desperately hoped he took my flippant final comment to him as facetious and not me being mean.

We got through his funeral and kept checking with Leo to make sure he was okay. All three of us suffered through powerful new emotions and terrifying nightmares. It was challenging enough to manage the burden of grief while also focusing on my part-time job and finishing my senior year. I had nothing left emotionally to worry about boys, so the overnight trip and amorous hotel moments quickly faded into insignificance.

A couple of months later, I got asked to prom by one of my classmates who said he'd had a crush on me for some time. Our relationship had grown lately from acquaintances to friendship to flirting. At last, I had a real boyfriend!

Prom was fun and I was happy. My boyfriend and I spent a considerable amount of time together with our favorite peer group between then and the end of senior year. Alex was part of that since he and my boyfriend were close. Neither of us said anything about our brief encounters during the Social Studies trip, not that it mattered.

To be honest, I'm not sure anyone knew. There was never an occasion to gush about it to any of my girlfriends due to the incidents following our return home, and I don't think he shared it either.

The secrecy was unprecedented given what commonly happened through the local gossip chain.

One thing I observed from being around Alex more was his quirk of being consistently inconsistent. He often broke dates with girls, but also with his crew he used to say he would do something or meet them somewhere, and just not show up.

In those pre-cell phone days, there was no way to track him down unless we drove out to his house. People ceased counting on him, even if they double-checked and he confirmed. Alex was the definition of "ghosting" before there was a term for it!

We were all in a whirlwind of preparing for the momentous changes of life after high school. Quite a few colleges had accepted me, but I really wanted to go to the state university where Stacey was enrolled. We already had plans to share a dorm room.

My parents nonchalantly broke the news to me after graduation that they couldn't afford the school I planned to attend, but they would help me go to a local college if I remained living at home.

I was LIVID. Having to tell Stacey our roommate dreams were ruined was horrific. I was ignorant about applying for grants or financial aid at the time. With only a small amount of money of my own, I had no recourse but to accept my fate.

As summer ended, I did my best to be supportive and upbeat for my friends and boyfriend while they finalized everything to leave our hometown. I promised to visit them as frequently as possible, mainly to escape from my parents!

Undergraduate classes started. My severe frustration with my situation should have spurred me to excel so I could pursue better options. Inversely, my pathetic grades after the first semester proved I was not ready to be responsible... In addition, my boyfriend and I broke up after the distance between us led to suspicion and arguments.

I dropped out of college and got a second shift job at a local retail store. It was decent pay, but mind-numbingly boring. As a perpetual night owl, I sincerely liked working afternoon and evening.

Then I learned about two of my high school classmates having an apartment nearby and holding parties on a regular basis. So, I created a new weekly routine where I would finish work at 10 or 11 p.m. and enjoy a few hours at their place until the festivities wound down.

Alex was an unpredictable partygoer one night, and we got to chat and catch up after a bit. He left college as well and was employed at his dad's construction company while living with his parents. Regrettably, neither of us had much of an idea about our futures. Most of us at those parties were in kind of a life limbo and burying our aimlessness in alcohol, loud music, and dumb decisions.

As our conversation wrapped up, I told him I was glad to see him, but I was going to make my exit soon and go to bed. He said he was done too; he had to work in the morning. He offered to follow me on the dark country roads to make sure I got home safely. Deer were a legitimate concern, so it was kind of him to ask. I accepted; we said our goodbyes and left.

We took the backroads leading to our hometown, and he got in front of me. As we passed an empty parking lot for the local fairgrounds, he pulled in and turned on his hazard lights. I thought something was wrong with his car, so I parked behind him and got out to see if he was okay. He didn't appear to be upset as he shut off his engine and strode toward me. When I asked what was going on, he flashed his smirk-smile.

"I've missed you, Tabby. I wanted some quiet time alone with you."

"Oh!" I said with an incredulous look on my face.

He laughed at my confusion as he pulled me against him. His familiar smell was intoxicating. This time I was more confident when his lips met mine, I'd leveled up with my ex-boyfriend! We leaned on my car as we made out, and I indulged in the feeling of our bodies pressed together.

The cold air compelled us to move into the safety of my car's passenger seat, warming ourselves while exploring each other's mouths and letting our hands roam.

We hesitated when another vehicle was passing and reminded us where we were. Someone could stop or call the police about two cars parked randomly in the middle of the night.

We then decided to go home in reality, but we took our time disengaging. Neither of us wanted it to end. He went back to his car and we parted ways. There were no future plans made or dialogue about what it all meant, which suited me fine.

That wasn't our only impromptu late-night tryst, several happened intermittently over the next two-year period. None of the occurrences were scheduled or on a regular cadence. When we ended up at the same place and the circumstance presented itself, we would find a way to coordinate our departures and have a backroads make-out session.

Neither of us asked for more or less; we weren't in love or even a couple, we were simply lifelong friends with (partial) benefits. We treated each episode like it was our final time together because we never knew if it was. It would probably end with one of us being in a serious relationship with someone else, which was okay.

Our nights never led to more than heavy petting, largely because we both lived with our parents and our cars were not exactly comfortable settings. In truth, sex seemed like a step too far in the direction of commitment, at least to me.

Letting hormones take over and releasing some sexual tension with a man I trusted felt pretty damn amazing, though. The secrecy also added to the attraction, of course. We didn't have to explain or define any of it, which made it easy and more erotic.

What did that say about me?

I considered maybe he was embarrassed to tell other people we were hooking up, but it didn't matter to me either. There was evidently something attracting him and bringing him back for more, and that's all I needed to know.

Part of my nature was to overthink and analyze situations ad nauseam, in particular when it came to the opposite sex. But with Alex, things were different. I was already aware of his unreliability. He did not always live up to expectations, and therefore I didn't apply any to him.

~ *Chapter 2* ~

TAG TEAM

Not long before I turned twenty-one, I decided I'd had enough of floating around and I was going to concentrate on finishing college. I had recently moved out of my parents' house into an apartment close to campus with roommates from work, so I enrolled in the spring semester.

I left retail for a job in a steakhouse with flexibility on hours so I was able to attend classes and study on whatever schedule I chose.

Restaurant life is a whole vibe of its own, especially near a college campus. It was difficult not to get swept up into the fun nightlife. The familiar routine of my shift ending at night and having numerous parties and bars to choose from was tough to resist, but I learned the hard way that showing up to class hungover was not a sustainable lifestyle.

I reached the elusive responsible point at last because I got to a solid place of work, classes, and studying, with sporadic nights out when my schedule allowed. My life was slowly but surely getting back on track, although I didn't have a precise blueprint of what I was going to do after college. For now, focusing on school and paying my bills were my only priorities.

Less than a year after I started at the restaurant, a new waitress was hired with the name Guinevere Beckett, who went by Ginny. She's one of those people who is ALWAYS perky and smiling – the kind you either roll your eyes at or love on sight. I liked her right away! It may have been because I wished I was more outgoing like her, or maybe because her laugh and smile were too infectious to deny.

She had tightly curled blonde hair different enough to be noteworthy. When I first saw her, I immediately thought of Little Orphan Annie's curls, but with a much better style and color. I asked her once if she got perms, which were popular at that time. She sighed and told me most people assumed it was permed, but hers was *au naturel* from her mom and grandma.

Our boss assigned me to be her trainer, so we spent a decent amount of time together in her first two weeks on the job. Ginny said she was taking a semester off school to figure out her next steps.

Her parents were very unhappy with her about quitting college, but I couldn't fault her for it. That uncertainty was something I understood way too well. In fact, it was one of many things she and I had in common.

When Ginny passed her server test and officially became part of our crew, a group of us decided to go out and celebrate. One of the guys was wildly excited to have her join us at the bar, but I knew his style. He had a bad reputation for watching girls get wasted and then swooping in as the "nice guy" who would gallantly escort them home safely, only to make sure they "repaid" his kindness before he left.

He was gross, and I held back on my drinking to stay observant and save Ginny from falling into his lecherous trap. Nobody said anything to her so she could enjoy herself without worry and just in case he was legitimately having fun with no ill intent.

I tried to give him the benefit of the doubt, but he kept true to form at the end of the night. Ginny drunkenly told me he was going to protect her by walking her back to her apartment.

I convinced her to come dance with me one more time to a popular song she liked and then needed her to come with me to the restroom. A couple of my female co-workers knew my plan and would preoccupy Mr. Jerk in case he got suspicious.

When the restroom line was long (it always was), I said I'd wait until I got home. Then I took Ginny out the back door of the bar and guided her back to her apartment myself.

She was too inebriated to remember her original offer, and I kept her talking so she wouldn't think about it. I made sure she got in her door and she swore to drink some water and take a couple aspirin. Proud of my good deed, I strolled back to my place.

Friends told me the following day that the nasty dude sat there waiting for close to half an hour before he realized what I'd done, and I claimed victory!

He and I got into it on our next shift together. He forcefully banged the door shut when he came in the employee entrance and asked someone if I was there. I made sure several coworkers were nearby to witness whatever was about to go down.

He strode up to me with his chest puffed out and his face red with indignation.

"What's your problem, bitch?" He was practically spitting each word.

The stench of his stale cigarette breath in my face was disgusting, but I widened my eyes and asked innocently, "What do you mean?"

"Don't give me your bullshit! You cockblocked me with your little girlfriend at the bar. What are you, some lesbian whore and got jealous when she was hot for me and not you? You tryin' to keep her for yourself?"

He sneered and got even closer, but I stood my ground and kept staring directly into his bloodshot eyes. I didn't say a word.

"It don't matter anyway. She wants me, and I'm gonna give her allll of it whether you like it or not!" He made a crass gesture in case I didn't get his drift.

When I still didn't respond, he started running out of steam.

"Whatever. Just stay out of my way from now on, cockblocking bitch," he finished weakly. As he strutted arrogantly past me, he shoved his shoulder into mine to assert his dominance. It was unexpected, but I retained my balance and didn't give him the satisfaction of making a sound.

Oh hell no. I marched straight back into our manager's office and told him everything I knew had happened up to this point. He was taken aback that no one had brought it up before, but I admitted that we were worried about repercussions or worse treatment from the dirtbag if he found out someone snitched on him. With the face-off a few moments ago, I reached my limit of tolerance and was willing to lose my job if it meant protecting others from the abuse.

Other women servers validated what I said, and he fired the asshole that same night. Several of us breathed a giant sigh of relief at an awful person being out of our lives and our manager listening to and believing us.

When Ginny learned what had transpired, she was shocked I would do those things for her. I explained that I was doing it for all the females we worked with, she had simply provided a tipping point for him to hang himself, so to speak. She vowed to take me out and buy me all the thank you drinks I wanted soon, and our friendship blossomed quickly from there.

We were nearly inseparable whenever we had time to be together. I let down my guard and trusted Ginny completely, despite usually still being wary about allowing people to get too close. I went so far as to give her a key to my apartment for her to crash after the bars if she didn't have anyone to walk her all the way home or the weather was bad.

My roommates and I got used to seeing Ginny sacked out on the living room couch in the morning. However, as soon as she heard us moving around, she was up, smiling, and ready to make coffee for everyone. It was a mystery to me how the perkiness came so rapidly and naturally for her, but I saw it in action so many times I knew it wasn't fake.

To her credit, the one near-miss with our sketchy former co-worker was enough to make Ginny careful and always go out with someone she trusted. I didn't have to be concerned when I was studying or wiped out because she had a wide array of friends to accompany her.

Women didn't often address it, but everyone had their own sexual assault memories or horror stories from friends. Those scars kept us vigilant against letting bad things happen if there was anything we could do about it.

In addition to her natural joviality, another thing I envied was Ginny's skill with makeup. Growing up a tomboy, I never had any interest in it, but now I wanted to try. She was a superb teacher, but no matter what she showed me, I was never able to duplicate it properly.

When she did my makeup, I was prettier and acted more poised. When I applied it myself, I ended up looking like, well, I should be standing on a street corner. It wasn't a huge deal to me, but I was disappointed I couldn't share cosmetics tips and products with her.

Borrowing from Ginny's closet would have been another dream come true. Alas, I was taller and a little bigger than her, so nothing fit me the way it should. When we were out together, she was the cutely-dressed, smiling, curly-haired perky girl who drew boys like moths to a flame. I was the quiet, boring sidekick with straight brown hair with no particular style, very little makeup, and discount store clothes.

Sometimes I ended up talking with the hot guy's friend if he engaged. Once they got to know me, I was more outspoken and wittier, but I was timid when I first met people. I joked on many occasions how I was the plain Jane wing-woman to Ginny's Barbie, which brought a lot of sympathetic laughs.

Whether we were out and about or having a laid-back night in, we invariably had enormous amounts of fun. Partying with Ginny was always an adventure, but I treasured our quiet evenings with just the two of us.

I specifically remember one night when we were going through outfits and planning on meeting people out.

We got so caught up reminiscing about past craziness; we flopped lazily on her bed and talked all night long instead.

I had been lamenting my tense relationship with my parents lately. My dad and I were still at odds about most decisions I made. My mom was frustrated that I didn't go straight through college so I would be graduating soon. It would have been ideal to spend more time with my brothers, but I avoided going home too often because it would consistently end in disagreement with one or both of my parents.

Ginny had already heard about my childhood and the strict Catholic rules I had to follow. I opened up more about how unfair and unhappy my father was all the time and how trapped and inconsequential I felt while I was growing up. My brothers and I hid a lot from our dad to avoid confrontations, and I never intended to be in a similar position again.

With brows furrowed, I declared, "I'm determined to finish college and build a decent career because I want the freedom to make my own choices. I refuse to feel obligated to answer to anyone else unless I want to. Any man who wants a serious relationship with me needs to be a calm and caring person who is willing to INTEGRATE our lives instead of making me conform to his." I bobbed my head firmly to reinforce how much I meant it.

Ginny applauded and proclaimed, "I hereby affirm your goals and, as your B.F.F., I shall do my best to assist you as much as possible in your endeavors." She pretended to land a stamp of approval on my leg, and we laughed hysterically at our ridiculousness.

She had only told me bits and pieces about her family. That night she shared how she grew up near the East Coast with her parents and two half-sisters from her dad's previous marriage. They were several years older than Ginny, but they loved her and she adored them.

When Ginny was in fifth grade, her parents started arguing. They each threatened to kick the other one out and sue for full custody of her, which made her feel like some kind of bargaining chip between them. With her dad being a lawyer already, middle school Ginny feared what would ultimately happen to her. She didn't want to lose either parent or her sisters.

Her mom and dad eventually did get a divorce and a customized joint custody plan. Her mom then moved with Ginny to the Midwest because Ginny's grandparents were old and having health issues. Without her sisters, Ginny was oppressively alone and angry with her mom. She had maternal cousins nearby, but she hardly knew them and it was nowhere near the same.

She saw her dad and sisters on many major holidays, but summer break was her favorite because she spent extended time with them. She dreaded coming back here for school each year.

When she was starting high school and her sisters were in college, she loved going to visit them and learn about boys and makeup and sorority life. Their college lives were thrilling and grown up, whereas she remained stuck in Midwest public high school.

Both of her sisters are 'wicked smart' according to Ginny. They excelled at prestigious universities and did all the right things to get hired into lucrative careers. They were now successful and busy professionals, which meant they had less time to spend with their little sister. They all still talked on the phone and had some holidays together, but their family gatherings had drastically decreased in recent years.

She vehemently wanted to move back there with them, but she doubted she could afford it. She also admitted to being intimidated by her lawyer dad and her sisters' notable lives as another lawyer and a computer whiz at a famous tech company. It saddened me that many of her school years had been so lonely and she perceived herself to be left behind and small compared to the people she loved most.

I was glad to be a positive part of her time living here, and I selfishly hoped she would stick around for a long time to come.

Ginny and I became continually closer. We even confided in each other about the concept of our future offspring. I hoped to have a daughter someday because I'd never gotten the sister I wanted. I planned to call my little girl Arica *(pronounced "ARE·i·ka" and not "AIR·i·ka")*, which I thought was a beautiful and unique name.

She agreed and said we should try to marry gorgeous, funny, rich brothers, so we'd be the fun aunts to each other's kids. She couldn't envision herself becoming a mom, but if it happened, she would dedicate everything she had to being a much better mother than her own. She wanted to understand her children as individuals and to provide them with all the love and support she was able to give.

No matter what we started discussing, we inevitably ended up on our favorite topic – dating and boys. One night she told me her mom had been obsessed with the Renaissance era and named her Guinevere because of it, which she kind of hated. She tried to avoid telling people her full name if she could help it, but sometimes it came up. Any time a boy made a joke about being her Lancelot, she immediately subtracted from his D Score.

I was instantly confused. "His WHAT?"

"Oh yeah, I guess I haven't told you about the Date-ability Score, otherwise known as D Score. My sisters used to tell me about some of the boys they went out with, and my sister at M.I.T. created the Date Worthiness Scale. They used it to compare Date-ability Scores for pre-date, first date, and afterward.

If his score increases over time, he's worth continuing to date. If the score keeps going down, it isn't going to work out, and you need to cut your losses. It's science."

I stared at her in disbelief for a moment and then burst out laughing so hard I was hardly able to breathe. That led to bad hiccups, which also made me laugh. I had never met anyone like Ginny and her sisters; I loved all of it!

From then on, the D Score became one of our primary subjects of conversation. As with high school, I didn't go out with a lot of men during my time in college.

(There was rarely time to hang out with my friends, for crying out loud.) I dated some good ones and a few not-so-good ones.

Ginny, however, made up for my share and her own, and she was constantly reassessing her previous assessment to assess whether the boy of the moment was worth continuing to assess. There were periods when it was exhausting to keep up, and other weeks where I thoroughly enjoyed living vicariously through her wacky and wild escapades!

It was never boring when Ginny left her apartment, and she was more than happy to tell me about anyone she met at the grocery store, the video store *(one of her prime places to look for new dating potential)*, the mall, or pretty much anywhere.

There were a few times when she shed some tears over a breakup, but seldomly. For the most part, she shrugged off the endings and was back to her normal self in no time. She wasn't mean or heartless about it, I genuinely believe she was trying to find a man who filled the missing pieces in her life and would provide a balance she craved.

A male co-worker once overheard us deliberating over Ginny's latest date and the D Score during a slow night at the restaurant. He shook his head at us and said, "I love you girls, but I would hate to be one of the contestants being rated on the Tabby and Ginny Show. You two are VICIOUS!"

We thought that was kind of overstated, but we did start being more prudent around other people. The next time we were together away from work, we decided we really liked his 'Tabby and Ginny show' naming of us. We brainstormed some other nicknames we could call ourselves.

She suggested The T&G Band, (formally known as The Tabby & Ginny Band of Bitchin' Badass Babes). Then we considered shortening it to TNG like Guns N' Roses had done.

She threw out the idea of just TAG, and I spontaneously broke out into hip hop from the original Tag Team. We belted out almost the entire lyrics of "Whoomp!

(There It Is)" together, collapsing into breathless laughter when we finished.

We concluded that TAG Team was perfect for us and we'd make it our karaoke song the moment we got the chance to go public with our newly-discovered awesome (not) rapping skills!

Ginny came home with me once for Easter weekend when she didn't want to go see her mom. I appreciated the buffer of someone new to distract my parents, so it worked out well for both of us.

She and I stayed up super late in my old bedroom talking about boys we went to high school with, who we had crushes on, and all the silly girl stuff that deepens bonds.

She went through my senior yearbook and pointed out the large photo of the drama club with Alex doing his goofy pose and me pretending to be my stoic and snooty character from the play. She thought it was great and said I should make a copy of it and frame it for my bedroom wall!

I briefly contemplated telling her about the weird path Alex and I took, but for some reason it didn't feel like the right time. Someday soon I would come back to it and regale her with stories of swatting mosquitoes in cornfields while making out with a guy I never thought would give me the time of day.

Postponing that divulgence ended up being an excellent decision – it saved me a lot of shame later.

~ *Chapter 3* ~

SURPRISES

When some high school friends were visiting during Thanksgiving break, we caught up over dinner. We were twenty-three years old, and most of them were college graduates and working their way up in "real" jobs. A couple were in grad school, one engaged, and another married. I judged myself as the loser of the group, but I held my head high and laid out my plans for finishing my degree and getting to the more successful point myself.

I called Ginny when we were dispersing and asked her to meet me at our favorite bar. She sensed I was feeling low, so she compensated with excessive perkiness. As soon as I arrived, she signed us up to play pool *(something I always enjoyed)* and had my preferred drink waiting for me.

Surprisingly, in walked Alex Yates. We grinned at each other and hugged. It was great to see him after more than two years. Ginny encouraged me to sit and catch up with him while she played pool with some other friends of ours. Alex told me he moved about an hour away and was dating a girl he had met at work. He was still trying to figure out where he wanted to go from here, but he was happier being away from our hometown and his family pressures.

I empathized with being in a similar "holding pattern" and shared my own parental woes as well as the disheartening ordeal I'd just had with the high school friends and feeling so behind everyone else. It was almost eerie how much we were living parallel lives, and I was reminded once again of all the things we'd had in common throughout our lives.

With him telling me about the girlfriend, obviously there was nothing going to happen between us. We still flirted discreetly while playing pool, harmlessly and mainly for nostalgia's sake. He and Ginny got along well, which was a bonus. Things had turned around nicely!

Before we left the bar, he asked for my phone number to call me when he got back to town, and I gave it to him. He didn't offer his, and somehow it didn't occur to me to ask.

To my amazement, he actually followed through about a month later when he was back in the area for Christmas. He called as I was heading out the door to meet Ginny and other friends, and he volunteered to join us.

After an hour or so, he showed up at the bar with a friend and wasn't in the greatest mood. He was quiet, frowning, and sitting by himself at first. I greeted him and asked what was wrong, and he confessed that he and his girlfriend had broken up the week before. They'd had a fight over the phone tonight about him coming to retrieve some of his things from her place.

Ginny and I tried to cheer him up. She ultimately got him smiling some, and by the end of the night he relaxed enough to dance with us and sing some horrible karaoke Christmas songs.

He asked if I would mind giving him a ride to his grandparents' house since he didn't have his car with him. His friend hadn't stayed at the bar long. That was fine with me, not knowing if it meant our old arrangement or if he was still too melancholy from his breakup for any of that. It was strange he wasn't staying with his parents, but I didn't push the issue because it was likely a sore spot for him.

I was Ginny's ride as well, so I told her I'd drop her off first and then take Alex home. We all chatted on the short trip to her place, and then he and I were alone and driving into the dark backroads like old times.

He had to give me directions since I only had a vague idea where his grandparents lived. It had snowed, so I was paying more attention to the road conditions than him. Randomly, he put his hand on my leg and asked me to pull over for a moment. I smiled to myself and was glad I was wearing a lacy bra and matching underwear in lieu of my old comfy ones.

However, instead of leaning over to me, he sighed and studied his hands on his lap. "Tabby, I'm sorry for depending on you when I felt lonely in the past. I hope you don't think I was using you, that wasn't my intention."

Hearing him admit it out loud caught me off balance. I touched his arm as a gesture of reassurance. "Alex, I was fully complicit in my participation. We both used to conquer some loneliness together. I have no regrets. Do you?"

I wasn't sure I wanted to hear his answer.

He finally met my eyes. "No, I don't regret being with you at all. And you've been more patient with me than anyone else. I can't tell you how much I appreciate that."

Tears blurred my vision thinking he was going to end everything – seeing me when he was home, our secret attraction and partial benefits, all of it. After being apart so long, I had lost some of my ability to read him like I used to.

I braced myself while I waited to see what he was struggling to say next. Instead of talking, he put his hand on my face and kissed me more gently than usual. I responded with the same, and somehow his vulnerability was a catalyst for the most intense it had ever been between us.

At one point he asked in a husky, breathless voice, "Do you want to go back to your apartment?"

"I wish we'd thought of that in the first place, but sadly I really should call it a night." My voice was also low and full of wanting.

We kissed long and sensually one more time. He gazed hungrily into my eyes and told me, "Next time I see you, we're going to finish what we've started. If you agree." He placed his lips lightly on the top of my cleavage, and I gasped at the exhilaration shooting through me.

"I don't think 'agree' is a strong enough term for it," I whispered next to his ear. He shuddered with pleasure when my lips grazed his neck and nipped his earlobe. As we ruefully separated, both of us laughed when we noticed the entire car was fogged over from our heated session. We situated our clothes in silence; our trysts usually seemed to end in regret for us running out of time and adequate space.

I followed his instructions to get to his grandparents' while reveling in the tingling I still sensed all over and through my body. Our attraction hadn't diminished – if anything, it was more powerful than ever.

After I parked in their driveway, he slowly said, "Tabby, I've also wanted to say thank you… for being one of the few… constant people in my life. I never would have guessed that you'd still actually like me after all this time."

I gave him a look like he was crazy and said, "Why wouldn't I like you? It seems quite obvious that I enjoy our time together. I'm glad we've stayed in touch for so long."

It sounded lame and insufficient for what I wanted to convey, but I couldn't think of anything better to respond in the moment. My head was reeling from the different way he acted tonight and his heartfelt words. Plus, I was bone tired from a busy day and week.

He gave me an adorable smirk-smile and a quick goodbye kiss. We wished each other Merry Christmas and Happy New Year, and he got out of my car.

Little did we know those would be the last kind things we said to each other for a very long time.

The restaurant was overflowing with customers during the holiday celebrations. Ginny and I rang in the new year together with a few work friends. She asked me if Alex had been in a better mood when I dropped him off after the last time we hung out. I said yes with my own smirk and told her that something had changed between him and me. We seemed to be venturing into new territory, and I was conflicted about whether I even wanted a relationship with him if it was an option…

She was astonished that anything romantic was happening with us. I hinted that there had been sparks before but no real flames until that night and promised to fill her in on all the details at our earliest convenience. A loud chaotic bar wasn't the most opportune place for a confidential revelation, so it stayed a secret once again.

Then college classes resumed. I focused on studying, and my life went back to my version of normal. In the middle of January, I caught the flu, which later turned into bronchitis. I was miserable and homebound for nearly three weeks.

At first, Ginny came over each day or two with the purpose of brightening my mood and making me smile. She comically wore a bandana over her nose and mouth and goofy gloves to avoid touching my skin when she handed me things. She came bearing gifts of trashy magazines, gossip from work, soup, and vitamins to help me heal.

Upon arrival, she would dramatically pretend to cover me with anti-cooty spray and tell me I looked decent for someone who couldn't speak an entire sentence without hacking up a lung.

It was hilarious, but I had to tell her to knock it off. They say laughter is the best medicine, but it made me cough too much and might kill me.

She talked to our boss at the restaurant and told him I was on my deathbed, and he shouldn't bother me until I let him know I was ready to come back. My co-workers weren't too upset about picking up my shifts because this was always the slow time of year before Valentine's Day anyway.

My roommates helped me get my class assignments and return papers due, reminded me to take antibiotics and drink fluids, and refilled my humidifier to help me breathe. It was undoubtedly a group effort to nurse me back to regular health.

In the second week, I noticed that Ginny hadn't visited in several days. I called and left a couple of messages on her answering machine to see how she was doing. I was afraid I'd gotten her sick after all, and I would have felt terrible if she were suffering alone.

I heard nothing back.

When I was well enough to drive, I went and knocked on her apartment door, but no one answered. I stuck a note in the door jam, but still no response. I was really starting to worry…

On the night before I went back to work at the restaurant, I was dreading getting through an entire evening after being ill so long and so severely. My call to Ginny for support went unanswered yet again. Whatever, I would see her during a shift soon and we would discuss her unexplained disappearance.

But when I showed up the next day and reviewed my upcoming schedule, I didn't see her name posted anywhere. I went to my manager and asked when Ginny would be in, and he told me she stopped by earlier in the week and quit. She turned in all her things and said he should mail her last paycheck.

EXCUSE ME?

My blood ran cold at the realization that my last connection to Ginny was now severed.

When he saw the stunned look on my face, my manager apologized for being the bearer of bad news; he thought I knew since we were so close. Yeah, I thought we were, too!

Depression crashed down on me like an avalanche. I trudged through my classes and work but had no interest in anything. The bare minimum was all I gave on my homework and studying for tests. Going out after work wasn't even a consideration; I went home and straight to bed. I picked up extra shifts at the restaurant both to compensate for my time being sick and to give me something to do besides sitting on my couch dejected and alone.

The sudden and significant change in my closest friend was incomprehensible. How could she simply ditch me like it was nothing? I dissected every conversation we'd had in recent history, scouring my memory for anything that hinted at why she now hated me. What had I done/said/not done/not said to cause her to reject me? If she let me apologize, I'd do it in a heartbeat!

I got angry with myself for letting someone in and caring enough to allow them to hurt me again. The protective wall I'd put up after the mean girls in high school discarded me should have stayed put. I was stupid to lower my guard, I swore it would never happen hereafter. My roommates voiced their concerns about my state of mind, but I told them I'd be fine in the end. I was heartbroken and inconsolable and needed time to recover.

After two long and detestable months, I finally started to rebound from my emotional stupor. Somehow, a guy in one of my classes asked me out. I needed to get out of my funk, so it was a welcome distraction.

Alex hadn't reached out since just prior to me getting sick, so I had no idea what our status was. My subsequent calls to him went unanswered, which was not surprising. I highly doubted he was waiting around and pining for me, so there was no guilt when I accepted Rich's invitation.

He was friendly and fairly good-looking, so what would it hurt to have a meal and learn more about him? Besides, who was I to pass up the rare date night? Of course I started to think about his D Score, but that was too painful and I sharply cut those thoughts off before they could turn into tears.

It was April and unseasonably chilly, so I struggled to find an outfit warm enough but still moderately attractive for a date. A fleeting thought crossed my mind of wishing Ginny were here to help me with makeup, but I buried that too and just went with some lip gloss and a bit of mascara.

Rich picked me up right on time, we made small talk on the way to the restaurant, and we arrived early. The hostess told us our table wasn't ready quite yet.

We went into the lounge area for a cocktail while we waited, and THERE THEY WERE. Across the bar sat Alex and Ginny, cuddling together over their drinks, giggling, and clearly the cutest couple that ever existed.

I froze. I stood there with my eyes bulging, mouth gaping open, unable to speak or move. Rich asked for my drink order, but I never answered him.

Thoughts rushed through my mind in rapid succession.

Well, at least she's not dead.

I guess he does know how to take a girl on a decent date.

He never wanted to be seen in public with me like that.

I've never heard him giggle; it seems unnatural.

Why would she keep this from me instead of being a fucking adult and talking to me?

Of all the guys she could get, and after all we've had together, this is how she treats me?

The last one was the impetus for me to move toward them, though I craved nothing more than to run far, far away and hide from the truth.

I walked slowly around the bar, feeling like an impostor in my own body, until I was standing directly behind their barstools. As they sensed someone and turned to acknowledge, their eyes enlarged and their demeanor changed to terrified.

I spoke first. "What. The. Fuck?"

Ginny stammered, "Oh shit, wait. Tabby, please let us explain. Don't be mad; it's perfectly understandable."

As she babbled, I noticed Alex was looking me up and down appreciatively. I felt a small glint of satisfaction that I had hit the mark with the alluring part of my attire.

The rest of me was filling steadily with rage, and things started to appear red around the edges. My heart pounded like it was going to beat right out of my chest. My fists clenched, and my fingernails dug painfully into my palms. It was nothing compared to the agony of this treachery playing out in front of me.

As I looked from one to the other, I saw the guilt written all over the faces I knew so well. Something inside me snapped. An excruciating ache of betrayal and loathing pulsed through my body. It was like an all-consuming fire, and I was clueless how to put it out.

Seething, I turned and walked toward the main doors on stiff legs – forcing myself to put one foot in front of the other. As I passed Rich, he tried to stop me and ask what was wrong. I think I said something to the effect of, "I'm so sorry, I need to leave right now," and kept going. He began following me, as did the two biggest traitors who ever lived.

The crisp air soothed me when I stepped outside, maybe the fire inside me wouldn't burn me to a crisp after all. Rich again asked if I was okay, and I requested that he start the car. I said I would be there momentarily to clarify everything. As I heard Alex and Ginny rush out to talk to me, I turned around and faced them again.

I hardly recognized my own voice as I coldly and furiously told them through gritted teeth, "I don't know when this started, or why, and I really don't care. What matters to me is that both of you stabbed me in the back, knowingly and unapologetically, and you have broken my fucking heart. Neither of you cared about me the same way I did about you, and I will never forget this. You are both shitty friends, and you fucking deserve each other."

They stood wide-eyed in shocked silence. They probably wouldn't have guessed I was capable of saying those things to anyone, let alone them. Surely they understood there was nothing they could reply that would make a difference. The relationships they each had with me were now irrevocably ruined.

I stomped to Rich's car and got in the passenger side, gratified to hear Ginny sobbing as I slammed the door shut. The vindictive part of me made a mental plea for karma to have a grand old time with the two of them. There was a moment of guilt for my hateful thoughts, but it was promptly overshadowed by the misery of being forsaken by two of my favorite people.

Feeling this infuriated was new to me, and I was surprised at how easy it would be to give in to it. Admittedly, the outrage hurt less than the profound sadness when I didn't understand why Ginny deserted me. Maybe I should latch on to the fury instead.

I apologized profusely to Rich for the drama and asked if we could postpone our date. He was fine with that and took me home. He understandably stopped sitting near me in class, and we never rescheduled.

Anybody who asked got the same brief explanation – Ginny and I had a disagreement over a guy, and we were no longer friends. Given her revolving door with dating, it was completely believable and further questions weren't asked. I had no interest in what assumptions people made; I just wanted to never speak her name or think about her again.

With Alex and my history being a secret, I was spared the torment of telling anyone what happened there.

As far as I was concerned, they were both dead to me.

~ *Chapter 4* ~

THE KIDS ARE ALL RIGHT

My pain and memories were immediately locked up tight and firmly buried.

A move to a different place and college marked a fresh start, where I completed my bachelor's degree and graduated in December at age twenty-four. From there came a stable role in project management, along with meaningful new connections.

A helpful therapist worked with me on some of my abandonment issues. We touched on the subject of the mean girls in high school, but mostly she focused on getting me to talk about my father. She raised the salient point that his emotional absence was likely the main cause for me to fear the same treatment from others around me. I did not reach the stage of telling her about Alex and Ginny before I changed jobs and she was out of network for my insurance. I should have prioritized finding someone else, but I naively believed I was capable of effectively managing my thoughts and emotions. Ha!

My colleague Kate Daley and I became friends. She was part of a group that regularly played darts and pool on the weekends. She invited me to come along with her a couple of weeks before my twenty-fifth birthday, and I began slowly meeting more people and learning dart games. My pool skills were rusty, but not for long.

A dashing and charismatic man had also recently joined the friendly competitions, and he introduced himself a few nights after my birthday. Max had a great smile that lit up his face and he laughed easily, especially when I teased him during pool games. We talked periodically and did some occasional flirting, and he asked me out about a month later.

We had a fantastic evening together; I even got the "butterflies in my stomach" sensation for the first time in my life. When we kissed on our second date, I knew I wanted to be his girlfriend and should hold onto him. Max is fun to be with; dating him was easy. The harder part was believing I could trust him.

It took me longer than it should have to let him in and give him the love he deserved from me, but my caution was hard-earned. Certain traits were still strictly prohibited in anyone I considered having a relationship with – plutonic or romantic. I was staunchly avoiding the heated fury of heartbreak and needed to make sure he wasn't someone who would yell or try to control me like I grew up with.

After a lot of self-reflection, I finally realized that my protective shield was partially to my own detriment. It might safeguard against anguish, but true love wasn't going to be available until I allowed myself to be vulnerable. I vanquished my inner demons and decided to give him a chance. Lucky for me, Max stuck it out until I was ready to make that leap.

Unlike the other men in my life, Max is a steady, reliable person with an exceptional sense of humor and an unmatched generosity. As a financial analyst, he is methodical and meticulous. In his personal life, his impatience is more prevalent, but he managed to prove time and again how much he cared for me and valued my input.

When he proposed, I asked Kate to be my maid of honor. She was the first woman I'd gotten close to since Ginny, although it took many months before I lowered my innermost barriers. Our in-depth conversations about the similar childhoods we'd experienced made us kindred spirits, and Kate's quick wit and dark humor were my favorite characteristics of hers.

Maxwell Louis Ganter became my husband on 9-9-99, which was a Thursday but too perfect of a date to pass up. We did things a little unconventionally by saying our vows at the courthouse with a small contingency of close friends and family and then holding our celebratory dinner and reception party two days later on Saturday night.

My parents were disappointed (yet again) by it not being a Catholic wedding ceremony, but they didn't belabor the point. I think they had resigned themselves to the fact I was not coming back to the church despite their efforts to persuade me. What Max and I did was so fun and low stress, I have zero regrets and wouldn't have changed a thing!

We got pregnant quickly, and our daughter Arica made us parents on June 16, 2000, when I was twenty-nine. Our son Dawson completed our family two years later on July 22, 2002, and we set down roots in a quiet subdivision of a Midwestern capital city with a highly regarded school system.

Max is just as wonderful at being a father as he is a husband, and we waded through the unknown waters of parenthood together. He is the yin to my yang and everything I didn't realize I needed in a life partner. Marrying him and raising our children made me happier than I thought possible!

Arica and Dawson did well in school and were both about as average as I had been growing up, which was comforting to me. Arica was my mini-me when she was little – she loved books, dressing up, animals, and art. She was so talented at looking at something and transferring it onto paper (or once, all over a wall in our house) to look strikingly like the original. She tried a few sports, but running around and getting sweaty wasn't her thing. She got good grades all through elementary and middle school and always had a lot of friends to keep her busy.

Dawson takes after Max's side of the family with his high energy and short attention span. He liked several different sports when he was younger but couldn't settle for one very long. He loved the movement and playing with his friends, but practicing the fundamentals was "too boring." Anything that involved repetition caused him to lose interest before the ball ever reached its target. Video games were only temporary fun. He liked to help his dad with small projects and was always good with numbers, so we had some hopes he might follow in Max's footsteps someday. It's hard to tell with our kid, he keeps us guessing!

When I was thirty-eight, social media was ramping up, and many of my fellow high school classmates connected on Facebook and Twitter. There were slightly more than a hundred students in my graduating class, and I'd known more than half of them since at least kindergarten, if not pre-school. It was interesting to see what people were doing as we approached middle age status!

A few of them began talking about our twenty-year reunion, and I volunteered to help with some of the decorations and table centerpieces. Arica and Dawson were young, but I had fun showing them old cassette tapes, floppy discs, and other 'artifacts' from my childhood.

Max chimed in at times and attempted to solve a Rubik's cube like he claimed he did in high school. Dawson also worked hard on it, but neither of them succeeded. I went through my yearbooks from junior and senior years with them and asked the kids to pick me out. They had trouble recognizing their mom as a teenager!

As everyone on the planning committee was reaching out to people who were not on Facebook or Twitter, I paid close attention in case Alex's name came up. Someone called his parents, but I was relieved to hear they never got in touch with them.

Not that I thought Alex would show up even if he were told, but there was no way I'd be able to remain calm and civil if he was in the room. It would have been a substantial let down if I had to skip the whole thing, so his silence was music to my ears.

In the weeks leading up to the event, I amused myself by daydreaming about how long he and Ginny were probably together and the reasons for the ugly breakup I projected upon them.

One possibility was that she got fed up with his unreliability and nonchalantly dumped him after he stood her up too many times. He regretted choosing her over me and knew he'd made a hideous mistake.

Another idea had them splitting up due to Ginny's tendency to date someone for a couple of weeks and then casually move on. I hoped Alex was hurt when she left him for the next best conquest. That's basically what he did to me, so c'est la vie, mon chéri.

I imagined that he ditched her when he found out how flighty and melodramatic she could be, and she cried desolately with no one to comfort her. It was morbidly entertaining to visualize her isolated and dejected without me or her sisters to talk to.

They might have gotten into a huge fight about me after I scorned them outside the restaurant, which would have been apropos. Regardless, I wished for them both to be miserably remorseful and miss me constantly.

In any scenario, I envisioned his D Score plummeting day after day, and it made me smile.

Whenever I accidentally flashed back to them at that bar being so precious together, I started to feel the angst building. Before the rage took hold, I would force myself to think about anything else. Somehow, more than a decade and nearly two years of therapy sessions had not entirely erased my anger.

As the reunion approached, I finished fantasizing about their tumultuous separation and mentally prepared myself to hear people talking about Alex without my face or body language displaying my disgust. Once again, I was incredibly thankful nobody knew about us. There was no way I wanted to explain about any part of our painful saga.

Stacey was coming from halfway across the country for the reunion, and we decided to make it a girls' trip. She and I were excited, and our husbands were happy to stay home. Enjoying some alone time with her allowed me to just be myself. Not wife me, or mom me, or responsible worker me – simply Tabitha the goofy, nerdy woman having a fun weekend with one of her best friends!

It was enjoyable to catch up with several classmates in person, particularly the ones who were avoiding social media and I hadn't talked to in years. I had such a great time, I barely thought about Alex at all.

As they grew and matured, Arica and Dawson got along well but were typical siblings. There were intermittent fights and tears and competitions for nearly everything. Even when they entered high school, our children authentically seemed to like being at home with us and told us quite a bit about their lives. I'm sure they both have plenty of secrets of their own, but that's to be expected. What's important to me is that Max and I have a much better relationship with them than either of us would have imagined with our own parents.

Their high school held an annual spring play, and Arica chose to work on it behind the scenes during her sophomore year. She might have been interested after hearing me lovingly reminisce about my acting days, but no matter her reason for joining, she was assigned to oversee costumes.

After learning how to sew and doing some research on historical dresses, Arica discovered fashion was her passion. She combined her love of drawing and her new obsession with fabrics and style to create breathtaking outfits.

Max and I were in awe of how naturally and effortlessly it all came together for her and skyrocketed her interest and enthusiasm. Fashion had never been something I was good at, but I tried to absorb more information as she talked about it.

As the saying goes, the days are long, but the years are short. Before we knew it, our daughter had concluded her junior year. It was time to begin preparing her to choose a college and leave our cozy little nest. She systematically narrowed down her list of potential schools based on their curriculum offerings and applied only to her top six choices.

Despite Max and I urging her to widen the net just in case, she insisted. If none of them accepted her now, she would find a way to meet their criteria and start next semester or the following school year. There was no convincing her otherwise, which I recognized as either her dad's tenacious perseverance or my bullheaded stubbornness…

Whatever it's called, it worked. She got accepted to four of the six, so she had to choose between New York City, Rhode Island, or Massachusetts.

We visited the two in New York City as a family during fall break of her senior year and had an awesome time enjoying the Big Apple. Both schools were so focused on fashion and artistic design I thought she wouldn't be able to resist the call of city life among art folks like her. I would have been thrilled to visit her there!

Over spring break, the four of us flew back out east to review the other two schools. We started in Providence to see the Rhode Island School of Design (RISD), and we walked around campus and along the river. The area was beautiful as the warm springtime sunshine was coaxing the trees and flowers to life. The history of the place was prevalent everywhere we went, and it had a quieter, more distinguished atmosphere.

We then took a train to Boston to visit the Massachusetts College of Art and Design and spent some time enjoying the landmarks and famous places. It was the smallest school on her list, but there are many colleges in the surrounding areas. Arica would have an abundance of fellow students to mingle with, which we thought she'd love.

To our surprise, she chose RISD over the New York and Boston options. She said it felt like a home-away-from-home as we were touring the campus. She was enthralled by the classical architecture mixed with the artsy ambiance, she had been inspired by every conversation she had with other students, and she couldn't wait to go.

Wow, our baby girl was going to college halfway across the country! It would be a monumental change that was starting to sink in for all four of us.

The next few months were a whirlwind of her prom, high school finals, and graduation, and of course getting everything prepared for her departure. Prom involved a large amount of shopping, complaining, scrutinizing, and FINALLY choosing a dress. She would have looked gorgeous in most anything in the stores, but she was persistent in finding something stylish and reflective of her personality in the way she wanted. It was a humongous relief when she told me she decided.

She had been working in the costume department of our local community theatre since her junior year, and they were sad to see her wrap up her time with them. They didn't get a lot of helpers with Arica's level of ambition! She wasn't paid much, but she loved it and it gave her a great head start for college. We gladly helped subsidize what she needed for her dorm room and food.

And then there was the clothing.

As a fashion aficionado who was going to be around many more like her, she was extremely particular about what she wanted to wear during her first year of college. Tragically, we were unable to afford the upscale apparel she truly desired. Nor could we rent a fleet of semi-trucks to drive her whole wardrobe and furniture to Rhode Island. Much to her dismay, she had the difficult task of limiting what she would take.

In her entire time in high school, she and I never argued as much as we did over her outfits in the month before she left. As a mom, I had an obligation to advise her to be practical and plan for walking between buildings when the weather was windy, rainy, cold, etc. You would have thought I demanded she cut off her own arm!

Her overly-dramatic outbursts flared up nearly once a day. I made every effort not to yell, but I wasn't perfect at that endeavor. My tone was primarily exasperation. Max and Dawson learned to be anywhere other than our vicinity when those exchanges took place. By the end of July, we were all counting the hours until Arica left for RISD...

But when the day came for us to load the rented box truck, we were a solemn bunch. Between that and our family SUV, we switched drivers and vehicles on and off during pit stops and after meals. We had all agreed to drive straight through the fifteen-plus hours and sleep when we arrived in Providence.

We crashed gratefully into bed after the long trip and took our time the next morning. We got Arica moved in and had dinner with her roommate and her parents. We'd had several video chats over the past six weeks, but it was a pleasant evening talking to them in person.

Then came the dreaded goodbye part.

Outside the residence hall, Max hugged Arica and reminded her about safety and calling us as much as possible. She was nodding and both of them struggled to hold back tears. Dawson gave his sister a quick one-armed hug *(boys!)* and told her to text him all the things he should know about college so he could decide if it's worth it.

When I stepped up, she squeezed me tight and immediately commenced crying.

I rubbed her back and said, "Sweetie, you'll be fine! You've been looking forward to this for months; you're ready."

"Yeah, I just can't believe it's here after all this waiting. Mom, I realize I've been a pain in the butt this summer, and I'm sorry I got so mad at you. I knew deep down your advice was right, but I didn't want to hear it. Thanks for helping me be more prepared for this."

It was my turn to begin crying. We hugged long and hard one more time before she wiped her cheeks and said she was tired and ready to go upstairs. Max took my hand as we watched our firstborn child walk into her dorm building and toward her beautiful future.

I wept all the way back to our hotel, up to our room, and into bed. My dear husband held me as my sobbing slowed to sniffles and we drifted off to sleep.

Dawson didn't start his junior year of high school for another couple of weeks, and Max and I had the week off as vacation time. The three of us leisurely drove back home, making a few stops for sightseeing and doing touristy stuff. Arica called a handful of times to ask if we'd seen something she couldn't find or to help her figure something out.

I teased her about abandoning me to be the only female in a house full of testosterone. Dawson implored her to stop calling because it was easier for him to guilt us into buying him things as our only child. We were happy to see her smiling and laughing. She seemed to be settling in quite nicely, but I believe there was comfort in our familiar and loving voices that made her feel more grounded.

At home, the three of us adjusted to a new normal without Arica in the house. Dawson switched his part-time job from a fast-food place to a grocery store that paid better and slid right back into his routine of working and school.

As our kids were busy with their own lives, Max and I were both dealing with the declining health of our parents. My father was showing signs of dementia. Max's mom was diagnosed with acute leukemia and sadly passed away less than eight months later. We navigated unknown territory with her death in December of 2018, and I did my best to be Max's support system during that difficult time. My mother-in-law had done a lot for us over the years and cared deeply for her entire family.

There's no way to prepare for the pain of losing a parent.

Arica flew back for Christmas as soon as her finals were done, so she was able to be home when we buried her grandmother. It was a challenging holiday with the recent loss, but it was also gratifying to have all four of us under one roof again to console each other.

Max's dad Louis did not do well with being a widower. They married when he was twenty years old, and he couldn't comprehend how to be alone. Max and his brothers banded together to take care of my father-in-law until he adjusted to his new reality.

Arica loved her school, classes, and making connections with quite a few classmates her first semester. She told us at Christmas that she wanted to stay out there over spring break and do some sightseeing with her friends. Her choice was sad news for Max and me, but she was too happy to say no.

Dawson's job at the grocery store lasted through Christmas. Something happened not long after the new year, and he abruptly quit without telling Max or me many details. Dawson was bored almost immediately, so we gave him some small home projects to work on. That was beneficial for everyone, but it wasn't enough. He stayed jobless for a month or so and then decided he couldn't stand having so much free time on his hands and no money coming in.

He started looking again and got hired at a landscaping company. They were ramping up for the spring season and badly needed physical laborers. Dawson liked it a lot due to the variety of tasks to do. In addition, it was hard work and actually tired him out! He seemed to be fine with the different types of weather, and he and his boss Sal got along well.

Meanwhile, my mom chose to be the sole caretaker for my dad as his mental acuity deteriorated. Leo was thankfully closer to her geographically because I struggled to help much while being two hours away. I already had an overflowing plate with maintaining a full-time job and finishing raising my children.

Arica arrived home for summer, and it was easy to see how she'd changed during her freshman undergraduate year. My baby was a grown adult! It made my momma heart burst with pride but also break a bit that she wasn't our little girl anymore.

She hadn't planned on working, but Max and I insisted she do something to earn some money and stay busy. It would have been lovely to spend every day with her while I still could, but we inevitably would have driven each other crazy. She landed a position in a higher-end clothing store to be around her beloved fashion and get a firsthand glimpse at the newest style trends.

Dawson finished his junior year of high school and took as many hours as he could at the landscaping company. We wondered if he would pursue college, but we decided to give our son more time to think about it before we began pressuring him to make any choices.

The months sped by with all four of us constantly coming and going. We commemorated both kids' birthdays in June and July, they were now nineteen and seventeen.

Dawson thrived that summer and entered his senior year as a tan, strong, tall young man with a lot more confidence. Arica flew back to RISD, and our routine went back to what the three of us were used to.

Max and I reached our twentieth anniversary in September – an impressive milestone! With everything going on, we chose to keep our celebration simpler. We took an extended weekend trip to Chicago for some fine dining, live theatre, museum visits, and a stroll along Navy Pier and the lakeshore. The weather was gorgeous, the lake was serene, and we entertained ourselves with people-watching and making up stories about some of them. It was an enjoyable getaway, and everywhere we ate made us feel special.

Dawson was doing very well in his classes, but we knew it was difficult for him to sit still and stay focused in school for so long each day. Max and I tried several times to subtly urge our son to vocalize his plans for the future. The suspense got the better of me the week before Thanksgiving, when I gave up on the hinting and passive comments and confronted him.

"D, what are you thinking for after high school? If you're going to go to college, we really need to move on that. Things take longer than you might realize! There's applying, waiting for the responses, maybe some visits to campuses where you are accepted, picking the one you want. Then there's paperwork to fill out and stuff to pay for.

It might seem like you still have tons of time, but it's already the middle of November, and that only leaves you with a few months until you should be making firm commitments before the deadlines hit. We want to support you, but first you gotta figure out what your next steps will be."

"Yeah, I know, Mom. I've been thinking about it a lot, and I still can't decide. I'm not sure college is for me, I have no idea what I would study if I went. I'm pretty good with computers, but I just don't see an office job as what I want to do for the rest of my life. I love working for Sal and I'm making decent money, but it's not my long-term goal to stay there. I hate being so indecisive, but I can't figure out what I want right now."

His face had a look of anguish for not giving me a better answer, and I struggled with how to reply. I flashed back to his younger days of bouncing around to different hobbies and never settling on one that gave him joy. This was purely his nature and we couldn't force it.

I hugged him and said, "Okay, sweetie. That's fine, thank you for your honesty. Let's not rush into something that may be a bad fit for you." He seemed relieved when I didn't push the issue any further, we left it there for now.

After reviewing the conversation with Max, we both felt helpless. Max is a doer – he examines, identifies a solution, and wants to act right away to solve the problem. I'm a planner, professionally and personally. In this case, neither of us had any advice about what to do next for Dawson. It came so easily for Arica, but now we had a gigantic question mark and no answers for our son.

Being a parent is a complicated journey.

D then told us after Christmas he wanted to take a gap year after high school to determine what he would do next. We agreed but also asked him to do some serious research into careers that might interest him. Whether he chose to go to college, a trade school, or find a profession that didn't require further education, he needed to commit to **something**. He was fine with our requests; he yearned to feel at least some of the passion he'd seen in his sister and a few of his friends.

Arica came home for the holidays, and at Christmas she said she had been hearing about a scary, bad new virus going around. It was making people much sicker than the flu and could potentially be fatal.

Max and I didn't know about it, so we chalked it up to rumors. We told her to be careful and try to avoid going out a lot if the illness was that prevalent in her area. She and Dawson both went back to classes after the first of the year, and things returned to normal.

Or so we thought…

When the COVID-19 pandemic hit nationwide, everything we were accustomed to came to a screeching halt. Our schedules were completely upended when school shut down in March 2020. Arica was panicking about trying to come home when so many flights were being cancelled, but we managed to book her a seat and got her back safely.

She and Dawson had just started spring break, and we thought they would resume classes as usual after that week. No such luck. When we got the emails about switching to virtual learning and the new plans of when everyone needed to be online each morning, we resentfully adjusted.

Then both Max and I were instructed to work from home until further notice. We had four people used to constant activities, suddenly with nowhere to go and no indication as to how long things would be this way. We were miserable for weeks trying to find a routine where all of us attended meetings and classes on schedules with no rhyme or reason at first. We all tried to carve out spaces in our house to be on the phone or video calls while not disturbing anyone else.

The kids were going stir-crazy without the in-person interactions at school and work and the freedom they'd taken for granted. Max and I were concerned about keeping our jobs if the economy tanked during the crisis. It was all frightening and chaotic.

Dawson didn't care much about missing his senior prom, but he **was** bummed he wouldn't graduate with the traditional pageantry and his classmates around him. His mental health worried me a few times throughout his final semester. Fortunately, we were able to keep our heads above water and, after a while, he seemed better.

Even though Arica despised being in the house 24/7, she and her friends established alternative outlets for gossiping about boys, TikTok videos, and celebrities' fashion choices rather quickly. She lamented that she was being cheated out of her college experience, but the video dates alleviated some of her discontent. Her grades slipped a tad, but we didn't feel justified in getting upset with her given the circumstances.

Max and I acclimated to grocery shopping online and bought masks for everyone. We checked in on grandparents and other family members periodically, and all of us did our best not to drive each other insane. We found ways to enjoy time together with board games, more frequent movie nights, and making dinner, but we also made sure there was ample time alone when necessary.

Dawson maintained decent grades despite the situation. For a kid who didn't care for school, he accomplished a lot scholastically! He graduated under unusual conditions due to everything being virtual, although his school did a respectable job of trying to make the seniors feel recognized and commended.

We still ordered him a cap and gown to take pictures, and we invited a few close family members to come celebrate in early June. We apologized to Dawson that we weren't comfortable hosting a party with all his friends. He understood it was beyond our control and was primarily glad to put studying and tests in his rearview mirror. Max and I were now parents of two high school graduates. Time sure flies!

Our summer was not exactly a fun one, yet it still sped by as it always does. Max and I visited our respective parents on many weekends, sometimes together. We convinced my mom to move my dad into an assisted living facility once the COVID dangers passed. Max took turns with his brothers to make sure their dad got out of the house some and kept up on bills and chores. Arica and Dawson were part of some of those trips, but we tried to spare them as much as we could.

Dawson started picking up hours at Sal's brother's excavating company. He was intimidated by the giant equipment and large-scale projects at first but was captivated by the powerful changes those machines made. We had a festive night for his eighteenth birthday in July with a few of his close friends, which was a joyful break from the fear and isolation of 2020.

Not long after that, it was time to get everything prepared for Arica to head back east for her junior year. The campus was going to be open for returning students who wanted to attend in-person, but some courses would be hybrid and others would be adjusted to smaller class sizes to maximize social distancing. They also warned that things could be closed again without advance notice if outbreaks occurred. As parents, we worried, but our daughter was confident she was ready to face the challenges and stay healthy.

Prior to the shutdown, Arica had already made plans to move into an apartment with three of her friends. Max, Dawson, and I all took some time off work, and the four of us drove out a week early to help her transfer her belongings.

We were able to enjoy some quality time together at last, it was great! Arica showed us all her favorite places on campus; we went sightseeing around Providence; we went down to Newport and the ocean; and we all relaxed and laughed like old times.

Arica took Dawson with her to a friend's apartment one night *(she avoided calling it a party in front of us, but we had our suspicions)*. They stayed overnight at someone else's place who had empty bedrooms before the curriculum resumed.

With both kids gone, Max and I treated ourselves to a lovely date night in Providence, ordering takeout from a fancy restaurant and eating delicious seafood down by the water. We talked about our college days, what we envisioned for Arica and Dawson in the next few years, and other topics except the responsibilities we left back home. It was a refreshing reprieve and lifted our spirits more than I could have hoped. We knew it was temporary, but we held onto the peace while we had it.

~ *Chapter 5* ~

Big Changes

The three of us came home and returned to jobs and elder parental care. Unfortunately, my father passed away not quite a month afterward.

We told Arica she didn't need to come back from school, it would have drastically interrupted her studying. In addition, last-minute flights were not easy to find (or afford). She voiced her guilt about not going to the services, but we convinced her it was okay not to juggle everything to make it work.

My mom was a heartbroken mess. It fell on me to help make arrangements and spread the news out to family, friends, and the community. My brothers took care of our mother while Max and I figured out what needed to be done with the morgue, their church, and the funeral home.

At the visitation, most of the attendees were relatives, many of whom we hadn't seen in several years. It was bittersweet to reconnect with my cousins, and we all pledged to do a better job of keeping in touch. Memories were shared that I hadn't thought of in decades. We even had some good laughs about our parents playing tricks on each other when we were younger. It was a nice reminder for me that my dad had once been more carefree than he was for the majority of the time I lived with him.

The next day was the burial, which was dreary and drizzly to match our moods. The priest graciously kept it short, and we took my mom back to her place. Some family members and a few church friends came over to bring food and condolences throughout the afternoon and evening. Nobody stayed very long, which was great since mom wanted to go to bed early.

Max and I spent the night with her; Dawson already left earlier in the day. Micah and his wife Elise would be there in the morning to keep my mom company for the next couple of days.

Max turned fifty in October, and his birthday was conveniently on a Sunday. Dawson and Arica arranged for her to fly home Friday after class, unbeknownst to both me and Max. D picked her up at the airport and walked in the house like nothing was amiss. Arica suddenly popped out from behind him, and they yelled Happy Birthday in unison – surprise achieved!

We'd also planned a small secret party on Saturday. We ordered dinner to be delivered from his favorite local restaurant. We timed it perfectly so when the doorbell first rang, Max thought it was the meal, only to find people walking in with presents and well-wishes! Max said he felt loved and celebrated, which was the goal.

The rest of fall presented new challenges for me as I did my best to finish everything for my dad's estate and help Mom figure out what she wanted to do next. After lengthy discussions with Max, we offered for her to come live with us, and she said she'd consider it.

At Thanksgiving, she wasn't comfortable driving the two hours to our house by herself, so Dawson volunteered to go get her. I think it really cheered up my mom to be around the bustle and noise and most importantly, her grandchildren.

Arica and I chose to drive her back home on the Saturday afterward. We told Max and Dawson it was girls only, no boys allowed! It was a fun road trip spending some valuable time with my mother and daughter, a lovely memory that will always be a highlight for me.

I called my mom on Monday to make sure she was doing all right. She said she'd had a very good time with us, but it reminded her just how alone she was in her condo.

She couldn't visit with friends much due to COVID restrictions, especially for older folks.

She asked if Max and I would still be okay with her moving in. I assured her we were, and she said she'd like to take us up on it. It would be a relief not to keep making the drive back and forth so often anymore. But it was also going to be a ton of work for the transition and organizing a brand-new living arrangement for all of us.

I told Max, and we started a checklist of things we'd need to do in preparation, as well as what we would ask my mom to handle at her own place. There were many concerns, but at heart I believed this was the best option for everyone. I texted my brothers the news, they were both supportive and said they'd help however they could.

By Christmas, we'd been able to check several projects off our list with Dawson's invaluable assistance. He was a trooper by coming home from work and digging into what needed to be done without complaint. I was grateful he chose to stay home his first year after high school, we would have spent much more time and energy without him.

Thanks to our son, we created a bedroom space on the first floor by adding a wall between the dining room and what we call the front room, which had never gotten a lot of use over the years. We ordered a Murphy bed set, and Dawson did the majority of the labor setting up. Max helped him with the heavy lifting and bolting it into the wall studs appropriately.

We also added another section of wall and a door to the open area to make it a proper room. It was gratifying to see them working hard and well as a father and son team, it had been a while since they'd had a mission to execute together.

Dawson sometimes had to stop and ask us questions, which caused him (and us) to learn a lot. He diligently watched instructional videos when none of us were exactly sure of how to do something, and he did an awesome job on following directions and figuring it out.

Meanwhile, I spent an enormous amount of time on the phone with my mom. We talked through the things she should pack for her first few weeks vs. long-term and what she wouldn't need once she got here. Leo and I worked together on getting her doctors switched to our area and instructions on how to change her address and cancel her utilities when the time came.

Arica was awestruck at Christmas by how much we'd done and praised our efforts. She said she wanted to help pick out some of the accessories like curtains, bedding, and rugs. That was fine with the rest of us for sure! She also ended up choosing the paint color, matching lamps, a watercolor painting, and a cushy recliner chair for the room.

She and Dawson went to the hardware store for the paint and supplies, and they knocked it out in one day since only the bed was in there so far. It was really starting to look like a cozy bedroom! Arica told us she was sad she had to go back to school before everything arrived because she was super excited to see it all come together. She made us promise to send pictures when we got it all arranged.

The hardest change to make was to expand our ground floor half bath into a full bath so my mom wouldn't need to go upstairs. Even in early 2021, it was still challenging to find a contractor who would take on new clients because of the pandemic. Thanks to referrals from friends, we finally reached out to one who agreed to tackle the job with our favorite local plumber.

Dawson took a vested interest in the renovation and would evaluate the progress every day when he got home from work. He made sure everything looked like it should and they were staying on track to complete things when they told us they would.

They finished near the end of January, we painted and tidied up from the two months of construction, and we felt like we were almost entirely prepared for the move. I had been to visit my mom twice to pack up and donate and clean, and Leo purged and cleaned a lot as well. He was working with a realtor he knew to get the condo ready to put on the market. We all decided the first Saturday in February would be the official moving day.

Dawson convinced a couple of his paternal cousins and some of his co-workers into helping us both load and unload the rented box truck. Max and I were able to do lighter physical work and be with my mom while the youngsters did the hard stuff.

Mom was very happy with her space! She kept expressing her gratitude and how phenomenal the bedroom and bathroom renovations were. We video chatted with Arica the next day so she could hear directly from her grandma how charming the room was.

It was a strange and slow adjustment period after adding my elderly mother to our daily routines. Max, Dawson, and I all helped her with tasks that were difficult for her while also finding time for each of us to be alone in the house for our own interests.

My fiftieth birthday was on a Saturday in March, and it came up fast on me with everything else I was dealing with. In the morning, Max brought me my favorite French toast for breakfast in bed, made by my mom and son. Dawson then entered the room with fanfare playing on his phone and presented me with a crown, scepter, and a light purple cape with a furry border. They deemed me Queen for the Day!

They came back to pick up my tray and dishes after I finished. Max handed me a card with a gift certificate for a massage and manicure at a local spa at 1 p.m. He and my mom came up with the idea together and wanted to treat me to a luxurious pampering fit for a monarch. *(I do love a good theme!)* They advised me to shower and come downstairs for more royal treatment.

When I descended the steps in my crown and cape, the three of them noisily wished me happy birthday! The kitchen and living room were festooned with fun queenly decorations, and I admired the cohesiveness of it all.

Dawson informed me the motif had been Arica's idea and handed me a gift. The card included a loving message from my daughter saying she was very sorry she couldn't leave school to be here and would give me lots of extra hugs when she was home soon. There were also some of my favorite chocolate treats, and D took a picture of me with all of them to send to his sister.

My mom beamed with joy when I thanked her for the French toast. She said she couldn't believe her oldest child was half a century old!

After spending a fabulous couple of hours at the spa, I was on cloud nine when I returned home. As I walked in the door, suddenly all the lights went on and a dozen or so people yelled HAPPY BIRTHDAY at me! I was stunned, and more so when I saw that Stacey flew in for this!

My brother Leo and each one of my friends and neighbors hugged me, Dawson and my mom passed out champagne, and Max entered with a beautiful cake. Everyone sang to me, including Arica on video with Dawson and Micah and family on video with Leo. Kate recorded everything on her phone because she always remembers important things like that.

I opened presents and laughed and had a fantastic time. People started saying their goodbyes, and Max told me the last thing on the agenda was a regal feast at my favorite restaurant. It was a delicious meal with most of my favorite humans, and I felt supremely loved.

I was impressed they were able to surprise me; I was blissfully unaware anything had been planned! Without a doubt, this birthday celebration was my best yet.

By the time Arica came home for spring break, we were in a moderately comfortable schedule with my mom as part of the household. During her week with us, Arica broke the news that she applied for a few different internships out east and was anxiously waiting to hear back from them.

If she got accepted, she asked if we'd bring some things out to her at the end of the school year. That way she could avoid coming back and then turning right around to start working. She might also need some business attire if they had a dress code. We of course agreed, and we were thankful she took the initiative to pursue the opportunities.

We'd been so entrenched in all the craziness, I hadn't even thought to suggest she look into internships. After she left, I confessed to Max that I was feeling like a bad mom. He scolded me that our children are now adults and we shouldn't have to do everything for them anymore.

He was right, but it's still difficult for me to turn off the parental mode.

Once I had time to think about it, I realized I was quite upset about Arica not being home over the summer. The past one hadn't exactly been sensational with the pandemic ruining so many plans, and I guess a small part of me thought maybe we'd make up for it this year. I sensed our time was quickly running out before she was wholly independent and we would see her less and less.

When my mom moved in, she still had her car. She was not in the best condition to be driving around, particularly in an area she didn't know too well. I had already committed to taking her to most of the places she needed to go. Max or Dawson were Plan B if I had a work obligation. Plan C was arranging an Uber or Lyft if necessary.

We decided to sell the kids' high school car and let them use my mom's instead. It was much newer and had more modern accessories, so Dawson was happy with the upgrade.

The next months were filled with work, taking my mom to doctor appointments, and helping Max with his dad on occasion. My father-in-law was doing a lot better on his own, but we still tried to assist around his house when we had the chance. He needed guidance on the landscaping and yardwork that my mother-in-law used to lovingly care for, and Dawson was well-suited for that.

Arica was accepted to an internship in New York City *(woo hoo!)* and she immersed herself in planning for it. As a result, she texted me regularly about her thoughts and what she should do about her living situation.

She was nervous that they offered her a stipend for an apartment, but it probably wouldn't cover her entire amount. Plus, she'd need to buy all her meals at New York City prices and send money for her share of rent and utilities back at school. Then she worried about figuring out how to use the subway because she couldn't pay for a taxi all the time.

I was barely able to keep up with her questions and concerns, so we arranged to talk on the weekend and put together a list. That way she could work on one thing at a time to make her feel better. She hadn't mentioned clothes again yet, which I was dreading. In the meantime, I told myself to remain optimistic that it wouldn't turn into a huge confrontation like before.

She and I worked out a plan of action she seemed comfortable with, and we scheduled time to talk the following weekend about what we accomplished.

How on earth did people figure out what to do about these kinds of obstacles without the internet? It was baffling to me when my evenings consisted of hours of NYC research. The upside was that my mom and I found a multitude of fun things to do. We decided we might spend some extra time there once Arica got moved in.

Dawson's work schedule began getting busier with the warm weather, so we saw less of him. He was now in charge of several crews and had some fairly important projects. It was great for his résumé and bank account but also exhausting even for an almost nineteen-year-old.

He wasn't quite as enamored as he used to be, but I didn't say a word and let him process his feelings on his own. He caught Max and me lounging on the couch one Friday night and sat down with us.

"I've been thinking a lot lately about what I want to do. I'm just not enjoying the landscaping work as much anymore, and battling the elements is getting old. I miss using technology and math and some of the software programs that challenge my brain. Sitting at a desk all day every day still isn't ideal for me either, so I'm trying to find alternatives.

When Dad and I were building the bedroom for Grandma Wilder and I was helping Grandpa G. fix up his house, I got really excited about those projects. Because of that, I investigated some options for construction and architectural design.

I don't want to go back to a lot of school, but I think it's possible to get into an apprenticeship program. I'm sure I'll do well on the entrance exams, I've heard they're pretty straightforward. My landscaping knowledge should help, especially the excavations where we prepared land for new buildings and parking lots. If I'm admitted, there's a counseling office I can go to and get advice on which program might be best for me."

Max took the lead, "That's fantastic, D! I can't wait to hear what you find out. Apprenticeship is a great idea, and your mom and I are here to support you if you need us."

"Thanks. I appreciate that, but I'm on it. I'll fill you in when I have more information."

I said, "We're really proud of you, D. This is stellar progress!"

When he left the room, Max and I high-fived to applaud our son finally having a plan in place!

Dividing and conquering the assignments, Max, Arica, and I got all the important details finalized for her summer internship. We made plans to fly out a few days after classes ended. Mom had never been to New York City; she was thrilled to be part of the trip. Dawson had too much going on with work, so he opted to stay home.

The three of us had a lot to take with us per Arica's detailed instructions on what she wanted for her summer wardrobe, including several of her own outfit creations from class projects. Her self-assurance in front of other fashion lovers was admirable!

We timed our arrivals so Arica landed about thirty-five minutes before us and waited at the airport. We went from there to our hotel to drop off our bags, and then to her new apartment and got her set up. After that, we walked to the nearest subway station, and Max showed her where she needed to go and which app to download to her phone.

Her apartment and work location were several blocks off the busy area of Manhattan, but it wouldn't take long for her to find her way around once she understood the city layout better.

The overstimulating aspects of the city seemed kind of scary for her, but I was confident she would do well here. Besides, it was only for ten weeks. If she didn't like it in NYC, she didn't have to seek a job here later.

We ate dinner at an eclectic restaurant near her apartment, explored the vicinity a little, and walked her home.

We slept well and called Arica in the morning. She was fine and wanted some time to acclimate to her new surroundings, so the three of us were on our own for a while.

We took the subway to Central Park and explored for a bit, then we started walking down Fifth Avenue and seeing all the famous shops. My mom wanted to stop and gawk at the things she'd only seen in movies and on TV. With her age and slight hip issues, it was slow going. By the time we got down to Rockefeller Center and Saks, we were all ready for a break. We had a late lunch and took an Uber back to our hotel to rest.

Arica called later and asked if she could come hang out with us at the hotel. My mom excitedly told her everything we saw. We then took a cab over to Times Square to see it all lit up at night, which was quite a sight. We went into a few shops around there and stayed for the Midnight Moment when all the screens are synchronized to show the same graphic, which was neat.

We took the subway to drop Arica off. Max reminded her that late night trains were on a different schedule, and she should never ride them alone at night anyway. She indulged him with a nod and smile, but I was uncertain whether she would adhere to his advice.

The following two days were much the same with the three of us sightseeing during the day and meeting Arica for dinner. Our favorite outings were going to a Broadway play, taking a boat out to see the Statue of Liberty, and touring the sobering but impactful 9/11 memorial and museum.

She said she was ready for her first day of work tomorrow, and we wished her well. We were staying one more day and then leaving the following afternoon.

She called us when she was done the next evening.

"This was the best day! Everyone was so nice and helpful, and I got lots of compliments on my outfit! It was reassuring to hear that from experts in fashion! One lady even asked where I got it, and she was amazed when I told her I made it at school. Can you believe it?"

We said we could not, although she paused only briefly for our response before eagerly continuing.

"My boss showed me around this morning, and I met quite a few of the people I'll be working with. I hope I can remember at least half of their names tomorrow!

Then I sat in on a meeting to hear the team's update from last week. I didn't get most of what they were talking about, but I know by the end of the summer I'll be able to understand it all!

We got busy and didn't go to lunch until late, so I'm not very hungry right now. Plus, I'm totally wiped out from today, my brain feels like mush. Are you okay if I'm not up for going out to dinner?"

I replied, "Of course, sweetie, that's completely understandable. We can come to your place and say our goodbyes, and then you can get some rest for tomorrow."

"Thanks, mom. I appreciate you and dad and Grandma Wilder coming out here with me and for being flexible when I have a lot going on."

The three of us packed up the next morning, ate brunch, and headed home. We were happily exhausted with tons of remarkable memories. It would be fun to go through all the pictures with Dawson and tell him about our adventures.

As always, summer came and went. We spent quality time with my mom and her sisters, as well as several members of Max's family. We hosted a Fourth of July party with friends and relatives, which also included an early celebration of Dawson's nineteenth birthday. My brother Micah, Elise, and their kids came to visit for Independence Day, and Leo joined us too. My mom was ecstatic about all three of her children being together with her and seeing her grandchildren from so far away. It was a much better summer than the past two had been, we were glad to relax and savor it.

Arica was having an amazing time in NYC, and she told us she was fine with getting herself back to school before classes started, so we didn't have to come out there again. She would just need to ship a few boxes home of things she wouldn't use during her senior year. It was hard to believe she was close to completing college!

In other awesome news, Dawson said he'd done a lot of research about apprenticeships and talked to Sal and some others about what they suggested. Consequently, he decided what he wanted to do.

He applied to the program of his choice and got accepted to start on October 1, and he was looking forward to it. Sal was sad to see him go, but he was very supportive and generously gave Dawson a small set of higher-end tools as a parting gift.

Dawson started his program and was instantaneously busy with projects and working more hours than we expected. He seemed to love it though, and we were grateful for his happiness.

Arica was planning to come home for Thanksgiving, but unfortunately, she was quite sick and had to cancel her trip. We hadn't seen her since May, which was the longest stretch we'd ever been apart from our kids. Max tried to remind me that this was practice for the near future, but that made it even worse!

The winter weather was harsh, and I was nervous that Arica's travel plans for Christmas would be disrupted. Luckily, her flight left before a snowstorm hit the East Coast and she made it home just fine.

Arica turned twenty-one over the summer in New York, but since we didn't get to celebrate with her, we planned a fun party while she was home. Several members of Max's family stayed the night on our couches and in the guest room. Dawson and one of his cousins were our designated drivers. Although they couldn't drink with us, they enjoyed it as much as anyone considering they witnessed all of us getting tipsy and hilarious!

Max's dad and my mom laughed heartily at different points of the evening, it was rewarding to be sharing this with our remaining parents.

We had a lovely Christmas and New Year's Eve as a family, even Dawson stayed home with us to ring in 2022. I suspect he missed his sister but didn't want to admit it!

I reflected on the past year and all it had entailed, which was a lot!

This time last year, we were finishing building the bedroom for Mom and getting ready to renovate the bathroom. It took weeks to get all the annoying drywall dust vacuumed up!

We moved Mom in and slowly but surely adjusted to having her as part of the household.

My 50th was so fun, that was definitely the highlight of my year!

Max and I took Mom out to New York City to get Arica started in her internship, which was a good time. The Big Apple never disappoints, and Mom really loved seeing so many famous things.

Dawson made some great decisions about his future, and he seems to be happy with what he chose.

We had to survive many months without seeing our daughter, but now she's home and my heart is full. I wonder what she's planning for after college. Will she want to come back here, or is she going to stay out east? Ugh, that's going to be so hard for me if she does. This year will bring some more big changes, I'm sure of that.

The colder winter made it harder for my mom to leave the house as much. Her hip was bothering her horribly, and she was petrified of slipping on ice or snow. As a result, she spent a lot of time in the house in her recliner or on the couch, which caused her hip to stiffen up more often.

By the time I realized how bad it was, it had been deteriorating for a while. We booked an appointment with her physician for some scans and to see what could be done. I scolded her for not saying something earlier, but she was stubborn *(where do you think I got that trait?)* and didn't want to burden us with something else.

Her doctor concluded that surgery was the best solution to fix the issue once and for all. We weighed the options of surgically repairing both hips at the same time or just the bad one first and seeing if that was sufficient. Regardless of what she chose, they didn't have any openings until late April. Being more than two months away wasn't optimal, but we scheduled it anyway.

Arica decided to spend her final college spring break out east, which didn't surprise us. The unexpected part was that she would be in Boston for some of it, visiting her new boyfriend! We knew she'd been dating someone, but we didn't realize they were in a relationship enough for her to go stay with him. She enthusiastically told us about their meet-cute in Providence shortly after Christmas break.

"So, I was standing in the coffee shop Saturday morning waiting for my drink, and the barista called out my name. She actually said it correctly, which was fabulous that she'd listened to me when I ordered. I took my cup and thanked her, and then I planned to leave.

But as I was walking toward the door, this quiet voice said, "Excuse me" as I passed a guy sitting alone at a table. I wasn't sure he was talking to me, but I stopped and looked at him to check. He smiled at me and said my name was unusual, like most people do, but then he told me it's his sister's name as well. This was the only other time he'd heard it, so he had to say something.

I was surprised, but I gave him my spiel about how it's more common than most people realize, Mom heard it in the '90s and loved it, blah, blah, blah. He introduced himself as Christopher, but he prefers to be called Topher and definitely not Chris." She chuckled fondly at his strong feelings about the nickname.

"Anyway, Topher invited me to join him for coffee, so I sat down and we started talking. He lives near Boston, but his job takes him to Providence and New York City quite often, so obviously we had a lot to chat about there. We never ran out of conversation topics, so we just continued until we ended up going down the street to have lunch together!

We've been texting a ton and video chatting after work, and he took the train down to Providence a couple of times on the weekend so we could go out for proper dates. He also tells me when he's going to be in town for work and we meet for lunch or coffee again or whatever he has time for."

She was more serious as she told us, "I really like him. I've been so busy with my senior project and working part-time that I haven't spent as much time with him as I want. That's why I plan to take half of spring break to unwind and let him show me around Boston. I haven't been there since we checked out the colleges, so it will be nice to get a better sense of it with someone who knows the city so well."

Max and I listened to her ramble on, both of us locked in our own thoughts. From our daughter who has been so focused on her classes and future career, hearing her this smitten over a boy was new for us!

When she finished, I chimed in with, "Wow, that's really exciting for you! Topher sounds great, I hope we get to meet him soon. It's my motherly duty to tell you to be careful in Boston, but also, have a wonderful time!"

Max added, "I second all of what your mom said, please text us when you get back to Providence. We love you."

After our call, Max and I glanced at each other in awe about her goofy girliness. We were happy for her, but I was simultaneously apprehensive about her spending days with a young man in a different city. I was all too aware of what could happen, and my maternal instincts were on alert.

Dawson was excelling in his apprenticeship, and he often told us over dinner about the new things he was learning. Max, my mom, and I asked him questions when we didn't know what he was describing, and he would patiently explain so we understood them. When we shared Arica's news with him, he was pensive for a few minutes.

"I wonder if he's the one and only for her. She's picky and doesn't get all mushy about this stuff, so it must be pretty serious." When he saw my shocked face, he laughed and told me, "Chill, Mom, she's smart and she won't rush into anything!"

Fortunately, Arica's trip went better than she expected, my worries were for naught. She got to meet Topher's sister Arica (who they affectionately call Ari), their parents, and even their grandfather. She adored each of them and couldn't say enough positive comments about them. She and Ari bonded over clothes and makeup, which made me briefly think of Ginny and me around the same age.

She and Topher had a terrific few days together, she loved seeing Boston through his eyes. I started to wonder if Dawson was wise beyond his years, at least about his sister.

My mom's mobility was getting worse, and I hoped her surgeon's office would call and tell us there'd been a cancellation and they could get her in earlier. Instead, my mom came down with a sinus infection the week prior to her scheduled date, and they wanted to postpone until her immune system was stronger.

Super.

They were able to fit us into an appointment at the end of May right before Memorial Day weekend, so we took it.

In the meantime, we had to figure out what to do about Arica graduating from college, getting her and her belongings back home, and what her next plans were. She had already asked us if we were okay with selling most of the furniture and bigger things to other RISD undergrads. There was an online marketplace for students enrolled in the school and it would save us a lot of trouble. We consented, it meant we didn't have to rent another large truck. With fewer big items, we'd only need a small trailer to tow behind our SUV instead.

As graduation got closer, I expressed my concerns to Max about trying to take my mom with us. She was stoked to see Arica walk across the stage in her cap and gown, but she clearly couldn't move around well.

Without being prompted, Dawson approached me one night after dinner.

He said if we wanted him to stay home with grandma, he would be okay. He didn't want to take much time off from his program, and he understood my mom would have a lot of trouble traversing the campus. I hugged him and told him he was the best son we could ever ask for!

My mom wasn't happy when I brought it up the next day, but she admitted it was the practical decision.

When Max talked to his dad, Louis said he had been thinking about making the trip out to see the campus and graduation. Arica was somewhat baffled by all the changes in attendance, but she was glad the three of us would be there.

"Mom and Dad, I have something to tell you. Topher is going to be attending, too. He's so nice to come support me, and I'd really like it if you and Grandpa G. can be on your best behavior around him."

I suppressed a loud guffaw and looked at my husband, who was having the same reaction.

I went first. "Don't worry, honey, we will make sure to ask him the most inappropriate questions we can think of."

"Yup, and I'll line up some primo dad jokes to make conversations extra funny. We can count on your grandpa for some awesome bodily functions, especially when it's real quiet around." Max was holding in his laughter as well.

"I'll practice my dinner etiquette and try to remember how to use the fork and spoon the right way. That's always so confusing!" I added in an innocent voice.

She gave an exasperated sigh and told us we were ridiculous.

We hung up shortly thereafter, and Max and I laughed so hard we had to sit down and catch our breath. We were quite proud of ourselves!

Graduation day was long and arduous, but also beautiful and a tremendous source of pride for us as parents. We only saw Arica for a few minutes before the ceremony, she looked gorgeous and so grown up. After all the graduates were done, we found her outside smiling radiantly into the eyes of a tall, handsome young man who was returning her gaze with the same affection. She nervously introduced us to Topher, and we shook hands with him and thanked him for being part of our daughter's special day.

I then forced everyone to take more photos than they wanted to. Topher was even kind enough to take many of Max and me with Arica, as well as her grandfather with us. We also took several that included him, but I consciously made sure we had plenty of good ones without him just in case.

Max and I had booked reservations at the same seafood restaurant where we'd had our date a year and a half ago. We surprised everybody with a fancy dinner along the scenic river and quite a few bottles of wine!

We got to know Topher better regarding his job as a law clerk, growing up near Boston, and his plans to become a lawyer. We heard more about Arica's senior project, her classmates she would miss the most, and what she was sad to leave behind in Providence.

Sitting across the table from the woman I raised, it was astounding what an incredible person she was turning into. Her boyfriend seemed smart and well-mannered, and he certainly doted on her. I was proud of her for so many of the choices she was making, she had an intensely bright future ahead of her.

Over dessert, my father-in-law entertained us with stories of some of Max's antics when he was a kid. Max defended himself against a few of them, but he laughed along with us. We ate, drank, and were very merry – it was an excellent evening!

The next morning, we picked up the rented trailer and filled it with everything Arica wanted to bring home with her. We went to lunch before our departure, and she kept looking forlornly at Topher as if this would be the last time she'd ever see him.

I was anxious about how the summer was going to go and what she would choose for her immediate future. How do you convince an almost-twenty-two-year-old to be patient about making life-changing decisions when the main thing on her mind is her first serious boyfriend and how to spend more time with him?

Their goodbye was exceedingly drawn out. Max ultimately reminded them that we had a long trip ahead of us and we wanted to put in as many miles as we could before dark.

The first day's drive was sullen. Arica was leaving behind a meaningful part of her life and a relationship she spent the first forty-five minutes crying over. Louis was in the back seat with her and at a loss as to how to comfort or distract her. When she fell asleep against the window at last, I breathed a sigh of relief at the quiet and lack of tension.

We stopped for dinner and a hotel to spend the night and finished our trip the next evening. We unloaded the trailer, turned it in right before they closed, and went home to have both our kids in the house for the foreseeable future. The four of us being together would be grand, but it was going to be an interesting period dealing with a lovesick Arica.

We held a combination Welcome Home/ Congratulations on Your College Graduation party the weekend after she was back. We had her wear her cap and gown again for some pictures of us with Dawson, my mom, and all the other family and friends who came by at some point during the day. It was pleasant, but our daughter was not as animated as she had been in Rhode Island.

That night, she and Dawson were draped on the couch viewing photos and videos on their phones while laughing and teasing each other. I didn't even say good night to them, I smiled and snuck upstairs to Max's snoring and let the kids enjoy their time together. They were still giggling around 3 a.m. when I got up to use the bathroom, which made me very happy and hopeful when I went back to sleep.

~ *Chapter 6* ~

MURPHY'S LAW

For the first two weeks, Arica seemed only half present. It was like a large piece of her was somewhere else and she was merely reacting to us when she had to. She slept late and watched a lot of daytime TV. I wanted her mood to be temporary, but the only times I saw her freely smiling and laughing were when she was video chatting with Topher in the evenings and on weekends.

She returned to the store where she previously worked part-time during the summer. They were happy to have her back and put her in a slightly higher position. She also had some phone dates with her college friends, she and Dawson went out with his friends a couple of times, and she reconnected with a few girls from high school.

Despite all those socializations, it was easy to see she wasn't where she wanted to be.

She and Dawson shared one car for a while, but it was obvious the arrangement wouldn't work long term. Our son brought up the subject one night at dinner.

"So, I've been thinking that maybe Arica can have grandma's car and I can buy my buddy's truck he's selling. It's not super old, he's taken immaculate care of it, and it's perfect for my job. I could use some help getting the paperwork done, but I can pay for it outright and won't need a loan, so that's easy."

Max and I were caught off guard. He asked, "Are you sure you can afford it, and it's in good shape? Should we have someone look at it? I can take it to the place your mom and I get our cars serviced to double-check." I nodded along in agreement.

Dawson replied, "Yeah, we can do that. I'm pretty confident it's ready to go, but a professional opinion is a smart idea. And yeah, I'm fine with paying for it. I've been working since high school and have only bought some clothes, a few pairs of work boots, and tools here and there. I feel like this is the right thing to do for everyone."

I gave him a grateful smile and said, "It sounds like you've thought this through and I appreciate that so much. It's a great plan; we'll see about getting it checked out as soon as we can and how to transfer the title if you pay cash for it. You'll also need to resolve the insurance part of it. Your dad and I can put Arica as the primary driver on the car when all that's done."

We accomplished the tasks for the vehicles in less than two weeks. It was a relief not to hear them negotiating about rides and schedules, and I think they both felt more like adults with individual wheels.

Arica and I tackled her résumé and job search plans. RISD provided her with resources to review, a career coach to contact, and they spent some time in class on what was needed, but she still seemed very unsure of where to start. With everything piling up at the end of the semester, she didn't have a vast amount of time to look for entry-level jobs. Topher might have also cut into her time, but I kept those suspicions to myself and just dove into finding her a position.

Then came the million-dollar question: where did she want to look for jobs? Her face made some strange expressions before she answered.

"Mom, I don't want you to be upset about this, but I REALLY want to find a job in Boston. I know I shouldn't base all my plans around Topher, but even if he and I don't work out, getting a job there would look good on my résumé no matter where I end up afterward. And if we are together for a long time, I don't have to worry about doing the long-distance relationship thing or moving around later." Her brow furrowed with concern as she finished.

"Honey, you can relax. Your dad and I guessed you'd say something like that. I'm glad you've thought about it rationally. It will be harder to interview, but we can come up with some short explanations you can give to companies about you moving there once an offer comes through. A lot of places are happy with video interviews these days, but if you must go interview in person, we'll try to figure something out." Her face eased, she smiled, and then she hugged me with tears in her eyes.

"Thank you SO much for understanding, I was afraid you'd want me to stay around here, at least for a while."

She hurried to continue when she realized how that sounded. "I enjoy being home, but I love the East Coast and all the places I got to see out there. New York City might be a little too big for my taste, and Providence now seems small, but Boston feels right with or without Topher. Oh geez, now I've turned myself into Goldilocks!"

We both laughed and I promised her I understood and we would support her decisions.

Next on the calendar *(it never ends)* was my mom's rescheduled hip replacement. We had diligently prepared the house and ourselves for her to be immobile for a bit.

The day before surgery, I was edgy and jittery. We ate dinner early so she could follow the rules about fasting for twelve hours, and then I couldn't sit still. Max asked me what I was so keyed up about, but I honestly had no idea. Maybe it was because none of us had been in the hospital for a very long time. Plus, sitting around all morning with nothing to do except wait didn't appeal to me whatsoever.

I finally settled down and got some broken sleep until my alarm went off at 5 a.m. We had to check in by 7 a.m., so I made sure Mom was awake and got into the shower to start our day.

The surgery went well, although it took a tad longer than planned due to some small complications. I paced the waiting room impatiently, tried to read, texted family and friends about her status, scrolled through my phone, and watched some of the morning news they had on TV.

Leo showed up around 9:30 a.m., and I was pleasantly surprised when Arica came to wait with me after she woke up. It was so much better to have people to talk to and distract me. Plus, Arica reminded me I needed to eat something, so we went to the cafeteria to find some lunch.

When the nurse came out to tell us Mom was awake and we were allowed to go see her, I was very ready to be anywhere besides that waiting room. She was woozy but overall fine, which was calming to see for myself.

The doctor came in later and told us they'd like to keep her overnight for observation, but she should be discharged tomorrow. We visited for another hour as Mom drifted in and out of consciousness, and then we all decided to head back to our house.

At dinner, we recapped the situation with Max and Dawson and made our plan for the next day. Max had the day off to get Mom to her bedroom and help during the day. Dawson said he'd get takeout on his way home so nobody had to worry about cooking.

It was a much better night of sleep, and I woke up ready to bring her back. Leo, Arica, and I arrived early but had to wait two hours for the release paperwork to be finished. The nurse pushed my mom in a wheelchair to the entrance and assisted us with getting her in the car. At home, Max and Leo got her inside to her bed while I parked and Arica brought everything in. We managed to do it all with minimal jostling or pain to my mom. Success!

Dawson arrived with our favorite Italian food, and everyone was pleased with our day. Leo left after dinner, and the four of us got mom into her recliner and set up a tray table to play a card game with her.

She and I were worn out physically and otherwise, so it was an early night for us. Max stayed up with the kids playing cutthroat games of Go Fish and War and had lots of fun.

We all chipped in to aid my mom over the next several days. She was doing well with her walking and exercises, but she still needed some assistance getting around the house and in and out of smaller spaces like the bathroom.

Everyone took turns playing a lot of card and board games to help her pass the time and be engaged. Euchre got us the most riled up – it was loud and wonderful to see my loved ones laughing, even if it came with some expletives tossed at each other!

Five nights after she came home from the hospital, my mom died in her sleep.

As Max and I were getting ready for work, my usual routine was to make sure she got out of bed okay and into the kitchen to eat some breakfast. When I opened the door to her room that morning, I immediately saw that something was off.

She was tangled up in the sheets with her ankles and feet hanging over the edge of the bed. Her left hand was on her chest and her right one was stretched out like she'd been reaching for something, probably her walker.

Rushing to her side, I shouted for Max. I shook her shoulder vigorously to wake her up, but I could tell it was useless. She was gone.

Of course, my yelling caused all three of them to come running into the room, and I promptly started sobbing and crumpled to the floor. This was so confusing…

Everything had been going so well, how did this happen?

We were doing all the right things!

Oh man, did I sleep through her calls for help? What kind of daughter does that?

Why hadn't I thought to install a button or something she could alert us with?

Max came over and held me after quietly telling Dawson to call 9-1-1. The rest of the morning is a blur in my memory… People coming in and out. Answering questions to the best of my ability. Trying to limit the crying so I could talk when necessary.

My phone sat ignored as it rang and beeped with calls and text messages I didn't have the time or emotional bandwidth to answer. Max kept up with some of it, but once word got out, the hometown grapevine worked its magic, and a tidal wave of virtual condolences poured in.

Max thoughtfully called my boss about what was happening, it had totally slipped my mind. Leo must have damn near broken the land-speed record with how fast he got to our house. Holding him while we both sobbed was a unique experience; I hadn't seen him cry since we were kids.

Arica and Dawson stayed in the background, and I sporadically remembered to check on them. They assured me they were okay and I should deal with what the authorities asked me to do and not worry about them *(Ha, if only it were that easy – my kids had seen someone they loved dead!)*.

It wasn't until late afternoon that the house was empty of strangers. I was finally able to sit down and face the onslaught of personal messages. It was heartwarming to read all the notes people were already sending. So many of them wanted to be helpful by bringing us food or helping clean up her things, but I couldn't conceive either of those possibilities at that point.

My aunts and uncles would all be arriving in the morning. Micah and his family would be here late tomorrow or early the following day, depending on which flight they could book. Max told me his dad and a handful of other relatives would be coming within the next couple of days as well.

Where all these well-meaning people were going to stay or what they would do was a mystery; but I couldn't be concerned about them right then.

My voice was hoarse from crying as I said to my family, "Thank you all for being strong for me today, I desperately needed your support. I thought we'd have at least five more years with her, but I guess it wasn't meant to be." I let out a choking sob.

"We were doing everything the doctors said to do, I don't understand how she made it through the surgery with flying colors and then poof! She's suddenly gone!" The tears flowed freely, and everyone surrounded me with hugs and love.

Once again, our children came to the rescue by asking a couple of their friends to bring us dinner. Despite having no appetite, I hadn't eaten all day and should get something into my stomach. More crying came when I saw the card games sitting on the counter near the table for evening play. Arica silently put them in a drawer while cleaning up.

I was on mental overload and went upstairs. I'm not sure what Max, Leo, and the kids did after we ate, but several people who came to see us the next day seemed to have assignments and were more helpful than I would have expected. I love my family.

Somehow, we got all arrangements made and set the date and time for the service and burial. It had been less than two years since we'd done all this with my dad, so it wasn't nearly as heavy a lift as it was the first time. Mom wanted to be buried with him, of course. Her services would be in my hometown where she spent the largest portion of her life, raised her children, and had friends.

We got the results back from the coroner, who deemed the cause of death a pulmonary embolism in her lungs from a blood clot. We were ignorant of what that meant, and I wish I had just taken them at their word and not looked it up. From what I read, she likely struggled to breathe for a few minutes and was potentially terrified. That did explain her hand on her chest and how it appeared like she had been trying to get out of bed but got caught in the sheet.

The blood clot was plausibly already in her leg and then loosened by the surgery. A whole new round of crying dedicated to feeling like a bad daughter started again.

Arica and my aunts picked out a beautiful outfit for my mom, and Leo said he'd drive it up to the funeral home the next day.

Days passed in a fog for me. Writing something profound for the eulogy was not easy for me. My brothers planned to speak as well, and they both had their speeches written in less than a day.

I was floundering with severe writers' block on this. There was too much to say in a condensed time frame, and how would I make it through without crying? The night before the services, I think I had a mild panic attack. The intrusive thoughts wouldn't stop about how I didn't deserve to pay her respects when I was the reason she died. Maybe I should stay home.

Max woke up around 3 a.m. and found me curled up on the couch wrapped in the comforter from my mom's bed. He sat down next to me and calmly stroked my hair.

"Tab, think about the joy you gave your mom in her final time. You included her in our family activities and even took her to New York City to be a tourist. We brought her into our home and cared for her the best we could for a year and a half. That's more than a lot of daughters would do.

You shouldn't beat yourself up when you spent so much of your own time and hard-earned money renovating our house to make your mom's life easier. You drove her to multiple doctor appointments and stayed with her for her surgery. We gave her the love and comfort of close family when she needed it most."

His kind and truthful comments helped immensely, and I eventually relaxed and fell asleep with my head on his lap.

The house was uncommonly quiet the next morning as everyone got ready to drive to the funeral home. Our two-hour trip was also silent, all four of us in our own worlds and me writing down my thoughts for the eulogy. The viewing didn't open to the public until 3 p.m., but we still had a lot to do, and family visitors would be allowed in starting at 2 p.m.

My brothers, aunts, and uncles met us there around noon, and we finalized everything. We set out the guest book, reviewed the pamphlets to verify all details were accurate, and made sure the flowers and photos were where we wanted them.

The kids and their cousins created some photo boards, which turned out beautifully. At one point, Arica nervously told me Topher was going to come later, and I nodded in acknowledgement. It would occur to me afterward how much he must care for our daughter to make the trip to be there for her. It was a long way and a significant commitment, especially considering he'd never gotten to meet my mom.

Family members started trickling in after the doors opened, and it was now time to do my daughterly duty of standing and greeting people and thanking them for coming. Making small talk at a time like this feels like torture, but it's expected, and I managed to keep up my end of conversations reasonably well.

Max's side showed up in full force, with people visiting who I hadn't seen in years. A sister-in-law later shared how Louis told everyone who knew me that my mom was as generous and caring as I am, and they would be disowned if they didn't show up. That man is a gem!

We had a short eulogy only for family at 2:45 p.m., with both of my aunts talking about their sister to those who were still there. I made it through without breaking down, but it sure was difficult. A lot of people left then, and it was only a few minutes before the second wave of visitors came through.

Topher arrived at some point, and Arica brought him back to the private room reserved for family. Max and I greeted him and thanked him for making the long trip. Dawson introduced himself, but that was about all we had to give.

He conveyed his deep condolences and how much Arica had lovingly told him about her grandma, and he wished he could have met her. If nothing else, at least she was very happy to have him there with her despite the circumstances.

A small number of people came by after 3, but the steady crowd started just before 4 p.m. It was then a consistent stream of my mom's church and local friends, former co-workers, and so on.

My boss and his wife dropped by, I didn't expect him to drive up. I told him how grateful I was for his patience with all my drama over the past few years. He graciously said he understood and had been in many similar situations himself. His wife and I had met at company gatherings, but I didn't know her well. She was kind enough to bring me a bottle of water and a fresh box of tissues when she noticed the previous one was low.

Some of my friends arrived later, which was extremely appreciated. I let go and cried with them when I talked about my mom's final days after the surgery. Another unexpected group was several people from my elementary and high school who'd had my mom as a substitute teacher.

And then, it was time for my brothers, me, and my nephew (he volunteered and really wanted to talk about his grandma) to do our speeches. The oldest child was scheduled first, and it required great effort to force myself to walk up to the podium and face all the people staring at me. They loved my mom, too, but how was I supposed to adequately summarize a lifetime in five minutes or less?

My paper was in front of me, but I had most of it memorized by then. I steadily made it through my address without crying and stepped away from the microphone. My concentration was so focused on getting it done I hadn't noticed how many people (predominantly women) were quietly sobbing during the last part. After all the worry and fear, it seemed I'd achieved a fitting tribute.

Leo came up and said he didn't know how on earth he was supposed to follow that, but his more lighthearted and funny homage was exactly what the moment called for. Micah and his son also did their jobs well, and the whole thing started winding down.

It seemed like we'd only been there for a short time, but it was already nearly 6:30 p.m. The doors would be open until 7, and we had dinner reservations nearby at 7:15. With us, Micah and his group, my aunts and uncles, a few close friends, some of Max's family members, and Topher, we were a large group of twenty!

The meal was good with lots of Mom stories floating among us. Arica and Dawson were at one end of the private dining room with their cousins from both sides. They were collaborating with Micah's kids to teach their Ganter cousins and Topher about the hot sauce challenge that had been established when they were young.

I contemplated stopping the chaos before it started, but they were having fun bonding after a hard day. All of them were old enough to deal with any repercussions from competing.

Max asked me quite a few times if I was doing okay. Surrounded by the family members I loved and reminiscing about my beloved mom was the best way this dreadful day could be ending. I confirmed I was fine.

And then I wasn't.

While we were discussing dessert, Arica and Topher came over to Max and me. They said Topher's parents flew out with him because he hadn't been on a plane by himself before. The three of them were staying in the same hotel as us and planned to fly back home tomorrow.

His parents were outside the restaurant right now and wondered if they could come in with us and pay their respects. Max and I were shocked that Topher hadn't said anything, but he explained. They knew some people in the area and went to visit them today so as not to interfere with our private family time during the services. We said of course they were welcome to join us and to enjoy dessert and a drink if they wanted.

Arica and Topher thanked us and disappeared for several minutes. We resumed our dessert debates at the table trying to decide on quantities. Dawson and the other cousins had to be reminded that they didn't need an entire portion each when Max rose from his chair.

I registered him saying, "I'm Arica's dad. It's great to finally meet you! We've really enjoyed getting to know Topher so far; he's a good kid."

As he finished, I turned away from the kids. I stood up to greet Topher's parents and smiled as they faced me. There was an instant sense of recognition, and then I heard her voice softly say, "Hey, Tabby. Long time no see."

Once again, I froze in place. Ginny and Alex were standing in front of me more than two decades after we'd last spoken. I panicked spectacularly.

"NO. No, no, no, this can't be happening. YOU'RE Topher's parents? **This can't be real!**" I was shouting, and the entire room fell silent.

Alex and Ginny's faces went from hopeful to disappointed, as if they expected me to just welcome them with open arms. As if what they had done didn't wreck me and caused me to push people away for years so they wouldn't hurt me first.

As if it hadn't put my relationship with Max at risk in the beginning. As if I hadn't spent a lot of money on therapy to at least come to terms with the pain they inflicted and to understand that not everyone would abandon me.

The fury fire started burning upward from my toes again, and I clenched my fists to keep from reaching out and throttling both of them.

"I can't believe you would choose NOW, one of the **worst days of my life**, to show up and act like nothing is wrong between us. YOU don't deserve to be in this room with these people who ACTUALLY love me and care about me! Get away from me and STAY AWAY ONCE AND FOR ALL!"

My entire body was taut with rage as I stormed out of the room and into the restroom. I hastily turned on the faucet and splashed cold water on my face to try to quench the heat inside me.

My mind couldn't form complete thoughts; it just kept spinning from refusal to believe this was happening to red-hot hatred I hadn't felt in over half my lifetime.

My shaking hands gripped the edges of the sink counter to keep myself grounded. *Seriously? The day of my mom's funeral? The audacity!*

Arica burst into the restroom in tears. "MOM, what the hell? I know today sucks, but how could you treat Topher's parents like that? They're nice people, and you screamed at them!"

With raw hurt in my eyes, I scowled at my daughter. "Did you catch any of what I said? Do you not understand that I know them and they cut me to the bone years ago? I've known Alex since pre-school. Ginny was the very best friend I've ever had. When we were in college, they treated me like garbage and completely broke my heart. Yet somehow, the universe decided to punish me even more by bringing them back into my life.

Today was the saddest I've ever felt, and I thought it couldn't get any worse. I was so horribly wrong." My head drooped and the tears cascaded into the sink as my brain caught up with the current state of affairs.

"How is this possible, how could you know them already?" Arica was genuinely confused. "I met him halfway across the country, he never mentioned that his parents used to live out here. Are you absolutely sure?"

My response was half-laugh, half-sob as I said, "Ginny's parents lived on the East Coast before they got divorced, although I didn't know specifically where. She came to the Midwest with her mom. I knew her dad was a lawyer, which explains when Topher introduced you to his grandpa.

Let me guess, Topher has two aunts his mom was super close with as he grew up? His grandma wasn't around? His dad didn't talk about his family much?"

Her silence and wide-eyed look of bewilderment told me the answer. Just then, Max opened the door slightly and asked if he could come in. I sighed and said sure. He entered slowly, seeming to be afraid of how to approach me.

"Care to explain?" was all he asked.

"Oh, I have a feeling that's all I will be doing for the near future. But right now, I cannot and will not be near those two people. I need some time to cope with this and reconcile my anger with the fact that my daughter fell in love with the son of the people I despise most in this world."

They both gasped, and Arica left. Max came over and put his arm around me.

"Tab, you are one of the kindest and gentlest people I've ever known. Seeing your face and hearing the despair in your voice just now scared me to my core. I can't imagine what they did to make you feel this way.

I love you, and I'll listen and back you up however I can. But right now, I need to go back into that room and do damage control. Topher's parents already left, so it's safe if you want to come back."

I nodded. "I'll be there in a few minutes when I can stop shaking. Is Topher still here?"

"Yes, he was waiting for Arica to return."

"Good. I want to apologize to him before he leaves. Please ask him to wait a little longer." Max kissed me and exited the restroom.

I cooled off with more water, tried to calm my nerves, and used several paper towels to dry my face. Dealing with Ginny and Alex was done for now, but I did need to ensure that Arica and Topher were okay.

Putting my hand on the door to our dining room, I took a breath and held it while I counted to five. All eyes turned to me as I entered.

"I'm so sorry for my raised voice with Topher's parents. To make a very long story short, there is a lot of history between us, and it was a huge shock to see them again after more than twenty-five years. After I have had some time to recover from my mom's passing, I'm sure I'll be able to approach this with a more reasonable attitude. Thank you all so much for being patient and understanding with me on this difficult occasion."

Max, Arica, and Topher stepped outside the room with me when I asked to speak with them. I was now embarrassed about my outburst, even though my feelings were legitimate.

"Topher, I'm so sorry for acting the way I did to your parents, I should've handled that better."

"It's okay, Mrs. Ganter, I know you've had an awful day. My parents told me just this morning they knew you in the past, but I had no idea it was so emotional. I wouldn't have brought them in here if I'd known." He sounded like he was close to tears himself.

"Please don't think any of this is your fault, I realize you didn't do it on purpose." I put my hand on his arm, and I saw both his and Arica's tense faces relax somewhat.

He continued, "I don't know if I should tell you this now, but… My parents wanted me to ask if maybe you'd meet them for lunch tomorrow at the hotel after you're done with… what you need to do. They really want to apologize if you'll let them."

He was clearly uncomfortable telling me this, but I'm sure he felt obliged to do what Alex and Ginny *(I suspected more her)* requested of him.

I smiled gently and said, "Thank you for relaying the message. I'm sorry you're in this awkward position, Topher. I will think about it and give you my answer in the morning. Can I have a hug?"

"Yes!" he replied enthusiastically, and we embraced. A look of relief passed between Max and Arica.

I turned to my daughter and said, "Honey, this is going to be okay. I'm sorry to you as well for the way I treated Topher's parents. I will explain another time. I love you so much." We hugged and I fought back more tears.

The four of us returned to the dining room and finished up with dessert and more chitchat. My brothers and I solidified the plans for the next morning. I also told them I was way too tired to get into it now when they asked me about the yelling. They vaguely remembered Ginny from when I used to talk about her a lot and the one time she came with me to Easter. They didn't seem to recognize Alex as being the same guy from my graduating class or they undoubtedly would have bugged me more.

I hugged everyone there and thanked them again for their support before we left for the hotel. Dawson was silent as we walked out to the car, but when we got in, he was clearly dying to ask about it.

"So, Mom, should I prepare any future girlfriends for their parents meeting you the first time? I don't think I've ever heard you yell like that; it was impressive! Do I get the inside scoop?"

His attempts at humor brought a much-needed smile to my face. "I'll tell you at some point, but not right now. I'm more exhausted and emotionally drained than ever before… And I'm glad I intimidated you with my anger, keep in mind what I'm capable of when people treat me badly!"

The fake menacing look I gave him made him chuckle as we pulled into the hotel parking lot. He and Arica were sharing the room next to ours, so we went upstairs together and said good night. She was not yet in there, so I figured she must still be with Topher. My natural urge was to text her and make sure she was okay, but I had done enough annoying things for the day.

Max and I didn't talk as we got ready for bed, but I mentally prepared how much I would tell him. It was surreal to be in this position as an adult looking back at all the developments leading to today. I still couldn't wrap my mind around the fact that Alex and Ginny had explosively re-entered my life after so long.

When we crawled between the hotel sheets and got comfortable, I took another big breath and gave him the twenty-minute CliffsNotes version of the story. I ended with how all of it was what made me so hesitant at the beginning of our courtship and how terrifying it was for me to trust anyone then.

When I finished, tears were sliding down the sides of my face which I hadn't even noticed. Max turned and propped himself on one elbow to look at me.

"Wow. Babe, I can't believe you've been through all that. I'm surprised you never shared any of it with me before, but I understand how it would hurt too much to re-live it. Now I get why you had such a visceral reaction to them tonight."

He frowned and continued in a perturbed voice, "It wasn't fair for them to completely blindside you like they did, especially today. Now I'M pissed at them for their insensitive timing."

I kissed him and thanked him for being so wonderful. Part of me was afraid he'd scold me for my poor behavior, but he listened first. For the trillionth time (give or take) in our relationship, I was so thankful I overcame my fears and let him into my life unrestricted. Choosing to be with Max was indisputably the best decision I'd ever made.

"What are you going to tell Topher in the morning?"

My answer was honest, "I still don't know."

"Well, don't think about it too long. Are you going to be able to sleep?"

"I sure hope so, every cell in my body felt like it weighs a ton."

We had to wake up relatively early again for the burial, so I needed to rest soon. We kissed, and he was softly snoring next to me in minutes.

Being alone for the first time that day, my internal dialogue went into overdrive.

How dare they do this to me? Why today when I was at my most vulnerable? Was that their intention — to kick me when I was already down?

Should I have known somehow? They've obviously had the information long enough to plan this ambush.

Did Topher tell us his last name? How did I not think to ask about it at some point? They've been dating for like six months, I'm sure if I knew he was a Yates it would have at least set off some alarm bells…

It makes so much sense now — Topher growing up near Boston and his single grandpa the big-shot lawyer. I guess Ginny got her wish to move back close to her dad and sisters.

Why would she steal the name Arica for her daughter? That was MY idea!

I can't believe they're still together! Should I meet with them and let them apologize tomorrow?

I noticed Alex's hair is escaping his forehead, I never would have pictured him bald. He's also gained quite a bit around the center, but who hasn't? Middle age sucks.

Her hair is darker than it used to be and noticeably gray at the roots, she must dye it. She still does a terrific job with her makeup.

Hearing her voice was like having a tooth pulled out slowly with no anesthesia. Damn it was traumatic when I realized who they were.

Do I want to hear their explanations? What AM I going to tell Topher?

What if he and Arica stay together and someday get married — what on earth would I do then? I wouldn't be able to avoid them, maybe it's easier to yank off the band-aid now. Would it provide some closure? Could I accept their apologies and move on?

Ugh, how can I handle more heartbreak right now? Like my mom dying wasn't enough, then my cruel past reared its ugly head in front of all my closest loved ones and made ME look like the monster.

Murphy's Law strikes again. Just when I thought it couldn't be any worse, ta da — let's open old wounds! Max is correct, it WAS unfair of them to just show up out of nowhere, particularly when I'm dealing with all this.

They absolutely don't deserve my forgiveness, but should I at least listen so I can finally get the truth?

Curiosity was the real problem. I fiercely wanted to know what happened from the time I was lying in bed with the flu until I told them to fuck off outside that restaurant. The uncertainty has been such a wide, painful blank spot for so long, it would be undeniably satisfying to fill it.

~ *Chapter 7* ~

Pandora's Box

It felt like my eyes were closed for approximately fifteen minutes until the alarm blared. I could sleep for a week straight. I groaned at the prospect of having to tough it out through the burial service before going home and getting the rest I needed.

Max wasn't exactly jumping out of bed either, but we both slowly started packing and preparing for the day. In the shower, the incident during dinner came rushing back, and to my chagrin it hadn't been a bad dream. Topher was waiting for my decision.

Dawson knocked on our door at 7:30 a.m., and Max let him in. We were finishing up, and our son commented on us being behind schedule, which was unusual. We grumbled at him, and I asked if Arica was ready to go.

"I don't know, she didn't sleep in our room last night. Topher is bringing her to the church."

"So where did she stay?" I knew the answer as I was asking it, but it came out anyway.

"They stayed in his parents' room; they got double beds as well. I texted her to make sure she was okay, and she said yes, she'd see me there in the morning." His voice sounded guilty for telling us, even though he hadn't done anything wrong.

I sighed. "Well, she's a grown adult. I guess we don't have the right to tell her where to sleep."

Max and Dawson both watched me closely to gauge my emotions, but I turned away and busied myself with packing so they wouldn't see my irritation.

Of course, Ginny and Alex **would** be perfectly fine with our children sleeping in the same bed. They had no morals, so why should their son? Yes, I knew that was petty; it's not like Arica and Topher hadn't had plenty of opportunities to spend a night together. I simply couldn't stand the thought of Alex and Ginny being the cool parents who let the kids do whatever they want.

Max and I zipped up our suitcases and the three of us went down to the lobby. While we waited for Max to pull the car up under the portico (it was raining lightly), I texted Arica: "Please tell Topher I will meet his parents here in the restaurant after I bury my mother. They will have 30 minutes to speak their peace, no more."

Normally I added emojis to my messages, but there isn't one yet to depict the jumble of emotions I felt all at once when I thought about having to sit down with those two in only a few hours.

As with my dad, the weather was unfriendly and the priest kept things blessedly short. They had generously erected a tent over the burial site, but the rain found us no matter what.

As the procedures were ending, I stood there looking at the headstone with my dad's name and dates that would soon include my mom's as well. A major chapter in my life was now closed, and I perceived a hole where their presence had been for over half a century.

My brothers came up on both sides and put their arms around me for a shared moment of tears and sniffles. It was just us now, a family of five down to three. I hope our parents believed they'd done well in raising us.

After several minutes, we started walking back to the church. It was time for everyone to go our separate ways, and I was scared it would be a long stretch before I saw some of them again. We did one more round of hugs, and people started putting up their umbrellas and getting into cars.

Max and I thanked the priest again and headed to our vehicle. He told me that Topher took both Arica and Dawson back to the hotel already, and the three of them were going to make themselves scarce while the parents talked over lunch.

Ah yes, it was now time for the reckoning.

I stared out the window on the short drive, thinking about what I wanted to gain from this. Presumably, I should get the explanation I've been missing, but what else did I hope to learn? Yikes, that list was loooooong.

I reminded myself to stay as calm as possible and not to allow the fire to take over. The rage had been festering for more than two decades, but only because I never faced it head-on and dealt with its ramifications.

Maybe this was my shot to put it permanently in the past so I could truly heal. I resolved to maintain my composure, ask the questions that had antagonized me the most if they didn't cover them, and hear them apologize without making (too many) sarcastic comments.

It might benefit me to keep my mouth shut and let Ginny talk as much as she wanted at first. She had a tendency to just start babbling and spill her guts if given the opportunity.

Max parked and asked, "Are you ready for this?"

I smiled wanly, "I will never be ready for this, but I know I need to do it."

He held my hand and then kissed it, "I'm really proud of you for facing them, especially in light of why we're here. You didn't deserve any of what happened to you, and I hope this provides closure for you."

"Thank you for saying that. I love you, and I wouldn't want anyone else by my side during my mom's situation and this mess. Please be my rock in there. Squeeze my leg under the table if I start spiraling – it might help me come back to reality." He agreed, we kissed, and we got out of the car.

Walking into the hotel felt like what I imagined death row inmates might experience on their final stroll. Somehow, we made it inside and to the restaurant entrance. They were sitting near the back and away from the other diners.

Max and I held hands as we wound our way through the tables to them. Mine was sweating already, and I'm pretty sure I was trembling. He took the lead and greeted them, shaking their hands before we sat down. I stayed silent.

The server was instantly beside us asking what we'd like to drink. We told her and she left.

There was an awkward silence. Ginny quietly started with, "It's nice to meet you, Max. Tabby, I'm really sorry about your mom." A slight nod was all I gave her in acknowledgement.

She closed her eyes for a beat. Knowing her mannerisms as I did, I could tell she was tempering her enthusiasm. My expression was willfully aloof.

She looked at me and smiled. "I wish it was under different conditions, but it's amazing to see you again. I know that's not mutual, but I'm honestly so happy to be sitting across from you right now. I can't describe how much I've thought about this moment and what would happen. It's such a relief that it's finally here!"

I met Alex's gaze, and he grinned. "Before we get into things, you should know that she hasn't stopped talking about you since the time you left us outside that restaurant. I'm grateful you decided to give us this time so she can get everything off her chest. And I am also glad to see you, especially back here in our old stomping grounds."

His smile broadened, and I was perturbed to realize I still thought he was physically attractive. Too bad his traitorous personality ruined it.

Ginny continued. "I'm not sure exactly where to start, but I'm guessing you're curious how Alex and I ended up in that restaurant bar the night you discovered we were together…" I nodded. "Well, when you were sick, I was trying to be a faithful friend and visit you and make sure you were okay. Plus, it was a good excuse to spend time with you since we were both usually so busy.

One night, Alex showed up at our work looking for you. I explained how ill you were and you probably wouldn't be back on your feet for a week or more. He was concerned and wanted to go check on you himself, but I didn't think you'd want him to see you like that.

So, I told him I could relay his message and tell you to call him when you had your voice back. He said okay, but it seemed like he was down in the dumps about something. I asked if he needed someone to listen to whatever was bothering him and I got off work around 8. He said yes and he'd pick me up at the end of my shift."

At this point, she took a drink and our server brought Max and my beverages. She asked if we were ready to order, and Max informed her we needed some time to catch up first.

"We hung out at the bar that night and talked until after midnight – mostly about YOU, Tabby. He was conflicted about what was between the two of you and if he wanted something more. It was basically the same thing you'd told me on New Year's Eve!" My glance turned to Alex, but he was staring at his drink and avoiding eye contact.

"I tried to play matchmaker and suggested the two of you schedule an honest-to-goodness date to get things out in the open. I didn't know much about your history together, just what you shared about there being SOMETHING, but you hadn't decided if you were interested in more.

I convinced him that you two were on the same wavelength and he should be open and honest with you as soon as you were better. Then we left and he drove me home. We exchanged numbers so I could have you call him when you were able to talk and in case he had any more questions or anything."

We waited while the server refilled Max's drink, and Alex shifted in his chair uncomfortably. It amused me to see this wasn't easy for him, it shouldn't be.

"He called me a few days later and asked if I would meet with him again. I said yes, so we went back to the same bar and talked more, but this time it was more of a getting-to-know-you sort of thing, and we were laughing at each other's imitations of our parents, stories from high school, dating mishaps, all that stuff. We were there again quite late and had been drinking, so we waited until he felt able to drive."

She swallowed hard and looked at her husband, and I assumed the part I didn't want to hear was coming next. In a lower voice, she kept talking but wasn't looking at me as much now.

"There was a puddle in the parking lot from when it rained earlier, and I was babbling on about something and almost stepped in it. Alex grabbed me and steered me around it, and this electrical bolt went through my body when he touched me like that. I knew what it meant, but I was NOT going to let anything happen. He should be with you, not me. I refused to be the horrible girl who stole her best friend's crush while she was lying on her deathbed!" I raised my eyebrows accusingly because that's exactly what she had done, and she blushed.

"We got in the car, and he drove me home. When we parked at my apartment, he put his hand on mine and thanked me for listening. We met each other's eyes and when he leaned over to kiss me… I… um… well, I gave in to the electricity. We got kinda hot and heavy in the front seat, but then I shut it down and told him this was wrong. I couldn't betray you like this, and neither should he. The two of you needed to talk first and figure out if there was anything worth exploring. I got out of the car and felt like the worst friend who'd ever lived."

Alex now appeared mortified when he heard it spoken aloud, and I was again satisfied to see it.

Our server refilled Ginny's drink, and we stated we'd be ready to order in five minutes or so. My message to Arica said I would only allow them half an hour, but I hadn't paid attention to what time we arrived or how long we'd already been there. Hearing the rest of the story was paramount, so who cared about the arbitrary time limit I set?

Max broke the tension, "Should we figure out what we want to eat? I'm starving!"

Alex chimed in with, "Me too. I skipped breakfast, and it takes a lot of fuel to maintain this studly body!" as he patted his belly.

Max chuckled, and Ginny and I rolled our eyes at each other. A smile began to form, but I caught myself. We weren't the TAG Team anymore. We hadn't been on the same side for a very long time. I grabbed the menu and concentrated on what I wanted for lunch.

After we ordered, Ginny went back to the story. "The next day, I was planning to come visit you with a CD I'd made of some of our favorite songs, but I started crying every time I picked it up and thought of my deceit. I wouldn't be able to fake it in front of you. I'd have to tell the truth, and you'd hate me. I didn't want to make things worse for your health, so I stayed home that day. And then the next day I went through the whole thing again and didn't go… I'm sorry I didn't give you any explanation; it was so hard for me to admit what I'd done to hurt you."

She wiped her eyes with the napkin, Alex put his arm around her, and she leaned into him for solace. It defied the odds that they were still together, but now I was seeing their devoted connection in front of me. They didn't even notice they were doing it, the reinforcement came so naturally after all this time.

"And then this idiot *(she tilted her head toward her husband)* called me AGAIN and asked if he could talk to me and apologize. I thought I was smart by meeting him somewhere instead of him picking me up, so a friend came with me to the bar after work. You remember Willa, with the really dark hair?"

I frowned, then nodded. "She was a lot of fun; she loved dancing and always tried to get us out on the dance floor."

Ginny smiled, "Yes, exactly! She was my wing-woman that night and I told her I couldn't leave with Alex. Well, Willa was doing her thing and almost forgot me, but she did keep to her word and took me home later.

Anyway, Alex apologized for rushing into things; he said it was totally unplanned and unexpected for him. We chitchatted, and then he opened up about all the stress he'd had the last several years. His parents were pushing him hard to take over the family construction business when his dad retired. That wasn't what he wanted at all, but he felt guilty for not being who they expected him to be. He got tired of all the arguing and went to stay at his grandparents' house for a while."

Everything she was saying tracked, and I again glanced at Alex to see if he remembered the significance of my driving him to his grandma's. At last, he looked me full in the eyes and mouthed the word "Sorry" to me. Ginny didn't notice, but Max saw it. She was still talking.

"He was utterly miserable, even his ex-girlfriend tried to persuade him to do what his parents wanted. He said you and I were the only ones who helped him feel normal and appreciated during that time."

My gasp of surprise caused her to pause while I took in the information.

To Alex, I said, "I didn't know you were enduring so much. Was that what you thought about telling me the night I took you to your grandma's?"

He nodded, "My intention was to tell you everything, but I didn't know how to start. My parents thought I was the worst son in the world, I hadn't finished college, and I was clueless about what to do with the rest of my life. I was such a major loser. More than anything, I wanted to keep enjoying our times together and not have you pitying me or being disgusted with my worthlessness. I knew you wouldn't tell me to do what they were demanding, but it was just so tough to come clean about what was going on… I hated myself back then."

His demeanor was genuinely contrite and dejected as he recalled his adolescence and our relationship.

Unbelievably, I was feeling a tiny bit sorry for young Alex. He'd seemed tortured, but I'd never pried him for answers.

Our server arrived with our food, and we took a break to eat. Max asked them a few questions about living near Boston, but I was only half-listening as I reviewed everything they'd divulged so far. The things I still didn't understand were why they'd never apologized or tracked me down after our confrontation. Perhaps those points would come out in the story soon.

When we were finished, Ginny took a big breath and went back to it, talking faster now. "The next day, he called again and said he wanted to see me again. I told him no. He showed up at work later that night and sat in the lounge until I was done. I said he was being outrageous and stalker-y, and I didn't like it. He smiled and told me I did like it and he knew it. The asshole was right, but I didn't want to admit it.

I was trying SO HARD to be a good friend to you, Tabby, but damn the pull of him was strong. I let him take me to the bar, he took me home, and I took him inside. It was over at that point; I was head over heels."

It wasn't easy hearing this, but I noted the affectionate way she talked about him and their journey to becoming a couple. I'd like to think I would have given them my blessing even if I was upset at first. Their secrecy robbed me of that possibility to be a good friend to them.

"Sometime in the following few days, my shame was at an all-time high, and I was dreading facing you at work soon. I spoke to one of your roommates on the phone and heard you were feeling a little better each day, so time was short. I could face you and my horribleness as your so-called friend, or I could take the coward's way out and avoid you. We all know which path I chose. Hell, I recklessly quit my job and had no way to pay my rent for a month. I was fully committed to being a spineless jerk!"

She had a sad and remorseful look as she hesitated. She stared into my eyes and said, "Tabby, you were right when you said I was a shitty friend. I was. I was so afraid of hurting you, and yet I caused much worse pain by hiding from you."

She reached across the table and took my hand. Tears were forming in the corners of her eyes. "I'm so sorry. You were the best friend I ever had, and I ruined it. I killed the TAG Team and stole one of the few guys you liked. I can never make those things up to you, but I want you to know that I deeply regret them."

A sob came out of me before I even knew it was there. Tears streamed down my face, and I let her hug me. Until that moment, I didn't realize just how much I needed to hear her apology.

The gravity of her words provided the long-awaited antidote for the pain I'd been carrying for twenty-seven years. A wound inside me began to scab over at last.

I excused myself to go to the restroom, where I freshened up and returned to the table. Alex was on the phone, and Max was texting someone. Ginny told me our kids were worried about us. We all chuckled at the irony, and the men finished reassuring Arica and Topher that everything was fine.

Ginny sighed. "There's a lot more to the story, but we can stop if you want. It's already been WAY longer than thirty minutes, and you're probably sick and tired of hearing me talk. That's totally okay."

Max looked at me and shrugged. It was entirely my decision to make.

"I'd like to hear more about how you two managed to stay together and decided to get married, and definitely why your daughter has the same name as mine." My eyes narrowed on the last part, and Ginny nodded as if she figured it would be a hot topic.

"Alex and I were like magnets at first – we could not stay apart for any length of time." They both smiled, and I had another momentary flash of anger before I remembered I requested this explanation.

"When you ran into us at the restaurant, we were in our own little love bubble and used to going wherever we wanted as a couple. I stupidly assumed it would be a complete fluke for us to run into you if we started eating at different restaurants and hanging out at bars on the other side of town. It was a dumb plan, and it obviously failed.

After you called us out and left, I was a mess for weeks. I cried all the time, didn't want to leave my bedroom, and detested myself for what I'd done.

Alex and I had our very first argument over whether we should go to your apartment and grovel. I shouldn't have listened to him when he talked me out of it, but we had already caused enough damage. I didn't want to pour salt into the wound too. And let's face it – I was scared to see you.

We decided to let you go so you could live your life without us holding you back. I guess that plan failed as well…

In the middle of my depression, I got sick and couldn't keep anything down. Alex was worried when I went several days barely eating, and he insisted I go to the doctor for antibiotics or something. Well, come to find out, I was pregnant."

That caused me to gasp involuntarily again, and Max put his hand on my leg in case I was feeling overwhelmed. I gently squeezed his hand to let him know I was surprised and not furious.

Then I was confused. *Wait, that was too early for Topher. Did they terminate the pregnancy or lose the baby? I don't think Arica mentioned an older sibling, did they give it up for adoption?*

She sighed again. "So, there we were, twenty-three and twenty-four years old, penniless and no life plans, and having a baby. We had no clue what to do next." Alex huffed his agreement, and she reached for his hand.

"First, I called my mom, and she was SO PISSED. I hung up on her in the middle of a tirade and didn't speak to her again for over a month.

Alex tried talking to his parents, but they basically told him he just kept making lousy decisions. They said they weren't about to raise their grandchild because he couldn't keep it in his pants.

So next I talked to my sisters, and they were surprisingly supportive. I was afraid my dad would be super mad, but they said they'd soften the blow and be at the house when I broke it to him.

We arranged a day and time for me to call, and Alex and I nervously gave him the news. He didn't take it well, but it wasn't as awful as I'd feared. He asked what we were going to do, and I admitted we had no idea. He offered for us to come back to Boston and stay in an apartment in one of the buildings he owned.

We talked about it, and both of us were kind of excited for a fresh start and a big city to raise our child in.

My sisters were willing to call in some favors to help us get jobs, but we wanted to try on our own first before we took them up on that. The morning sickness was still making me terribly nauseous, so Alex took over on getting us packed up. My dad paid for a moving truck, and we got it loaded and went east."

Max got up to use the restroom, and Ginny said she would like a break as well. That left Alex and me, and we sat in awkward silence for a long moment.

After the pause, I said, "I'm sorry again for your parents treating you so badly. Now that I'm a mom, it makes me even more mad when I hear about how some people have to grow up. I put up with a hefty amount of shit from my own parents, but we eventually got to a decent place. You've always been a good person, and you deserved better."

"Thanks, Tabby. It means a lot that you're able to say nice things to me right now. I really was a shitty friend too, you hit the bullseye there. You were nothing but kind to me, and I took advantage of that."

I decided to lay all my cards on the table with him. "You know, I don't think you and I would have ultimately worked out as a couple, but there was definitely something between us. We had so much history and so many things in common, and the physical attraction didn't fade over time like I thought it would. I played it cool like I didn't care what happened, but I did actually like you and wanted you to like me back. It was devastating when I realized that you chose her over me, particularly since you hardly knew her, and only because of me. I just think you should know that."

He blushed. "The attraction was mutual. I don't know why I was so secretive about the two of us. I suppose I wanted you to myself and not have to explain it to anyone. I had to justify so many things with my parents and try to keep up the façade of 'the cool funny guy' or whatever.

Being with you was EASY and stress-free and I needed that so much back then. I never meant to hurt you, and if I could go back in time and change anything, it would be to treat you better and talk to you more. I'm sorry I was such an ass to you, and I wish Ginny and I had handled the whole thing so differently."

Tears were falling down my cheeks again as Max and Ginny returned to the table. They could tell something had transpired between Alex and me, but they didn't ask questions.

Our server offered another drink refill, and we all said yes. We'd been there quite a while, I wondered if she was getting frustrated. There were very few customers in there, so I didn't feel too bad. I would make it worth her time – I always tried to be a higher tipper, and I suspected Ginny did as well. Once you've worked in restaurants and had to pay rent and bills that depended on tips, it changes your perspective.

Ginny dove back in. "To make an already long story shorter, we started making a home for ourselves in Boston. It was a dream come true to have my sisters there for support, and Alex and my dad got along well, which was an enormous relief. My dad got him a low-level job at the law firm, and Alex took it so he didn't offend my dad. It wasn't great, but it was money and we could start working on buying stuff for the nursery.

We were trying to make it on our own and not depend on my family for financial support, but it was also such a help when we had nothing.

We had a son and named him Hudson. All of our doctor appointments had been fine, but Hudson was born with a heart defect, and he had to stay at the hospital in NICU for almost a month."

She took a drink before continuing. Alex held her hand. "The first two years with Hudson were so hard. He was in and out of procedures to keep his little pumper working properly, and we were constantly afraid we'd lose him.

When he was home, I barely slept because I always wanted to make sure his heartbeat was steady throughout the night. I could actually kind of relax when he was in the hospital. At least they had him hooked up to monitors and the nurses would be alerted right away if something was wrong.

When he was around eighteen months old, things started to change for the better. His heart was beating stronger and more regularly on its own, and the doctors were encouraged that we might be out of the woods. He was under tight observation for several more months, but then they felt comfortable letting him be less monitored.

They warned us that he shouldn't be overly active, but we were able to start living a more normal life. We celebrated hugely on his second birthday for many reasons, including me sleeping through the night again.

Alex and I decided to make it official and get married soon, so my sisters took it upon themselves to plan it. They went way above and beyond!" She laughed at the memory, and Alex smiled too.

"We would have been happy with a small ceremony with a few friends and our immediate family, but they didn't stop there. Lisey and Jade invited extended family members, a large portion of Alex's relatives, and my mom and her side. It was crazy!

We had an amazing wedding, and by then my mom had somewhat resigned herself to being a grandma and me moving back east, so she was supportive as well. It was weird to see her and my dad in the same space together; they hadn't spoken to each other much at all since the time I was going back and forth after the divorce.

Hudson was the happiest baby, and it was so fun to see everyone we knew and loved smiling with our son. Even Alex's mom and dad enjoyed themselves and told us they would like to visit more often, which was a welcome surprise."

The server gave us our checks, and we handed her our credit cards. She promptly ran them and brought back the receipts. She thanked us for coming in and said her shift was ending. She was leaving, but we could stay as long as we wanted. She seemed relieved we were out of her hair!

Ginny and Alex whispered to each other, and now he took over the story to give her a break from talking. "So, we were married and living in her dad's apartment building, and I had a job that paid our bills but not much more. Then there was a stack of medical expenses. Every birthday and Christmas we just asked for money to help pay it down.

Ginny had the full-time responsibility of keeping Hudson entertained but not letting him do too much cardio during the day. We were in a good place overall, and then she got pregnant with Topher. We were both obviously worried about his health, but we tried to stay calm and make sure the doctors checked everything they could to determine if there would be problems.

Fortunately, Topher was born with no complications, and we were a family of four. We weren't sure if we were going to have any more children, but Ari decided to surprise us. We learned Ginny had another bun in the oven when Topher was almost eight months old. It was a juggling act to take care of all three of them while limiting Hudson's exercise; I don't know how she did it.

I was trying to move up the ranks in the law firm without using Nick's influence too much, and she was home with the kids. It felt like everything was going in slow motion and a speeding train at the same time."

He looked at Ginny to see where he should go from here.

She resumed with, "To answer your question about Ari's name, I did do it on purpose. When the doctor told me I was having a girl, there was no doubt in my mind about what her name would be. Like Alex said, I never quit thinking of you, and I wanted to honor you as the reason we were together and building this family. Naming her Arica was my way of proclaiming I still loved you while knowing I would probably never see or talk to you again. I didn't tell Alex why I insisted on the name until later because I didn't want to hear any objections from him." He gave her a meaningful look, and she rolled her eyes at him.

"Okay fine, I'll be honest. I wasn't planning on telling him at all, but one night my sister asked me how I picked it. We were sitting in her backyard drinking margaritas when all the kids were asleep inside, and I was tipsy. I let down my guard and told them the story of you and I having girl talk in your apartment and how much you loved the name.

It was a symbolic way to prove I missed you and hated hurting you. I didn't know if you had children or specifically a daughter, so I wanted at least one Arica to be in the world because of you.

Alex was annoyed I hadn't been truthful with him before that, but I don't regret a thing." Her chin stuck out with defiance when she said the last part, and Alex shook his head.

I was tearing up yet again at the thought that if I hadn't had my daughter, Ginny still cared about me enough to make sure the name I loved was given life. Max handed me a napkin, and I wiped my eyes.

Alex said to Max, "This is what I've put up with for twenty-seven years. The two of them have been inseparable even when they weren't together."

Max laughed, and I was slightly aggravated that the two of them were hitting it off so quickly. It was irrational to think of my husband as a traitor just from being amused by Alex, but my emotional state was certainly not at its peak.

Ginny turned to her husband and shook her head with a dismayed look. I didn't know what it meant, but he picked up the story in a monotone voice.

"Life went on, I was working and we were raising three kids, one of whom had health limitations and regular doctor visits and gave us a few scares over the years.

We got the boys through high school, and Hudson graduated from college. He was living in an apartment closer to Boston with a friend he had known since middle school. He called us on Friday to catch up, and he told us he wasn't feeling that great and planned to rest a lot over the weekend. Ginny reminded him to make an appointment with the doctor just in case, and he said he would call them on

Monday. He and his roommate were watching Sunday Night Football, and the roommate went to bed at halftime."

Alex swallowed hard. "He found Hudson the next morning in the same place on the couch. Hudson's heart gave out some time in the night. He peacefully went to sleep and never woke up."

I choked out a sob and an "Oh no!" and put my hands over my mouth and nose in shock.

Ginny had her eyes closed and was wiping her cheeks with a tissue, and I could sense the pain reflected in her clenched jaw and pursed lips. Even Max had tears in the corners of his eyes and a stunned look on his face.

The memory of finding my mom the morning after she passed and the image of her struggling to get out of bed popped into my mind, and I was crying yet again.

We were all silent for a minute or two, and then Alex wrapped it up.

"For the past three and a half years, we've been healing as a family and thought it was enough. Then along came Topher with a whole new craziness." He sighed and flapped his hands in exasperation. "From trauma to drama, and here we all are."

We paused to take in their tale of heartbreak. This was all so intense, I wasn't sure how much more I was capable of handling today. "I am so sorry for your loss. What you've been through is unimaginable." Max nodded his agreement.

I took a drink and remembered one of my questions. "I'm curious. When did you figure out my Arica was bringing us all full circle?"

They both giggled, which brought another flashback to that fateful night in the restaurant when I saw them across the bar. It still seemed odd to hear Alex giggle.

Ginny had innately rebounded from the sadness about Hudson's death and responded cheerfully. "We knew pretty soon after they met that Topher was interested in a girl, but he didn't tell us much to begin with.

After a month or so, he said he had an errand in Providence and planned to meet up with her again. We inquired about her name. He laughed and told us that ironically, her name was how they started talking because he heard the barista call out Arica and saw it written on her coffee cup. It was surprising, but I didn't put too much emphasis on it at first.

After he met up with her a couple more times, we could tell he was captivated, and we asked more questions. He said she was originally from the Midwest and had moved to Providence for college.

Her last name didn't ring a bell of course, but when he talked about her parents, I became suspicious. When he described which area she grew up in, I was almost convinced. I mean, how many people from that part of the Midwest would name their only daughter Arica? I did some social media research," Alex's reproachful look returned. She stuck out her tongue at him, which made us chuckle.

"Okay, online stalking, maybe," she continued, "and I tracked you down on Facebook. I saw your married name and started crying immediately. When I showed Alex all the evidence, he verified my findings. We were absolutely dumbfounded this was happening." Max smiled, and I huffed.

"So, then I didn't know what to do again. Topher had no idea, I promise. Alex and I talked about it at length and debated when we should act. We agreed that if the two of them stayed together, we needed to find a time to face you and apologize.

When Topher told us about your mom, Alex was sad because he remembered her from when she taught at your school. We read the obituary just to confirm 100% that it was really you. Alex wanted to come back here with Topher to pay his respects, so we booked tickets for the three of us.

He also decided to visit his parents and see if he could smooth things over with them. They never forgave him all the way for not taking over the business, but they had warmed up a little more over the years after their grandchildren were born. They always send birthday cards and Christmas gifts for them and usually a note to us.

We visited them once or twice when the kids were little, but life got busy and we haven't been out here for years.

Anyway, we told Topher we'd accompany him so he wouldn't be alone, and we'd rent a car to visit family. Topher didn't understand how close his grandparents were to where your mom's services were held, and we didn't tell him. He was too focused on seeing Arica to think of much else.

We didn't share that we knew you until the day we flew out here. The poor kid had no clue he and his girlfriend had opened Pandora's box!" We all laughed, the ludicrous nature of the situation was too great not to be funny!

I asked, "I have one final question. What possessed you to choose last night to approach me?"

They nodded and Alex answered, "That was yet another of our disastrous decisions, apparently. We truly couldn't figure out the right time, and we thought maybe after dinner would be kind of low-key and safe. We didn't expect you to be thrilled to see us, but we couldn't have anticipated your feisty reaction!" He flashed a smirk-smile at my blush of embarrassment.

"We didn't know if you had an idea of us or not, we were flying blind on what you were aware of. We didn't want to ask Topher and throw a wrench in the works."

"No, I was oblivious! It's weird that I never asked about his last name, although I'm not sure I would have suspected even then. Yates isn't uncommon, and I would have just thought it was the universe messing with me. I mean, it WAS, but I wouldn't have predicted on THIS level." The three of them chuckled in response.

My burning questions had now all been answered. *Where did we go from here?*

Max was the one to bridge the gap of silence again. "When do you guys fly back east?"

Alex jerked. "Oh shit, I haven't thought about that in a while!" He abruptly pulled out his phone. "We're okay. It's almost 2 now and our flight leaves at 4:30. We have to go soon, but at least we're not late."

They were potentially wondering what I was feeling. I carefully said, "I'm genuinely glad I heard your story; it gives me a lot to consider. You've revealed many very unexpected things today, and I do appreciate your candor. With my mom and this, I'm going to need quite a bit of time to grieve and think and wade through a TON of feelings." Max squeezed my leg in a consoling manner.

We all stood up and stretched, and Ginny asked if she could give me another hug. I accepted, and we held each other for a minute. "I'm sorry about Hudson," I told her. "I'm sorry about everything," she responded. We both smiled, and it was soothing. Today was a step in a positive direction.

Alex hugged me as well, and I received one more smirk-smile. "I'm glad I don't have to worry about you finding us and smothering us with pillows in the middle of the night anymore."

"Don't be too confident, I still have to process twenty-seven years of anger. You might want to continue sleeping with one eye open until further notice." He chuckled and said he'd missed me and it was awesome to see me again.

Max shook their hands and thanked them for sharing so much with us. He expressed his condolences about their oldest son and said he'd take care of me.

We walked out of the restaurant and saw our three children sitting together waiting for us. Their inquisitive eyes searched our faces to determine the mood, and they received four smiles in return. Arica and Topher got up and hugged us all.

Dawson introduced himself to Ginny and Alex. I forgot they hadn't technically met yet. I suddenly wondered what their Ari looked like. Maybe I'd ask Arica if she had a photo…

We all said our goodbyes and headed out the front door of the hotel. Arica and Topher predictably hung back and were fawning over each other. In fairness, it may be some time until they'd be reunited. Ginny and I both had a look of "whatever" and I smiled again.

It was way too easy to fall back into the habits of the TAG Team, but I couldn't risk getting so burned again. Going slow was imperative to find out if I could trust her on any level this time. Besides, there was no guarantee that our kids would stay together, so the issue might resolve itself without me having to worry about it long.

Geez, I had SO MUCH to think about… It made me tired just acknowledging it. We managed to get the two lovebirds separated, and Max drove the four of us home. We had a fairly quiet dinner, and Max and I both went to bed early. I was afraid my brain would want to replay things and start analyzing, but fortunately I was wrong. I told Max good night and was out cold.

~ *Chapter 8* ~

AFTERMATH

The next few weeks were strange. It was disorienting not having my mom there to care for, talk to, or play games with. Grief hit me at random times – sometimes with prolonged crying, others were a quick pain at a memory and then gone.

About a week after we were home, I gave the kids a watered-down version of what I'd been through with Alex and Ginny. They were sympathetic, even though I'm not sure they fully comprehended the depth of the hurt I endured. I was grateful for their innocence; I didn't want my beloved children to ever have to face such a debilitating level of deception. Sadly, the truth is that someday they would likely understand all too well.

Dawson excused himself hurriedly after our conversation, but I asked Arica to wait. This was a delicate subject I didn't want to ignore or blow out of proportion.

"I know my actions with Topher's parents upset you, and I want you to know I feel bad about that part of it. It's clear you really like him, and I don't want to come between the two of you or jeopardize your future because of my past. The saying that 'blood is thicker than water' is appropriate here because your happiness is much more important to me than my anger. I'm just going to need some more time to figure out how to deal with all of it."

"Mom, it's okay. Now that I know the backstory, it makes sense. What they did to you was cruel, and you didn't deserve to be treated that way. They seem like they regret it, but I get this is new and you haven't had a chance to think about it yet. You were already overwhelmed emotionally; I wish the timing wasn't so terrible."

Through my haze of tears, I smiled and said, "Thank you for understanding, it has been a lot. I really can't believe this. Of all the young men you could have met, it turned out to be him."

She laughed. "Topher and I have discussed that! We feel like maybe we're meant to be the bridge to healing that helps everyone leave the bad blood behind and find some peace. That sounds cheesy and kind of egotistical, but it's so absurd when you think about the odds of this happening.

Mom, I do like him. Possibly even love him. But if seeing or talking to them is going to hurt you so badly, Topher and I will do our best to keep you apart. We don't live close enough for it to be a huge issue. You'd really only have to see them at major events like our wedding and stuff if we stay together. We'll do that if you want, we have a plan."

"That's a generous thing for you to offer, sweetie. It means a great deal to me." I cleared my throat from the sobs threatening to take over. "But I don't want it to be that way. Putting that stress on the two of you isn't fair, and I love you too much to expect you to take on such a heavy burden.

I will find some way of getting over this. Whether it's therapy, screaming into my pillow, or otherwise, I need to recover from all of it. I locked up the past and threw away the key, but it found me again and there's no escaping it now. As an adult, I have better resources and knowledge, and I want to set a good example for you and your brother on overcoming adversity. This is my opportunity to take the high road."

She hugged me. "I love you, mom. You deserve to be happy, too."

I cried on her shoulder and told her I loved her more than words.

My inquisitive brothers received a more colorful depiction of the scenario, and they were astounded to realize it was the same Alex from my class who caused all the uproar. They offered to fly out to Boston and give them a "brotherly beatdown," which had me cracking up at our group chat!

Max gently told me that he and the kids would leave Mom's bedroom as it is until I was ready to take the next steps of clearing it out and gathering up her clothes and possessions. In the first month, I couldn't fathom purging her things that reminded me of her smell and presence.

Arica celebrated her twenty-second birthday not long after, but with her missing Topher and me mourning my mom, it wasn't exactly the jubilation we normally tried to hold. The same goes for Dawson when he turned twenty in July. They each invited a few local friends to join us for dinner, and we did the cake and presents thing. It was low-key and bittersweet.

Our son was doing outstanding work in his apprenticeship and the on-the-job training. He was humble about it, but he did share with us some compliments he received at various times. He seemed to be enjoying it too, which was our foremost consideration. We were feeling more optimistic now that he had discovered something to build a future on.

Arica had been sending out résumés for more than two months, and she was getting frustrated at the lack of interest from companies. She was anxious to get back east, but with no job prospects, it wasn't financially feasible for her to make the trip very often.

Max and I explained to her more than once that we spent a large amount of money on her schooling, living arrangements, and flights back and forth. We would pay for travel and hotel when she lined up interviews, but not just to go see her boyfriend.

Despite all that, she began ramping up her pleas to go out there again in late July, whining about it being months *(less than two, but who's counting)* since she last saw Topher, and she loathed being so far apart.

She even resorted to full-on drama a few times with crying, begging, and relaying in detail how miserably lonely and bored she was here. It was over the top, but perhaps I should have been more sympathetic. At the time, young love somehow didn't seem so important when there was so much else in life *(like death and former enemies)* to deal with.

In mid-August, I got a text message from an unknown sender, which I didn't read right away. On my lunch break, I opened it to likely delete and block it. However, it was not spam. "Hey Tabby, this is Ginny. I hope you don't mind that I got your cell number from your daughter. Alex and I would like to fly her out for Labor Day weekend to go boating with us. Topher has REALLY missed her, and we thought it would be fun to have her join us for our family tradition. She can stay at our house. Is that okay with you and Max?"

Arica and Topher had been laying it on thick from both sides… My response was a quick, "I'll talk to Max and let you know." She came back right away with several symbols for happy, applause, boats, and two hearts, I assume for our lovestruck children. Of course she loved emojis as much as I do. I resisted the strong urge to reply in kind and waited to review it with Max.

Over dinner, Arica was discreetly trying to feel out whether I would address the text message. Her tactics to get what she wanted were irritating, so I decided to let her squirm a little. We all cleaned up, and Max and I went into the living room while the kids did their own things.

Arica lingered more than usual, doubtless attempting to overhear us talking as it pertained to her. Instead, I blathered on about work until she got bored and left to video chat with Topher. Max commented on her being clingy all evening.

"Well, there's a reason for that, and we need to talk about it," I told him.

"Oh boy, I can't wait to hear this…" he responded suspiciously.

"I received a text message from Ginny today asking if we would be okay if they flew Arica out to Boston over Labor Day to go boating with them. It's apparently an annual custom for them, and she would stay at Alex and Ginny's house. Ginny mentioned how much Topher missed

Arica, so they've **both** been pushing hard for her to be out there."

Max shook his head at this revelation. "Wow, they are persistent, I'll give 'em that. I suppose if Alex and Ginny are offering, I'm fine with it. What do you think?"

He was not expecting me to unload, but my thoughts tumbled out one after another… "I guess so as well. I just wish she would hear back from any of her résumé submissions. I'm afraid the longer it takes, the more tempted she's going to be to move in with him. I wholeheartedly don't think that's best for her. She should learn how to be independent first!

I know that's not what we're talking about here, but it's my worst fear that she'll recklessly jump into something she might profoundly regret later.

Or what if she ends up like Ginny, pregnant so young and it changes their entire future? Ginny's family is rich and all, but it's not Nick's responsibility to also subsidize his grandson and our daughter.

Part of me wishes we could afford to move her out there and pay for an apartment until she lands a job, but we can't. She needs to figure out how to do it herself anyway — that's a life lesson everyone should experience.

She's so passionate about her career in fashion, I really want her to be able to pursue that and find out what she's capable of!" The tears were welling up, crying seemed to be my default state in those days.

Max's surprise was evident, and he was speechless for a moment. "How long have you been holding all those thoughts in? Holy cow, babe, that's a lot to worry about!"

My shoulders slumped after I released several of my fears. "Yeah, well, still waters run deep, as they say. My brain never lets up, and I remember how impulsive I was at her age. It scares me. We can give her the good news now, you can tell her." He kissed me.

We called Arica in, and she sat on the couch with a cautiously hopeful look on her face. Max gave her the answer she was waiting for. She screamed and hugged us both hard before running back to her room to call Topher back.

Dawson came in after the scream, but we reassured him it was his sister's exuberance that she got to go to Boston again in a couple of weeks. He smiled and said that was awesome, then went back to his room. We heard Arica excitedly making plans and laughing freely, which made me feel like a slightly better mom.

We hadn't seen this side of our daughter in quite some time. She was non-stop talkative and bubbly and excited about her Labor Day getaway. We drove her to the airport early on Friday morning and Max took me back to work from home. He went to his office, so I had a rare quiet day all by myself in the house. I brought my laptop out to our back patio to soak in the sunshine and breathe some fresh air while being on calls.

Arica texted that she arrived just fine and Topher's mom picked her up. My reply was positive emojis and telling her to have fun, although I bristled at the thought of her and Ginny having quality time together. I pushed it aside and focused on work.

At just past 4:00, I turned off my laptop. I opened a bottle of wine and decided to relax until Max and Dawson got home. With Merlot warming my insides and the late summer sun warming my outsides, I let my mind begin to wander.

For the first time in weeks, my thoughts didn't go straight to my mom. Instead, I entered the dark side to think about the Alex and Ginny dilemma.

I should sit down and dissect all the information they shared at that lunch, minus the sad parts about Hudson.

I know they didn't hold back, everything she told me lines up with my memory of what happened.

Yet somehow her knowledge of how much she was hurting me, makes it worse. She was so cowardly!

Why was she so scared to tell me? It's not like we had ugly blowout fights or anything, I barely even got irritated with her during our friendship.

And why did Alex convince her not to tell me the truth? Because he didn't want to face me being hurt or angry? He was a major gutless asshole, too!

How can I trust them with my precious daughter when they might still be like that? What if their son is like that, too?

Ugh, how am I going to put this all behind me for good?

Should I go back to therapy? Maybe it's a smart idea considering I need to get past the grief of my mom's sudden death and the unexpected resurgence of my worst nightmare AT THE SAME TIME.

I'm madder at Alex than I used to be. It sounds like he was the one who pursued my best friend despite her telling him I had feelings for him. He admitted it was mutual and he treated me horribly, but it still stings that he dropped me like a hot potato as soon as he did. He's the one who caused everything to go downhill.

I never dealt with the heartbreak of losing Ginny like I should have. My state of mind went from severely depressed to even more severely pissed off, but then I shoved it all way down and carried on. Losing her was exponentially worse though because she was a MUCH bigger part of my life.

If someone said I had to choose between the two of them back then, I would have given him the boot without a second thought. There was a lot of backstory and potential for a future relationship, but deep down I knew he probably wasn't my forever partner. I liked him and wanted to see if we could be more than we were, but I loved Ginny like the sister I never had.

Am I a bad person for not readily accepting their apologies and forgiving them? It was more than twenty-seven years ago, should I be able to shrug it off like it was nothing more than stupid young people doing stupid things to each other?

It was easy to feel sad and sorry for them in the restaurant, but we still haven't addressed a lot of things. I have to play nice for Arica's sake, but there's no way I'll EVER trust them again. Letting my guard down this time is definitely a bridge too far. Fool me once, shame on you. Fool me twice, shame on ME. Once bitten, twice shy. Okay, enough of the clichés…

Yeah, I think I'll make an appointment with my therapist after the holiday. Is Dr. Feldman still practicing? I hope so, I liked her and I wouldn't have to start all over.

Wow, I finished my glass of wine in record time…

As I went in to pour a refill, I thought of suggesting to Max that we go out for dinner tonight, just the two of us. We hadn't had a date night since before my mom passed, and it was way overdue. I went back out to the patio and switched gears to finding a local restaurant with a tasty menu and maybe a shorter wait.

When I heard the garage door opening, I went inside to greet my loving husband and tell him my idea. He beamed and said it sounded like a fantastic Friday evening. He kissed me and went upstairs to change clothes. I texted Dawson he was on his own for dinner as I finished getting ready to leave.

During our date, I told Max my thoughts about going back to a therapist to deal with Alex and Ginny's big reveal. He wasn't a fan of psychotherapy, but he appreciated it helped me in the past.

He took a couple of bites and mulled it over. "Babe, I hear what you're saying, but would you consider talking to me about things and seeing if we can make some progress together before you take that step? I know the situation already, I was there when they explained and apologized, and I understand you better than anyone. I'm willing to try to help you work through the emotions as best I can and offer a mostly objective point of view."

His proposal came out of nowhere, so I took a few minutes to dwell on it.

"Okay, I guess we can give your idea a shot first. But I need you to be respectful if I don't think it's working for me. And I still might need professional help dealing with losing my mom and feeling like it's my fault."

He looked appalled. "Your fault! Why on earth would you think that? A blood clot went to her lungs. There's nothing you could have done to prevent her death!"

"Well, why didn't I hear her struggling to breathe and get out of bed? Why didn't I think to install some sort of system so she could press a button for a siren or alarm or whatever? If she'd been able to alert us, maybe we could have helped her long enough for the paramedics to arrive."

It occurred to me that I hadn't spoken my guilt out loud before. I fought back a sob, I had no desire to embarrass myself in a public place.

Max softened when he understood. "Tab, you can't beat yourself up over the what ifs. I did that, too, after my mom died, and it would have driven me insane. It's not worth it. It was your mom's time to go, and you had already done so much for her. You can't allow your conscience to get away with this. Be happy for the time we had with her."

He was right, and maybe it was feasible for me to start chipping away at the guilt if I convinced myself to focus on the practicality he was laying out for me.

We came home to an empty house and went back out to the patio to have more wine before we went to bed. We made love for the first time in several weeks, and I felt hopeful about life in a way I hadn't for a long while.

The next day was Saturday, and the three of us slept in. Max and Dawson were rustling around in the kitchen, so I went downstairs to join them. We had brunch and talked about what we should do for the rest of the day. There was a local Labor Day festival we hadn't been to in years, and we decided to go after everyone had taken a shower.

Before we left, we received a text from Arica in our family group chat that she was amazed at how the Becketts spent their weekend, complete with a photo of a stunning yacht. I guess Ginny's telling me they were "going boating" didn't mean fishing or a leisurely pontoon journey, but a luxury excursion with all the trimmings!

The name on it was "Beckett's Bona Mobilia" and I had to look it up. It's a legal term which means 'movable goods, personal property.' Nick's pretentious but appropriate titling of his yacht made me smile; it was exactly on par with what I knew of the man. Even without meeting him in person, I believed I had a pretty good idea of who he was.

Max, Dawson, and I had a fun time at the festival, eating more than our fair share of carbs and unhealthy fried foods and shopping for gifts. We got home late in the evening, and Dawson changed clothes and said he was going out with some friends.

Max and I once again spent some time on our back patio drinking and admiring the clear and starry sky. At one point he said, "It's been a hell of a year. Who knows what the rest of it holds, but I could really use a break from the constant go-go-go. Between everything that happened with your mom, Dawson and his apprenticeship, Arica meeting Topher and all the craziness that followed with his parents, we need some calm. I've come to realize I like quiet and boring. It's soothing!"

I replied, "I would love that as well. I don't know what's going to happen when Arica gets back, but I sure hope we can make it to the end of this year without any more massive surprises." We clinked our wine glasses and took a drink.

As we leaned back against the cushions, I stared up at the night sky and saw a shooting star streak across my vision. My wish was for the tranquility we craved. Max had been refilling his glass and didn't see the star. It was mine, and I begged it to honor my request.

Sunday was a lazy day at our house, and Monday was the holiday. The three of us didn't have much planned besides picking Arica up at the airport a few minutes after 8 p.m. We decided to stop for a late dinner on the way home. Her flight was delayed slightly, so we met her at baggage claim around 8:45.

We were all famished by then and headed to a nearby restaurant. Arica told us all the details of boating with the Becketts, with colorful descriptions of Ginny's sisters and Nick, and Topher's cousins. She gushed about Ari and how much they had in common besides their names. She was entranced by their family dynamics, yacht traditions, and how they all got along.

The rest of us quietly listened to her while we ate, and then she recognized she'd been dominating the conversation. "I'm so sorry, tell me what you did this weekend!" she exclaimed.

Dawson spoke up, "Mom and Dad had a date night on Friday, I hung out with friends, we all went to the festival on Saturday, and yesterday we were lazy bums. Now you're caught up."

Arica spontaneously started crying. We were confused, but she tearfully told us, "I am terrible. I've been so selfish talking about my wonderful holiday. I didn't mean to sound so superior!" We appeased her by saying she had every right to be excited about it. We weren't upset; she should not feel guilty in the least.

She smiled a little and told us she loved us and she wished it were easier for our family and Topher's to all be together. Max must have seen my jaw tighten because he gently squeezed my leg. We all ate in silence for a bit after that.

The ride home consisted of Max and me listening to our children in the back seat sharing memes and videos while laughing and making fun of things we didn't understand. I was happy to hear brother and sister enjoying each other's company, but also bitter that we were steadily losing Arica to Boston and her boyfriend's wealthy family and fancy lifestyle.

Coming to terms with my past needed to happen sooner rather than later because their relationship didn't appear to be ending any time soon. Plus, my resentment was still hard to keep contained.

We were all tired the next morning, but Max, Dawson, and I had to return to our normal work schedule. While we were preparing dinner, Arica was quiet and subdued. I wondered if she regretted coming back home. She excused herself after eating and went to her room to video chat with Topher as usual. When they were done, she came out to the living room where Max and I were in our own virtual worlds on our phones.

She sat down and said, "I just wanted to tell you that I greatly appreciate your support in letting me go out there this weekend to spend time with the Beckett family. I feel like part of Topher's world, and I love that because he and I are sure we belong together!

His parents, aunts, and grandpa were asking me what I envision for my career, so I gave them an overview. I also shared how frustrating it's been applying with no responses, and they were very sympathetic. They all told me they'd reach out to their network to see if they could find a decent option for me.

I don't know how long I'll have to wait or if anything will ever come of it, but I'm so grateful that they're all willing to help me however they can. They did say they'd fly me out there if something becomes available."

My look of annoyance must have been obvious because she continued quickly. "I know you guys have also said you'll send me, and I love you for that. I'm sorry it's been super expensive for you to keep flying me to the East Coast from here, and I don't want you to spend any more than you have to from now on.

I've saved up some money from my jobs that I can use when I need to go out there, and I want to try to do this as much on my own as possible. Topher and I are not looking for a handout or an easy button, we just want to be together."

Max looked at me, but his facial expression wasn't easy to read. I turned back to our daughter and smiled. "Honey, this is a pivotal point in your life, and again I'm glad you're facing it with rational thought and sincerity. Hopefully, someone in Topher's family is able to give you a leg up, because it sure seems like applying blindly to job openings isn't getting us anywhere.

Job searching used to be easier. As a recent college grad looking for your first full-time position in today's market though, it's not exactly a walk in the park. Unfortunately, your dad and I don't know anyone out there. We can only provide advice on your résumé and interviews and a place to live while you figure it out. I wish we were able to do more."

Arica was sniffling now, and through her tears she told us, "I know you want to help me; I know we're not the richest family in the world; and I know you're fearful that Topher will hurt me like his parents did to you."

Her words stung, and I started crying as well. "I won't deny that, it scares me."

"I really think he loves me and wants a future with me, and I need to find out if that's true."

The three of us hugged, Arica and me sobbing abundantly.

Max shook his head at us. "You may not realize it, but you are like two peas in a pod. We will figure this out. Arica will get offered a job; it will all work out for the best. Can you both try to be patient?"

She and I snickered and dried our eyes. Arica went back to her room. Max held me on the couch for a bit, and then we went upstairs to bed.

As I was preparing to go to sleep, my conscience notified me that I hadn't thought about my mom in several days. Was it a positive thing, or did it make me a horrendous daughter?

Right when I was feeling like I was ready to rest, my adrenaline shot up and I cried again. Would I ever be able to get past the grief and guilt of my mother's death? It sure didn't feel like it then.

With our lives in a relatively less chaotic period and a semi-regular schedule, I began spending more time with my friends. Kate had been a steadfast supporter when my mom came to live with us. She got me out of the house a few times so I didn't forget I was still Tabitha and not only a caretaker for the people I love. I need those traits in a friend!

One night with lots of wine at the ready, I finally gave her the full synopsis of my past with Alex and Ginny and why I reacted the way I did when I saw them again. She was aghast.

"I can't believe they did that to you. Those bastards! I also can't believe you never told me this before. That's a hell of a load to carry all by yourself for so many years."

I shrugged. "It was ancient history, and I didn't ever want to think or talk about it. It was too painful."

"Yeah, I suppose that makes sense. Damn girl, between your upbringing, the mean bitches in high school, and these two assholes, you've been through some SHIT."

"Ha! You're not wrong. When you put it all together like that, it sounds worse. Maybe that's why I didn't make as much progress in therapy as I should have. I never told her about Alex and Ginny either. I wanted to fix the problem without openly acknowledging it."

"Um, that seems pretty counterproductive if you ask me. But I'm not a therapist, so don't actually ask me." She shrugged, and I laughed.

"Max never even knew until I explained that night. Between the two of you, you've heard almost every single thing about me. I locked it all up tight as can be and never intended on opening it again." I sighed heavily in dismay.

Kate had a gentler tone when she asked, "So how do you feel about it now? You're probably going to have to deal with them again."

A disgruntled sound came out as I said, "I don't know! I have so much processing to do, and I don't want to think about it!

I really can't wrap my head around the fact that they're back in my life. They were supposed to be miserable and regret what they did to me for the rest of their lives. Now I learn that they're still together, they seem happy, and I'm somehow expected to just welcome them with open arms and pretend like nothing happened. None of it makes sense!

Arica had no idea, so it's not like I can be upset with her. It would be different if she knew and still decided to date him, but that's not the case. Now she's too deep in love for me to expect her to walk away, which means I have to find a way to cope. Of all the guys in all the big wide world, she chooses the son of THEM." I spit out the word like it was poison in my mouth.

Her eyes were huge. "I've never heard you get this worked up before, even about your dad. There's more to unpack than I realized. How can I help?"

I smiled and brusquely wiped the tears that were welling up. "Just listening to my complaining. You're always here for me, that's enough. More importantly, I know you'd never do anything like they did to me, and that's my primary criteria for friends as an adult. That, and having a high tolerance for wine."

We clinked our glasses in solidarity.

It bothered me that in the case of interacting with Alex and Ginny again, I couldn't come up with a plan. I ALWAYS had a plan…

For several weeks, I went out with various ladies. It was revitalizing to re-connect, laugh, and talk about things other than my own issues. I started feeling more like myself again.

Even before she moved in, I had unconsciously dedicated copious amounts of time and effort to constantly worry about and assist my mom. It hadn't felt like an overbearing burden while I was doing it, but both of my kids' lives were busy as well.

The extensive list of responsibilities had significantly decreased the time I had to spend with the other women in my life, and I'd missed them. Someone brought up the possibility of a girls' getaway trip next year, which sounded heavenly to me!

With friends who had also lost parents, I shared my fears about neglecting my mom in her final moments when she needed me the most. Everyone I talked to attested that I had done more than was expected of me. They unanimously concurred that I shouldn't punish myself for something I couldn't have prevented anyway. The guilt was a natural reaction to sudden loss and a part of grief, but I deserved to forgive myself and let it go.

Between them and Max, the sympathy and comfort helped me to begin the slow healing process from her death.

In addition to those conversations, Max said he was ready to listen whenever I wanted to discuss Alex and Ginny. Of course I didn't want to dive into it, but we made plans to sit down one Friday night when Arica and Dawson were out doing their own things. He opened a bottle of my favorite Merlot and set two glasses on the coffee table.

I took a big drink, sighed, and looked at him. "I don't know where to begin. What am I supposed to talk about?"

"Well, how about what you were thinking as they were telling their story. It was information overload! You said it filled in a lot of blanks, but you didn't tell me how you felt afterward."

"Okay. I've taken the time to analyze some of it, so I guess I can start there…

When Ginny was talking about the weeks while I was sick, I was irate. Obviously, they had to connect somehow, but it was infuriating that they met up so many times despite me being the common denominator.

They had fun together behind my back knowing I was confined to my bed. It was like they took advantage of my weakness and were laughing at me. And the worst of it was that she just let the attraction take hold of her like she did with the plethora of boys she went out with on a regular basis."

The last part had a harsh bite to it, and Max raised his eyebrows at me.

"Fine, I was always a tad jealous that she could get any guy she wanted. I was the sad, ugly friend who tagged along with her. I didn't date much, as I've told you, and it wasn't fair at all that she decided to seduce one of the few I liked."

"I'm not so sure it was her doing the seducing based on their story," he pointed out.

"Whatever. She certainly didn't try very hard to stop it." My defensiveness was high.

"Are you upset that he was actively pursuing her and didn't let up when she told him they shouldn't betray you? You seem a lot more pissed at her than at him, which doesn't balance with you losing both of them mostly due to HIS actions."

"Yes, I'm actually angrier at him now than I was then. It bugs me that he told her way more than he ever talked about with me, especially after he said he appreciated me being there for him through all our years together. He'd only known her for a few weeks, and it was suddenly like I'd never existed! I AM mad at him, but losing him wasn't nearly as painful as losing her."

As the words came out, I choked up a little, and the inevitable tears started.

"Alex was my friend for almost my entire life. We were attracted to each other, but I honestly don't think our personalities would have stood the test of time in a real relationship. Even if we weren't meant to be a couple, though, he still should have cared about me and my feelings.

Ginny was the closest thing I ever had to a sister, and I thought our bond was unbreakable. For her to not only choose to be with Alex when she knew I liked him, but also to completely abandon me was absolutely heartbreaking. There was no warning, no explanation, no apology, NOTHING. It wrecked me for a long time."

The last sentence was half-garbled through my heavy crying, but he understood what I meant. I got up and brought the tissue box back to our spot on the couch while wiping my eyes and blowing my nose.

"Yes, she admitted to being a horrible friend and a complete wimp for not telling me. But it still doesn't make up for what I felt then and how I feel when I look at her face now. The betrayal fills me up like it did twenty-seven years ago, and it HURTS." I clenched my fists as I said the last part.

Max said softly, "Nothing can change the past, Tab, you know that. But now you're aware of what happened from their side, and you need to figure out how to move forward with the knowledge. It would be different if you didn't have to see them again; you could take all the time in the world to process this and overcome the pain.

But in our case, you don't have that luxury. Our daughter loves their son, and vice versa. I'm sure you can be civil with them and 'fake it to make it,' but that doesn't solve the issue of you healing from the emotional trauma. What do you think WOULD help you?"

I threw up my hands in frustration. "I don't know, that's the problem! The apology helped some, and the petty part of me was glad they had a hard road for quite a while because they didn't deserve easy and fun. But I'm still in agony. I don't trust her for ANYTHING. I really don't like when it feels good to have our little moments of eye rolling and knowing what the other one is thinking. She's not worthy of that from me anymore! She hasn't earned the right to be back in my life or know MY daughter and spoil her!"

My voice rose steadily throughout this diatribe, and Max was somewhat flustered. "Okay, okay. I understand where you are now."

After a moment he hesitantly asked, "Have you thought about what you would say to Ginny if the two of you were alone and you could put everything out on the table?"

It was a valid question. "No. In actuality, I don't know what I want to say to her. I've associated her with extreme heartache and anger for so long, I never pondered what it would take for me to forgive her or treat her like just another person. It's like trying to envision the entire universe, it's too much for my feeble human brain!"

He smiled at my lame attempt at a joke and continued. "Maybe that's what you need to decide. What would it take, and how do we get there? I believe Ginny would be open to it if she knew what you needed. From our brief time together, I could see that she still cares deeply about you, and Alex confirmed that she never stopped. It might not be what you want to hear, but I think you should take it into consideration."

His justifying her feelings was annoying, but I couldn't deny his rationale.

In a quiet voice, I admitted, "I was astonished when she told me about why she used the name Arica for their daughter. I wasn't expecting that answer at all, and it was possibly the nicest thing anyone's ever done for me. No offense."

"None taken, that was extraordinary. I'm glad you're able to appreciate what she did, I think that's a huge step in the right direction!"

"Thanks, Dr. Ganter. I'm so pleased you think I'm making progress."

He laughed. "Maybe that's enough for tonight, I don't want to push you too hard. Are you all right with picking this back up another time soon?"

"That's fine. Seems like I need to do some more examination about what I just said. When it's thoughts in my head, I can shove them back into a closet and shut the door. Now that I've heard it and still reacted so strongly, I obviously have plenty more to deal with. I hate that we're having to do this, why couldn't it have stayed in the past?"

I put my head in my hands and cried for several minutes. Max held me and told me he loved me and we'd get through this together. Wiping my face, I took a swallow of the wine I'd scarcely touched so far and curled against him.

"Let's watch a dumb movie or something, I want to laugh." We chose one of our old comedic favorites and drank our wine while chuckling at the familiar and hilarious jokes.

~ *Chapter 9* ~

Difficult Decisions

Near the end of September, Dawson mentioned during dinner one night that he was wrapping up his first year of the apprenticeship. I chided myself for not realizing it earlier, but he brushed it off.

"No biggie, Mom. I was just keeping you updated. I've decided I want to be a CEM, which is a Construction Engineering Manager. One more year of this program and my experience should help me land a good starting job. I know I'll have to earn my way up from the bottom, I'm fine with that. It sounds like I'll still get to supervise crews and projects and do a lot of hands-on work on the job sites. Plus, I can use my computer skills in an office. It's kind of the best of both worlds!"

He smiled, and we all told him how proud we were. I studied him closely and saw how much of a man he was now; inarguably not my baby boy anymore.

His smile faded and he continued at a slower pace. "There's something else."

My stomach tightened and I put down my fork to give him my full attention. I was curious where this was going…

"Some friends of mine from the program have an apartment together that's a lot closer to where I work. One of them is leaving to live in Florida at the end of the year when his classes are done. I was thinking about taking his spot and moving in with them." He nervously looked back and forth between his dad and me.

Max spoke first, "Wow bud, that's all awesome! You've found a career you're excited about, and you might move into your first place away from home. Great steps for you!" He patted our son on the back and Dawson exhaled in relief at the reaction.

"Absolutely fantastic, D!" I added. "I love hearing the enthusiasm when you talk about your future! And we're happy to help and make sure you have everything you need."

He was beaming, and I returned his radiant smile.

Arica teased, "Aww, my widdle brudder is all growed up!" and pinched his cheek. He playfully acted offended and swatted her hand away. We all laughed together and finished our meal, letting Dawson tell us more details about his plans. A lot of what he said was a foreign language to me, but watching his face light up when he talked was all I needed.

If only my mom were still here, she would have loved to see him so happy.

Max and I were now barreling toward empty-nester status, and I wasn't quite sure how I would handle it. Who was I if I didn't have someone to take care of?

That weekend, Max and I were alone again. He gave me a thoughtful look. "Do you want to talk about the elephants in the room some more?"

I smirked at his reference and said, "I probably should. I've thought a little more about it since our previous session. Let me take my contacts out and I'll be back."

When I returned, I saw he had lit the fireplace, placed a box of tissues next to our spot, and once again poured me some wine. He knew me too well. I sighed woefully and began.

"You asked me a complicated question last time about what I would say to Ginny if I could unleash my feelings. I was kind of surprised I'd never contemplated it before, but I've always imagined the worst when I thought about them.

I'd daydream about them having a humongous fight and breaking up because she wanted to date around or he was an unreliable shmuck who just didn't show up to stuff. They deserved to be as emotionally damaged as I was, so that's what I conjured up in my head. I'm not proud of that, but it's the truth.

She gave us her side of what happened and how she was a wreck after we parted ways. She claimed she has missed me ever since, but it still doesn't feel like it compares to what I went through. She and Alex traipsed off to be with her sisters and dad, and I was left back in the same place all alone. They had each other, I had no one.

She has no clue how I desperately used to park near her apartment to try to catch her coming or going. How many nights I cried myself to sleep wondering what I did wrong. How much time I spent going over and over and over our conversations to figure out what I said that made her leave and never come back."

Tears were running down my face, and I took a drink. "Obviously she knew I was enraged when I said what I did outside the restaurant back then, but she still doesn't understand what I went through in the time between. A big part of me wants to tell her every tiny detail of that painful few months so she can grasp exactly what she did to me."

Max was nodding along with most of what I said. "All of that is totally understandable, Tab. You've never had a chance to express your feelings from when it happened. Then you suppressed them for so long it just became one immense glob of anger instead of lots of individual emotions like hurt, sadness, grief, and so on. I get it."

When he put it that way, I could envision it. "You really are good at this!" I kissed him and continued.

"You're exactly right, I lumped it all into rage because it was easier. If I didn't think about the details or separate the abandonment and dejection, it didn't hurt quite as much.

When I saw them after dinner this summer, I swear every single feeling and insecurity I had during that time came rushing up and punching me in the gut. Those emotions had been sealed tight for so long, I'd kind of forgotten about all of them until Ginny was standing in front of me."

Shaking my head, I ruefully conceded, "I am so fucking tired of dragging it all around with me."

"So how do you lighten the load and move on?"

I shrugged. "Isn't that what my therapist is supposed to tell me?" He chuckled.

Putting my next thoughts into words took me a minute. "The friends I have now, like Kate and my former co-workers, fill the gaps Ginny used to. She's unfortunately going to be in my life for at least the near future, but I want to convince myself I don't have to be besties with her anymore.

I would like to see her as just a regular person and not the Ginny I loved from our TAG Team days. That friendship is dead and buried, and I don't have to let her in close enough for her to hurt me again. I only have to see her as Arica's boyfriend's mom."

"That's an excellent goal, but does it realistically solve the underlying problem? Don't you think they owe you the opportunity to tell your side of the story, too? Telling them what you went through isn't to punish them, but to help you release the pain and convey how much they meant to you back then. That way everything is on even ground, and nothing is left unsaid about that time of your life."

Silence briefly ensued while I ruminated on this. "Okay, I understand what you're getting at. But how do I say, 'Hey, let's sit down again so I can make you feel like absolute shit by taking you step by step through my pain and anguish from twenty-seven years ago'?"

Max gave a small shrug. "I'm sure we can come up with a nicer way to say it; you don't have to go in guns a-blazin' with the intention of making them feel worse. Tab, if telling them, in particular Ginny, would help you move forward without the weight of this anymore, isn't it worth it to try?"

"Maybe? I don't know. They already apologized, so what more would I expect from them?"

"They were remorseful for what they know they did, not what they put you through specifically. Ginny got sick, it turned out they were pregnant, and their lives went speeding full steam ahead. Yours didn't for quite a while, but they haven't heard your journey.

Besides, what happens if you don't tell them now and Arica and Topher break up in a few weeks or months? You may never have this possibility again, and it's almost a gift for you to be able to say all the things you've kept pent up for so long. Not everyone gets to do that."

"I guess." It was extremely difficult for me to think of it as a 'gift,' but it would be liberating to FINALLY get everything off my chest.

He rested his case with, "Right now you're still carrying it with you, but leaving the past where it belongs is the only way you can truly be free of it, babe."

His logic was solid, and it was hard to disagree. Damn him for being so insightful.

Luckily, we didn't have to wait too long for Topher's family to make good on their promise.

Shortly before Halloween, Topher eagerly told Arica that his aunt was connected to someone in the fashion industry. Several conversations with multiple people happened, and there was a company looking for an entry-level assistant that would like to talk to her.

There was much high-pitched excitement as she told us the minute we got home from work. She barely sat still during dinner as she weighed all the possibilities this could unlock for her.

Topher said he'd be at his aunt's house the following night for Arica to gain more details and ask some preliminary questions. She practically ran back to her bedroom after we ate and cleaned up to call him back and make more plans.

As I was putting some laundry away upstairs, I heard her say, "Thank you so much, Mr. and Mrs. Yates. I can't WAIT to be out there with all of you!"

I rolled my eyes and felt a wave of anger wash over me at the thought that Ginny would soon be able to spend a lot more time with my daughter than I would. Great, one more thing for me to deal with…

The next evening, Arica told us not to count on her for dinner, she'd find something to eat after her call with Topher's aunt. She shut herself in her room and was on the phone for well over an hour before she came downstairs. She was quiet, which I was not expecting.

"Hi honey, how did the call go? Do you know more about the job opening?"

"Yes. Topher's Aunt Lisey explained how she reached out to her friend and it all went through the grapevine and led to her hearing about this position. She admitted she doesn't know much about fashion, so I couldn't ask any detailed questions. From what she told me though, it's pretty basic." Arica sighed and looked pitiful.

"If she's right, then I had more responsibilities during my internship in New York City. I told her I'd love to talk to them, of course, and she's going to have them email me tomorrow."

She flopped on the couch with a dramatic huff. "I just hope it's more than what she described, because I'm willing to work my way up from the ground floor, but I don't want to start in the BASEMENT!"

Max and I stared at each other to see who was brave enough to approach it first. He held his hand out toward me, and I gave him an annoyed look in return.

I had no idea what to say, but I went with my gut. "Well, it sounds like there's a LOT more to learn when you talk to them. Don't forget that interviews are two-way dialogues. They want to know more about you, but it's also your time to find out if the position is what you're looking for.

Don't make any assumptions yet. Try to keep an open mind and figure out what questions you want to ask to help you determine if it's the kind of role you want."

Max added, "Yes, and like you said, most of us don't know what you do about the fashion industry, so maybe Topher's aunt wasn't defining it well. And if this isn't a proper fit, another opportunity **will** come along."

Arica replied from under a pillow, "I get it. I'm trying to stay optimistic, but I was so hopeful it was going to be top-notch. Plus, I'm nervous because Toph's family *(now she's calling him 'Toph'?)* put themselves out there for me, and I don't want to make them look bad. I can't just turn down a job because I'm picky and risk making them mad. Beggars can't be choosers."

"I'm sorry the call wasn't what you expected, but progress is still positive." I tried to sound sympathetic.

She sighed in defeat. "You're right. I'm going to have a small bite to eat, and then I'm sure Toph will call when he gets back to his apartment. Love you both, thanks for listening." She hugged us and went into the kitchen to find food.

Max and I shrugged at each other. We'd had a short break from the maelstrom, but we were back again. It hit me that both of our kids might be on their own by New Year's if things continued at this pace.

Ouch, I was really NOT ready for that.

Two days later, Arica had her video interview with the company. Max and I hurried home from work to find out how it went. She was on the couch watching TV, but she shut it off and smiled at us.

"It went well, better than I expected. It's not the greatest job, but it's a foot in the door; I'm trying to focus on that part. The best thing is I would be working in a store that's only fifteen minutes or so from Topher's apartment, so I could rent a place near him and we wouldn't have to go far to see each other."

"That's wonderful!" I said, mainly referring to the better than expected part. "Did they tell you how long until you'd hear back from them?"

"They said they'll be talking to some other applicants the rest of this week, and they plan to let us all know in the middle or end of next week if we'll be continuing."

"Okay, that's not too bad," Max replied. "I understand how hard it is to wait, but I'm glad you feel good about it!"

"Did you send a thank you follow-up?" I asked. She nodded. "Fantastic job, honey! Congratulations on your first post-college interview!"

Max and I went upstairs to change out of work clothes, then back down to start dinner. The three of us were all lost in our own thoughts when Arica's phone rang. She must not have recognized the number because she answered it with some formality. She replied to a few questions as she was walking to her room for privacy. We went back to food preparation.

She came back to the kitchen as Dawson walked in the door, and said, "Cool, I can tell you all at the same time." Her eyes were sparkling with excitement.

"That was another company, one I applied to like a month ago. They were asking if I was still interested and if I had some time to interview soon. After we got off the phone, I went back and read the job description, and it's exactly the kind of responsibilities I'm looking for! I scheduled to talk to the hiring manager on Monday morning." She had a shell-shocked look on her face; I don't think it had sunk in yet.

"Awesomesauce, sis!" Dawson said. "How did today's go?" She gave him a recap as they walked back upstairs together.

"This is happening fast," I told Max quietly, "I'm not ready for her to leave us forever."

"Let's not get ahead of ourselves, babe. You and I both know that an initial interview doesn't guarantee anything. We should prepare more for consoling her if neither of these leads to an offer. She's going to be crushed if that happens."

Over dinner, Dawson amused us with a funny story from work, and Arica said she researched the hiring manager for her next interview on LinkedIn. She was a bit intimidated by how advanced the woman's career was. We reminded her to be grateful for those kinds of people, they could teach her so much.

I advised her to reach out to her RISD counselor for any advice or connections at either company that might help, and she said she would send an email right away. It was a productive family consultation where Max and I felt like helpful parents, and our kids learned a little more about how to navigate through the "real world" they were entering.

Before I went to work on Monday, I kissed Arica on the forehead and wished her the best of luck for the interview. Dawson yelled "Break a leg!" as he walked out the door, and Max gave her a small pep talk before heading downstairs for breakfast. I texted her near lunchtime to ask how it went, and she sent back a simple thumbs up emoji.

She was working that afternoon and evening, so it was close to bedtime when we saw her. Max and I pounced the moment she came in, asking her what happened and if she thought she answered their questions well. She was tired, but she summarized the conversation. It sounded like a positive one, and we told her we were proud of her.

It was an excruciating two days until she heard anything back. From there it got chaotic fast.

The first company decided to move her forward to talk to the hiring manager, and they made an exception for her to interview virtually again right before Thanksgiving.

Then the second company emailed that they ALSO wanted to meet with her again! They asked if she would be able to come out and interview in person if they provided a hotel room for her. She called me at work afterward to catch me up on everything.

I suggested she call the first one back and see if they preferred her to come in person as well and she could coordinate the two interviews on consecutive days after the holiday. I sent a text to Max to give him a heads-up on what we were dealing with.

Arica was a ball of restless energy that evening. The first company was thrilled that she was willing to travel, so she would knock both out while she was there. We booked her a seat to fly out early the first morning before her afternoon interview. The second one was the following morning, which gave her plenty of time in between. She wanted some time with Topher afterward, so she would stay an extra night and come home in the morning.

Since the second company was paying for one night's hotel, I mentioned without thinking that we just had to figure out the second night. She looked at me to see if I was kidding, and I blushed when I realized she would be staying with her boyfriend. More like both nights if I was being honest with myself.

I sighed and told her never mind, and Max and I left so she could call Topher and tell him all the exciting developments. They were still video chatting when Max and I went to bed. Ah, to be young and in love on a Friday night and never running out of things to talk about...

The four of us spent Thanksgiving at Max's dad's house with his brothers and families plus a few other close relatives. It was a loud, rowdy day with lots of laughter, teasing, and more food than anyone could eat. I had a great time, but with it being the first major holiday without my mom, there were several moments of tearfulness as well.

Arica and Dawson played board games with their cousins, which us adults had jokingly dubbed the "Ganter Survivor Games" long ago. For some reason, they always evolved into competitive yelling matches as some ganged up together, others complained about the alliances, and individuals turned on each other. Everyone ended up walking away with no clear winner. It was all in good fun, by the end of the day they'd be back to deliberating some current issue or laughing over the latest TikTok challenge.

During the loudest part, I took a video and sent it to my brothers with the caption, "This is why I'm half deaf and I drink," and wished them a Happy Thanksgiving. They both planned to visit at Christmas, but it was still strange not talking to them then.

We were all off work Sunday, so we decided to go out for a family dinner. We chose a fancier restaurant than normal, and it felt special to be dressed up and enjoying the evening to celebrate Arica's interviews and Dawson's successful first year in his apprenticeship program. Arica wore one of her original designs, which made her look like a movie star in my humble opinion. It was a stellar meal with the ones I love the most.

Arica flew out to Boston on Tuesday morning, and Ginny drove her to their house to get ready. Ginny also dropped her off at the interview location so she wouldn't have to deal with traffic on her own and find parking. Afterward, Topher picked her up to have an early dinner and then go to her hotel.

Arica texted our family chat when she landed safely and said the interview went very well. She and Topher were together, and all was fine. We were impatient to hear all the details, but we knew she wanted time with her boyfriend since she hadn't seen him in a while.

I had to admit, the transition from having her home and talking to her every day to her being out there and in her own world again was tricky for me.

She sent us a quick note the next morning after her second interview telling us the hiring manager was splendid and she loved the potential, but that was all we heard from her. She later had dinner with members of Topher's family.

Ginny texted me after they ate that Arica was such a wonderful person and seemed excited about her opportunities. She said Topher really hit the jackpot and everyone adores our daughter. I sent back a few heart emojis and shared the sentiment with Max.

Our daughter let us know that her flight was on time Thursday morning, and she was at the gate to leave soon. That evening, she was visibly tired but in a bright mood.

From what she disclosed, both interviews went exceptionally well, and the companies were impressed with her. She was ecstatic that she'd been able to meet with them in person, she said it went a long way to converse face-to-face and walk around the workspace with them. She finished by telling us she regretted not taking the following day off from her local job because she was utterly exhausted.

We told her if she didn't feel up to it, we were willing to call and tell them she was sick so she could recuperate. She smiled in gratitude and hugged us all.

I tried to reach Arica the next morning to see if she was awake since her shift started at noon and she habitually set her alarm two hours before. When she didn't answer by 11 a.m., I searched for the number to her store and called, finally getting through to the correct department. I told them my daughter wasn't feeling well and needed to sleep off whatever germs she had acquired.

She may be a responsible adult, but I still couldn't pass up a chance to be a caring mother! I texted her to rest today, I'd excused her from work. She didn't respond until nearly 1 p.m. and thanked me profusely.

When I got home, she hugged me immediately and voiced her appreciation again for saving her job. She had set her alarm but had not actually turned it on, so she just kept sleeping. She panicked when she woke up and saw how late it was, but relaxed after she read my text messages.

Score one for mom, I'll take it.

It was a quiet weekend with Arica working and D out doing his own thing, and Max and I had some time to talk. We calculated the timeline possibilities if Arica received an offer soon, plus Dawson moving into an apartment. None of the scenarios appealed to me. When he could tell I was getting frustrated, Max changed the subject. We avoided the Alex and Ginny topic; I had too much else on my mind with our children to focus on old wounds.

On Wednesday of the next week, the first job emailed Arica to tell her they had one more person who wanted to talk to her. It would be virtual, and they were hoping to meet with her on Friday morning. She adjusted her local job shift to start later to accommodate the interview and to grab a quick bite to eat beforehand.

The second job emailed her on Friday as well, but in the rush, she didn't see their message until after business hours. She left a voicemail rather early Monday morning, and we were back to waiting again. Arica called me after lunch, and she was almost screaming into the phone that the second company wanted to offer her a job!

It was a slightly different position than what they told her at the beginning. They were sending her an updated job overview, but it was hers if she wanted it. I told her how proud and excited I was, and I couldn't wait to hear the whole deal that night.

Yikes, we would now be moving both of them out at the same time, and my chest tightened at the thought. My parental anxiety would have to be addressed later. It was year-end crunch time at work, and I needed to concentrate.

Over dinner, Arica explained how the role had been altered after the hiring manager figured out Arica was more knowledgeable than expected. They wanted to give her more responsibility than they'd originally planned, which was terrific news.

The downside was that she would now be working in the corporate office instead of one of the stores, and the headquarters was located more than thirty minutes north of downtown Boston. Topher lived about twenty-five minutes southwest of downtown, which put an hour between them on a regular day. She could look for an apartment partway closer, but it would still make it difficult for them to see each other much during the week.

I gently remarked that most dating couples spend time together on the weekends anyway. She nodded, but it was clear she wasn't thrilled about the location part of the job modification.

We talked about what she would say to them to accept the position, what she should do with the first company, and when would be a reasonable start date due to the holidays. There were so many choices to make in a relatively short time frame, our daughter was getting a crash course in big decisions.

Dawson was quiet while listening to everything happening with Arica. After dinner I asked to talk to him when she went upstairs to fill Topher in on the details.

"I don't want you to think that this changes anything for you, D. We will still help you move in a few weeks when you can get in. Have you thought about what you'll need? Do you know when you'll add your name to the lease?"

"Well, the other guys are fine if I want to move in as early as the twenty-ninth, but I can be flexible if Arica's stuff is happening then and you and Dad need to go out with her. I'm just moving a half an hour away and have friends who can help me, hers is massive and more time-consuming."

I hugged him and thought yet again about how caring and considerate our kids are. We did something right with them! "I appreciate your adaptability. Once she figures out exactly what this company wants her to do, we'll also plan for your move."

"Thanks, Mom. What are you and Dad going to do when you suddenly have the house to yourselves all the time? Will you be okay as empty nesters?"

"I'm going to rent out your rooms for egregious amounts of money so I can quit my day job, and I think your dad has some plans for our alone time." I waggled my eyebrows at him, and he snickered.

"Gross, Mom. I'm sorry I asked!" We both laughed.

The next morning, Arica called to tell me that the first company offered her a position as well! They were hiring three people in the same role for different stores, and she was one of them! I was almost speechless – she received offers from the only two jobs she had interviewed for!

During my drive home, I mentally prepared myself to offer logical advice without emotional attachment. Our daughter deserved the best plan of action for HER future. Only time would tell if it also included Topher.

That evening, we spent a lot of time going through detailed comparisons of both companies. Company 2 ended up with more pros and fewer cons. Max asked, if she took Topher and his family out of the equation, what would she choose?

Arica admitted that she was more excited when she thought about the second company and the possibilities there. We already perceived it to be the better option, but we let her come to the conclusion on her own. We all sat in silence for a moment, and she nodded to herself.

"I really do want to accept that offer over the other one. If Topher and I are meant to be together, then an hour apart isn't a big deal. We've been doing a long-distance relationship for the majority of this year, so maybe one hour will seem like nothing. I just need to talk to him about how to make sure his Aunt Lisey isn't upset about the first one."

She leaned back in her chair and sighed. "Making life decisions is stressful. Does it ever get easier?"

Max and I laughed hard and assured her that no, it absolutely does not!

She thanked us for the help and went upstairs to have a serious discussion with Topher. Max and I exhaled heavily. I got up and grabbed the bottle of his favorite whiskey and began mixing us each a drink.

He smiled. "It's like you read my mind, babe. I think we did well and she got to the right place in her own time. You were great at being practical and not leading her too much."

"Thanks, I was trying hard to stick to the facts. You were smart to remind her to take him out of the picture so she could make an informed decision. I was glad you said it because I wasn't sure how to. This parenting thing is not for the faint of heart." We clinked our glasses and drank.

As we were getting ready for bed, I had a revelation. Christmas was only a couple of weeks away and we were not done with gifts yet. Mentioning it to Max, he said it was shaping up to be a strange holiday for presents. We might be buying things for our kids' lives as adults instead of the fun stuff we preferred to give them. I was both impressed by where we were and overwhelmingly sad that a major section of our family life was ending.

Arica and Topher talked until late into the night. A couple of times her voice sounded slightly annoyed, and I wondered if they were having their first argument over how to resolve this dilemma. I worried a little that she might change her mind about the job just to placate him. Thankfully, that was not the case. She texted me the next morning to tell me she called the second company and accepted the position.

I congratulated her and said I couldn't wait to hear more details. She also forwarded me the email she sent to the first company with her gratitude for their trust in her abilities, but she had taken another offer. She did very well on her professional communications based on what we'd talked about the night before, and I was so proud of her.

Arica worked that night since she had a busier schedule during holiday shopping, so we wouldn't hear more until late. Max and I were already in bed but awake and waiting for her.

She flopped down between us to give us a summary. The salary was enough for her to afford a small apartment and utilities. She and Topher had been looking at some together. He didn't want her to be in certain neighborhoods, but she wasn't finding too many in her price range that he was happy with. *(I assumed that was what they disagreed on.)*

The company asked her to start on January 23 since they had to get through the busy season as well. Once everyone was back from New Year's and things slowed down, it would be the right time to focus on getting Arica oriented. I was relieved. The later date gave us more than a month to get our ducks in a row. Plus, it wouldn't interfere with Dawson's move.

We thanked her for updating us and said good night. Max glanced at me before turning off the light and I told him I was fine. Wrapping up for the year at work had worn me out, so I fell asleep in moments.

For months, I had procrastinated cleaning out my mom's room and going through her belongings. My brother Micah and his family would be staying with us soon for Christmas, as well as Leo. That meant the bedroom would be utilized.

It was time.

Over the course of several days, I methodically packed up her clothes and organized them in storage totes. Her jewelry and other treasured keepsakes went carefully into smaller containers. Everything was then stacked neatly in a corner of the room. Her shoes and some bedding and pillows were donated to an area homeless shelter.

It was an emotional journey, but in the end, it gave me some much-needed closure.

Arica was going to take Mom's dresser, mirror, nightstand, and lamps to Boston. Dawson asked if he could have the recliner, which was fine with us. We arranged for the mattress to be picked up and discarded. I couldn't bear the thought of anyone sleeping on the place where she died. Max and I purchased a new one and borrowed Dawson's truck to bring it home.

We talked to our children about Christmas presents and moving schedules and made a plan. Instead of items under the tree, Max and I would provide each of them with the essentials for their apartments. In return, they would only give us small gifts and save their money for food and bills and such.

Max rented a trailer again to haul behind our vehicle for Arica's move, and he scheduled her car for a maintenance check to make sure it was ready for the cross-country drive.

Dawson took us to his soon-to-be residence, and we analyzed what they already had and what he should purchase for himself. I couldn't help but notice the blatant bachelor pad ambiance with hardly any artwork or pictures on the walls, mismatched furniture, lots of electronics, and nothing decorative.

His roommates seemed apprehensive about parents poking around, but Max and I tried to make them feel at ease. We even offered to provide Dawson with the makings for some homemade food to cook. They liked the idea, although our son didn't seem delighted that we were setting him up to make meals for everyone!

It hadn't occurred to me that Dawson had never moved before until he said something about not knowing where to start. We encouraged him to look for any sturdy boxes at work to use for packing, and Max and I would try to acquire some from our workplaces as well.

I also made him a checklist for the tasks to do and so he didn't forget any of the items we'd identified for him to take with him. As was his personality, once he had a project and defined milestones, he diligently worked toward crossing things off the list.

Both of my brothers arrived at our house on the twenty-third. They were puzzled at the amount of boxes, totes, and cleaning products stacked up in various rooms throughout the house. When we told them what was going on in the next few weeks, they generously volunteered to help while they were here.

Elise and my nieces were excited to hear all the details about Arica's upcoming move and job and boyfriend. Max made final arrangements for his brothers and dad to all be here for Christmas lunch, which was going to make for a VERY full house.

Leo was in charge of preparing our mom's lasagna recipe for our traditional Christmas Eve dinner, and it was a beautiful meal with a lot of love and stuffed bellies. Afterward, the cousins went to play video games, and we adults sat in the living room with drinks in hand. We stayed up later than we should have, but it was such a jolly night I didn't want it to end.

There were several moments of me wishing my mom was there, too, but I believed she was looking down on us fondly and rejoicing that her favorite people were together.

I'm not entirely sure how we fit everyone from my side and Max's immediate family around the tables and fed them all the next day, but we did. It was an incredible Christmas. Gifts were exchanged, hugs and hilarity abounded, and a few card games sprang up at various times.

On the morning after the holiday, everybody in our house was sluggish and sleepy. Not much was done by anyone, and we wore pajamas most of the day.

The following day, we were all feeling closer to normal. The men helped Dawson pack up a few more things for his move, and I heard them all laughing at stories from their own bachelor days.

Elise, Arica, my nieces, and I hopped into our SUV and met up with Kate to go shopping. We also hit a couple stores with after-Christmas sales and stopped at a coffee shop for a little caffeine pick-me-up. Our lunch was at a restaurant that Max and Dawson thought was "too girly" for them. We drove Arica to the local store where she'd been working to turn in her notice, and we all cheered when she came out. The entire day was so much fun!

That was another entertaining evening of playing games and teasing each other. Leo was leaving the next day, and Dawson had to go to work in the morning, so it was our last night of being carefree.

Before Leo left for home, I brought him into Mom's old room where Micah and Elise were staying. I told the three of them how I'd consolidated all her clothes and favorite things into the totes. I'd taken out what I wanted to keep from her, and they were welcome to any of the remaining items.

They both said they'd look through the stack, even though Leo wasn't overly interested in this activity. I offered to ship Micah anything they chose if it was easier. My daughterly duties were then completed, and yet another chapter of my life was now closed.

~ *Chapter 10* ~

THE NEST EMPTIES

On the twenty-ninth, Dawson, Max, Micah, and my nephew packed Dawson's truck and our SUV with everything he was taking with him to the apartment. Both vehicles were loaded to the brim, so we ladies stayed at my house and let them take care of it. D had some friends meeting them to help unload and set up so they could conquer it all as efficiently as possible.

Max and the other two didn't return until late afternoon, and my tears welled up when they walked into the house without my son. After twenty and a half years with him here, our home felt so empty in his absence! My sister-in-law kept me company while the men were upstairs taking showers, and Arica and my nieces started making dinner for everyone.

I tried to remind myself that this was for the best and what should happen, but it was small consolation to having my baby boy living with us. Arica was uncharacteristically quiet after we ate, and I made a mental note to check in with her soon to see how she was feeling about all this.

The next day, Micah and his family were leaving to visit some friends and other relatives in the area. They'd be gone until the evening of the New Year's Eve festivities.

Ginny texted me in the morning to ask if we could talk about the details of Arica's move. I grumbled about it, but Max gave me a look, and I begrudgingly replied and said I'd be free all afternoon. She called me just after 2 p.m., and in true Ginny style was perky and energetic about everything being planned.

"Tabby, we're beyond excited to have Arica out here, and we want to help as much as we can! I know you guys plan to look at apartments first thing, and we've mapped out a few that we think would be great neighborhoods. Do you want me to send you the addresses?"

I said, "Yes, that would be helpful. Thank you."

"Hooray! So, it sounds like you have a hotel lined up, but, um, Alex and I wanted to offer for you to stay at our house if you want." She sounded nervous about asking.

"It's small, but Topher's old room is now a guest room, and the girls can bunk together, or your Arica can use our pull-out couch if she prefers. It's entirely up to you and Max, though."

My mind was quickly trying to come up with excuses for not being in such close proximity to them for multiple days, but I was drawing a blank in the moment.

After a brief pause, I said, "Let me talk to Max about it. Maybe the three of us can stay in the hotel until we find her a place, and then he and I could use your guestroom for a couple of nights before we leave."

"That would be awesome too! No matter what, we want to have you over for dinner at least once while you're here! And I'd love for you to meet my sisters. They've heard so much about you over the years, they want to see you for real! And my dad might be around, but we usually make plans without him, and he joins if he can. And for sure Topher is going to take some time off work to be with us. I CANNOT WAIT to have you all here on our home turf!"

She literally squealed. She was extra ramped up about this, and I couldn't help but smile. She certainly hadn't lost her zest from when we were friends in college.

I replied with, "We really appreciate you being so accommodating for Arica to move out there. It's comforting that she already has people who care about her and she'll be supported when we can't be with her as much. And thank you for your charitable offer about a place to stay, I'll let you know what we decide."

"Of course! We love your daughter, and we're here for whatever any of you need. I hope you all have a very Happy New Year, and we'll talk again SOON!"

I wished her a Happy New Year as well, and we hung up. Max stared at me expectantly, and I filled him in on the conversation. He was satisfied with how I'd handled it and thanked me for being cordial. He commented that it would be nice to save a little money on the hotel room, but our accommodations were entirely my decision.

When I went upstairs to go over it with Arica, I found her crying on her bed. She increased to weeping as I entered the room. I sat down next to her and simply rubbed her back for comfort.

"Mom, I don't know why, but the tears just keep coming randomly this week. I'm not upset, I'm actually super happy to be starting this great job soon and being with Topher and doing adult things in a big city." She paused to blow her nose and wipe her face.

"But I also feel so BAD!" She cried again, and I waited. After a minute she slowed down and was able to talk again.

"It was hard when D left yesterday, and I saw how sad you were. And now I'm leaving you too, and I hate that it's going to be even worse for you and Dad when we're BOTH gone.

Plus, I still feel guilty about bringing people back into your life who hurt you. You're my mom and I love you, and sometimes I think I should break up with him and find someone who is just normal and doesn't carry so much heartache with him."

"Oh goodness, honey. Please don't worry about me. Your dad and I will be fine, and I will be okay with Alex and Ginny. You deserve to see what's possible with Topher if you care about him. Leave the rest of it out."

She sniffled some and thought about it. Then she continued. "To be honest, I'm also terrified about screwing up this job if I don't know what I'm doing. THEN what am I going to do? I'll be in desperate trouble if I'm unemployed out there. It might be months and months until I find another job; it was already a long time for this!

Or what if Topher and I split up and I have NO ONE out there who knows or cares about me? I have a few friends around, but not like GOOD ones. I don't want to be miserable AND alone!"

The sobs returned, and I pulled her into a hug so she could cry onto my chest. It had been years since she'd curled up into me like she did as a child, and I savored the moment of closeness.

Finally, I softly said, "Arica, you have become one of the most independent and ambitious young women I've ever known. You're going to LOVE being on your own and succeeding in your career. You've been living and breathing fashion from when you were a sophomore in high school, you know your stuff.

And if you're unsure of something, you ask. That's why having an experienced boss is such an advantage – she will teach you. Of course you're going to screw up occasionally, we all do! But that's also a valuable way to learn, and you just make sure you don't repeat the same mistakes again.

As for Topher, if it happens that you two aren't meant for forever, it will be okay. If you're ever feeling too alone, I will arrange to work remotely and come stay with you for as long as you need. Your dad and I will ALWAYS be here for you, all you have to do is tell us what's going on."

She cried for a few more minutes, and then it diminished to sniffles again. She sat up and faced me, "Thanks, Mom. You and Dad are the best support I could ask for, I'm just totally overwhelmed right now. I didn't think it would be this rough when D moved out; but I already kind of miss having all four of us here together. It's sad to think we might not all live in the same house again; that's a crucial turning point."

My tears started to fall as she voiced my biggest sorrow. "Oh, I'm sorry. I didn't mean to make you depressed too."

"No need to apologize, that thought has been like an enormous red flashing light in my head for weeks now. My heart will miss you eternally, but my head understands this is how it's supposed to go. You and your brother should leave the nest and fly like eagles!" I did a soaring gesture with my hand to emphasize.

We both chuckled and she made a cawing sound more like a crow, which caused us to laugh harder through our tears.

Max was coming up the stairs just then, and he poked his head in the doorway. "Everything all right in here? Did I hear a dying bird?"

She and I laughed again. He started walking away, but we called him back for a group hug.

"Are you okay, sweetheart?" he asked her, and she nodded.

"Mom came to talk to me while I was in the middle of a sad moment. She helped me feel better, and I was trying to imitate an eagle flying majestically away from the nest." Max was confused but amused, and Arica and I giggled once more.

∾

As we went through New Year's Eve Day, I mulled over the previous twelve months.

Arica met Topher and graduated college.

Mom had surgery, then died less than a week later.

We buried her and I was forced to interact with Alex and Ginny after more than twenty-seven years.

I had to reconcile our past and my suppressed anger with the fact that my daughter and their son are in love.

Arica went through the stressful process of interviewing for her first full-time job and accepted a great offer.

I packed up Mom's belongings and got rid of them.

We moved D into his first apartment.

We're merely days away from moving our daughter halfway across the country again, likely for good.

How on earth have I emotionally survived this year? I shook my head at the gravity of everything that had transpired.

Micah called and said they were on their way back and could stop and pick up food if we ordered something.

They pulled in right at dinner time, and we all had a delicious meal to close out 2022.

Much to our surprise, Dawson walked in as we were finishing up! He razzed us for not asking what he wanted. I was happy to see him and gave him a long hug.

He hung out with us for an hour or so. After snacking on a few of our leftovers, he said he was on his way to ring in the New Year with some friends. Max and I reminded him to be extra safe and call us if he needed a ride. We knew he wasn't old enough to legally drink alcohol, but we were also not born yesterday.

The eight of us watched the ball drop to welcome 2023, celebrated with champagne and some fun props I'd bought, and finished up not long after midnight.

Another year with fresh challenges and opportunities was now upon us.

Micah and his family had an evening flight out on New Year's Day. They spent most of the morning packing up and stuffing everything back into their rental car. It was wonderful having them with us for the holidays, and I enjoyed getting to know my nephew and nieces better.

The house seemed abnormally quiet after they left. Even Arica commented on how her footsteps were echoing and she anticipated voices at any moment. I texted Dawson to check if he was okay, and he replied that he was tired *(hungover?)* but fine.

The next day, we sat down at the kitchen table and laid out a calendar. With Arica's job starting on Monday, January 23, Max and I were taking two full weeks off work. We were burning a lot of our vacation time right at the start of the year, but we were both long-time employees and had days to spare.

We would leave early on Saturday the fourteenth *(less than two weeks from today!)*. On Sunday we had appointments to visit two of the apartments, and three more on Monday. If we didn't like any of those, we had a backup list and would keep looking on Tuesday. If there was one that stood out from the rest, we would go back and talk to them about signing the lease.

Our goal was to have her moved in somewhere by Friday night. She talked to our five top choices and made sure they understood our situation. All of them had availability and were able to comply with our compressed timeline.

Arica would have the weekend to settle in and start arranging her things, and she should be ready to go for her first day of work. Max and I would stay for a day or two more in case she needed anything, but then we'd head back home and not have to hurry.

When we'd all confirmed the logistics were solid, I looked at our daughter and said, "Honey, I'm very proud of you and how you've handled all these life changes. It's an exciting time for you!

I do have a favor to ask. While we're out there with you, I'd like you to stay with us and not at Topher's. We have many things to accomplish in a short time, and it would be best if you were readily available. We can certainly include him in the visits if he wants, and dinners, but can the three of us *(I motioned to her and Max and me)* please stick together at least until you're moved in?"

She smiled. "Okay, I can do that. I greatly appreciate you both for helping me get started out there, and I'll have lots more time with him soon enough. He's taking a few days off, too, so I'm glad you're cool with him joining us for the walk-throughs."

Max reminded me the following day that we were supposed to decide about sleeping arrangements and let Ginny know what we planned. I grumbled once again, but we sat down and designed an itinerary.

We would sleep at the hotel until we were able to move Arica in because it would be less navigating around the backroads. We also had to park the cumbersome moving trailer, which would be much easier in the hotel's lot than in someone's driveway or along a residential street. After we returned that, we would have more flexibility to stay with them.

Ginny loved the agenda, there were many heart and party emojis involved in her response. She also added,

"Dinner at our house Sunday night, my sisters are coming too!" I replied with a simple "Okay, sounds good," and my stomach tightened when I thought about coping with that much Ginny the first full day we were there.

Dawson spent a good deal of time with us on Thursday night before the big trip. He also came over the next evening, and Max left work early to stop and get the trailer. It was dark when he got home because winter days are short. We still managed to load it to the brim by bedtime. We packed Arica's car with a lot of our luggage and personal items while still making sure it wasn't too full that we couldn't see out the back window.

Despite only having a brief dinner break, it was after 10 p.m. by the time we finished. Morning was going to be here way too soon, so we called it a night. Dawson said goodbye and good luck to his sister, and when they hugged, I noticed tears in both their eyes. Of course that started mine up as well, and Max put his arm around me in knowing support.

The three of us left only fifteen minutes after our target departure time, which I considered a win. We switched up drivers during pit stops, and there was a stretch of the trip where Max was driving, and I was in the passenger seat. He broached the subject of my tolerance for the upcoming interactions.

"Babe, are you prepared for being around Alex and Ginny quite a bit this week? It's going to be stressful finding a good apartment for Arica and tough leaving her there, and they'll be part of everything. You okay with that?"

He was focused on the road and didn't see my grimace. "I'm as ready as I can be, I guess. Back when I was seeing my therapist, I'd get stuck on things sometimes. She would suggest journaling as a way to get it out of my head. Then I'd read it aloud in our next session and we'd talk about it from there. It usually did help me get unstuck and dig down to the root of the problem so I could work on it.

Taking her advice, I started writing about my history with both Alex and Ginny. The happy times are worth remembering too, instead of only the worst of it all. There were a lot of fun memories!" Recalling a few of the incidents with her made me snicker.

"It was a productive exercise, and I'm glad I did it. Hopefully, it will ease me toward my goal of seeing them as regular people. There is good and bad in everyone, and that's what I need to keep in mind when I'm with them."

"That was a great idea!" His excitement and broad grin boosted my confidence. "Maybe some time you could read part of it to me."

My cheeks warmed with a blush when I thought about the Alex portion. "Yeah, maybe!" I replied.

"Do you plan on having your talk with Ginny or both of them while we're there? I can entertain myself elsewhere or be right next to you, whatever you want."

"I don't know, there might not be time for that with everything else going on. If the opportunity arises, I'll try to work up the courage to say something. I guess I'll just have to cross that bridge if or when I come to it."

"Okay. I'm glad you're considering it. I think it would be really helpful for you, but I understand how intimidating it probably is." We left it at that.

We successfully reached our hotel in Boston just after 11 p.m. We tiredly brought in our overnight supplies, took quick showers, and crashed until 10 the next morning.

As we sluggishly arose, I saw I had text messages from Ginny. Arica also had notes from Topher, so the Yates family was evidently very excited to welcome us. We told them we arrived safely and were now up and around and would have lunch in the hotel restaurant soon.

Topher met us there halfway through our meal; Arica was overjoyed to see him and have him join us. He was more than happy to be our chauffeur for the day so we could relax and not worry about traffic or getting lost, and Max and I were relieved to be exempt from the driver's seat.

We finished eating and then it was time to leave for the first appointment. We piled into his older but still swanky BMW and away we went. I had a fleeting thought about what twenty-three-year-old drives a Beamer, but I let it go because I knew who his grandfather was.

The apartments we saw on Sunday afternoon were decent enough, but smaller than Arica had hoped. On a scale of 1-10, we gave the first one a score of 4 and the second one a 6.

We finished earlier than expected, so Topher took us back to our hotel. He timidly asked if we minded if he and Arica went and had some time together until dinner, and we told them to have fun. Frankly, I was counting on some nap time, so I was okay with her being out. I was going to need my strength to endure dinner at Alex and Ginny's house tonight.

Max and I woke up half an hour before Topher and Arica were to return. He took a shower; I freshened up and changed clothes. I texted Kate that I was going into the minefield, and she should prepare herself for crazy messages later. She wished me well and sent a .gif of landmines exploding. After several deep breaths and telling myself I could do this, we went downstairs.

They picked us up as planned, and the four of us rode through back roads and darkness to Alex and Ginny's house. Topher gave us a rundown of his family members, and I wondered what everyone looked like and whether I would be able to see any resemblances. Back when we were friends, Ginny showed me a photo taken prior to her parents' divorce, but that didn't count.

Approximately twenty-five minutes later, he was pulling into the driveway of a neat ranch house in an established and well-kept neighborhood. There was a stone walkway to the front porch and flowerbeds that would conceivably be full of color in the spring and summer. They literally had a short white picket fence around the yard, and I had to smile at the "iconic American dream" vibe.

We all got out, and within seconds I heard the screen door bang shut as Ginny came rushing out to greet us. She squealed in delight to see the four of us walking toward her, and she hugged each of us as we approached. She was almost shaking with excitement.

"Eeeek, it's actually happening, you're really here!" she exclaimed. "Come on in, dinner is about twenty minutes from being ready, and my sisters should be here soon!"

Alex opened the door and welcomed us with a smile as we entered. We walked into the living area, which spread across the front of the house. The space was divided into two segments on either side of the door – one had a brick fireplace with a large TV above the mantle and two couches, and the other had four individual oversized chairs around a coffee table and a bookcase in the corner.

Alex took our coats, and we tugged off our shoes. Ginny asked Topher to stir something on the stove, and then she turned to us.

"Obviously, this is the living room where we spend a lot of our time together, as well as what we jokingly call the den. In reality, it's just a place to sit and read or the kids to do homework."

As we passed a hallway on the right, she pointed and said, "Down that way is the guest room, Ari's room, and a bathroom if you need it while you're here."

She then indicated to the left as we entered the kitchen, "Our bedroom is around that corner."

The kitchen was larger than I expected, with plenty of space to move and prep food. Off to the side was a long table with many chairs for tonight. Everything was tidy and homey. Along the back of the kitchen and dining area was a sliding door to a three-season room with windows surrounding it, patio chairs with plump cushions and blankets, and a space heater.

Ginny gestured out there and told us, "If it's not super cold after dinner, we can sit out there and catch up if you want, the heater keeps it comfy. I'm out there all the time to drink my wine and be by myself. We've lived here for close to twenty years now, and it may be small, but we've made it our own and we love it!"

She beamed at us and said again, "I am THRILLED that you're standing in my kitchen, I've been looking forward to this for so long!"

Alex chimed in with, "If you're wondering whether she'll be this giddy all night, the answer is yes. It's best if you just go with it, there's really no other choice."

I chuckled and said, "Yeah, I know. She's always been like this, I don't understand how she's kept it up all these years!" Ginny smiled broadly at all of us, clapped her hands in happiness, and walked over to Topher at the stove to make sure he was doing what she'd asked.

Alex said to us, "I'm on drink duty, do you guys want something? We have tea, juice, soft drinks, white and red wines, beer, whiskey, and other various alcohols. What's your poison?"

Arica asked for a Sprite. Water and a glass of red wine sounded good to me, and Max asked about the whiskey selection. He and Alex went to a cabinet and started going through the options. My daughter came up next to me.

She said quietly in my ear, "Mom, I'm so glad and proud that you're doing this. I'm sure it's hard for you, but it means the world to Toph and me that we're all having a family dinner together tonight. I can't wait for you to meet his aunts." I put my arm around her and thanked her for the encouragement.

Just then, a beautiful young woman came into the kitchen, and I finally got to see the other Arica. Her makeup was flawless *(no surprise there, she had an excellent teacher)*, her dark blonde hair with wavy curls was a mix of her parents, and her outfit was both flattering and practical.

She introduced herself to Max and me, and I recognized a lot of adolescent Ginny in her facial expressions and movements. She talked more like Alex though, with his slower cadence and a joking comment sprinkled in when you least expected it.

Ari Yates was an interesting combination of the two people I used to know so well, and it only took a few minutes before I felt comfortable and wanted to spend more time with her. When she had a moment to greet our Arica, the two of them smiled and embraced. They appeared to be close already, and I was surprisingly pleased with that.

Alex brought Arica and me our requested drinks, then he returned to evaluating different whiskey characteristics with Max. Meanwhile, Ginny, Topher, and Ari were working on the finishing touches for dinner. As we were all chatting, the front door opened and a trio of rambunctious people entered the house.

Ginny's sisters had many similar features, but I didn't see any immediate physical likenesses to their younger half-sister. They were clearly familiar with the house and being here, because they barely slowed down to put their coats and purses away as they were walking toward us. Their eyes were locked on me, and I smiled uncomfortably.

"Oh my goodness, you must be Tabitha, the invisible fourth Beckett sister! I'm Jade, it's so nice to finally meet you!" Ginny's middle sister gave me a crushing hug.

"We started to worry that Ginny made you up in the beginning until Alex confirmed you were a real person! I'm Lisey, we're glad you're here!" and the oldest hugged me as well.

Jade's husband stepped up and stuck out his hand for me to shake, "I'm Rod Fletcher, it's great to meet you after everything Ginny's told us. Welcome to our neck of the woods!"

Alex introduced them to Max, and more hugs and handshakes were shared. The obvious intrinsic traits that Nick's three daughters possessed were the fast talking and unending enthusiasm. It was like a tornado of perkiness!

Jade and Lisey checked in with Ginny, greeted Topher and Ari, then hugged Arica and welcomed her back to Boston. They got a couple of drinks, gave Alex a hard time about having the easiest job of the day, and turned back to me. It felt like I was under a microscope with both of them scrutinizing me.

They called Arica over and asked us about our trip out there, how the first two apartment visits went, and if we picked one or were ready to see more tomorrow. They apparently knew all the details, this was a close-knit family without a doubt. I understood how Ginny would have missed this when she moved away and had nobody.

We told them it went well but we would continue the search the following day, determined to find a place that ranked at least an 8 on our scale.

Then I said to Lisey, "I wanted to thank you for helping Arica get that interview. It was a good opportunity, and we are so grateful for the support system she already has out here."

She beamed. "Of course, I was glad my network had someone useful in it. I genuinely don't know anything about the fashion industry except that it gets way too much of my hard-earned money!" We all laughed. "Arica was worried about me being offended if she didn't take it, but it was nothing like that. It sounds like the job she chose was better for learning and long-term advancement, which is the important thing."

I asked if the sisters had any children and found out that Lisey had a son and Jade had two daughters and a son. All three of Jade's were grown and spread out, with her daughter Mia living near Portland, Oregon.

"It's like she couldn't move far enough away from us," Jade said with a sigh. "And then she had the audacity to have a couple of adorable kids we don't see very often, which hurts my heart. I'm an excellent Gigi; I would spoil them rotten if they lived closer!" It was easy to imagine her fawning over grandkids.

Ginny loudly announced that the meal was ready, and we should pick a chair and park it. Dinner was comparable to Max's family gatherings, but in this case, it was the women who were the loudest and most talkative instead of the men.

The sisters fired questions at all of us. Alex and Ginny kept the food coming and opened more wine bottles as needed, and Arica and Topher were in their own little world and giddy about everyone being there because of them.

It was such a laid-back evening, it didn't take long for me to relax and immerse myself in the conversations and get to know more about the Becketts overall. Several funny stories were told about family gatherings gone wrong, past women Nick dated for short periods of time, and how too many lawyers could be either positive or negative depending on the situation.

As dessert was finishing, Jade and Rod said they hated to eat and run, but they needed to get going. Both of them had to work in the morning and had a half hour drive home. Lisey said that since they were her ride, she guessed it was her time to either leave with them or plan on hitch-hiking. Everyone laughed and began gathering plates and glasses to help clean off the table.

The sisters pulled me aside to tell me how glad they were that I'd forgiven Ginny for her heinous behavior in the past and joined them all tonight.

I cringed internally at their comment. Forgiveness may not be something I was even capable of, but I kept my mouth shut because I didn't want to ruin the mood.

Instead, I smiled and thanked them both for their kind words and said I'd loved spending the evening with them. We all hugged again and said our goodbyes.

Ginny had told me so much about them, it was heartwarming to see they'd all stayed so close over the years. I also repeated my appreciation for their support of my daughter. A strange feeling came over me that if Ginny and I had remained friends, I might have been tempted to move out here with her and be part of this crazy, fun family.

When the three of them left, it immediately felt quieter and emptier. The seven of us finished cleaning the table, wrapping up the leftovers, and refilling wine and whiskey glasses.

Topher and Arica said they were going to go watch a movie in the living room, and Ari excused herself to her room to study. She was in college to be a graphic designer, and unlike me, she was perfectly content staying at home and taking classes locally.

Ginny asked if we would like to sit in the sunroom. I said sure, and Max said he was going to use the bathroom and would join us in a few minutes. Alex came out with us and brought our wine bottles so we wouldn't have to come back inside to refill. I curled up in a chair and pulled a blanket over me, which made it cozy and warm with the space heater.

Alex went back in to grab something, and I started chatting with Ginny about her sisters and some of the common features I saw between all of them. We laughed about their quirky personalities, and she told me a little more about how they helped her and Alex when they first moved here.

As she was finishing her story, I noticed our husbands were standing in the kitchen talking and laughing. They didn't look like they had any intention of coming back out with us. Max caught my eye and made a hand motion to mean I should have my big vent with Ginny. I was annoyed at the men for what seemed like an orchestrated affair, but I'd also had enough wine by then to feel a tad bolder than I might normally.

I looked Ginny full in the face and started timidly with, "So, I've been thinking a lot since you and Alex told me what happened from your perspective. Can we talk about it?"

"Of course! You sitting here across from me means that you've at least gotten to a better place with everything, and I'm happy to listen to anything you want to tell me."

"You might regret saying that!" I said with a wry smile. "When Max and I discussed it, I realized that you don't know what I went through. I'm not even sure how much Alex told you about our history together."

"Not a lot," she confessed. "I tried asking a few times, but he just gave me vague brush-off answers like 'you two were kind of attracted to each other but never seriously got together' and stuff like that. He's frustrating when he doesn't want to talk about something."

Nodding, I replied, "I figured, he's never been much of a sharing person about his emotions. Which is part of why I was so mad – he talked to you like he'd NEVER opened up to me. But I'll get to that. I think I need to tell you everything from the beginning, and that way there are no more blank spots between us." She nodded her approval.

"But please let me get all the way to the end before you respond. There might be a few hesitations when my feelings are strong, but I have to keep plowing through so I don't lose my nerve. I'm not doing this to hurt you or make you feel worse, but so I can feel heard and maybe put all this behind me for everyone's sakes."

"Oh boy, I think we should fill our glasses up to the top first." I smiled and let her pour the rest of a bottle into mine. Then I began to pour out my heart...

Starting at the beginning from grade school, I talked about the interactions between Alex and me throughout the years: the field trip kiss and my confusion, him being part of the crowd I hung out with before graduating, running into each other after high school, then the back road rendezvous times. It was awkward to tell her too many details regarding her now-husband, so I abbreviated my descriptions of our nighttime trysts. I stopped when I got to the part about moving out of my parents' house and making the decision to go back to college.

"I need to use the bathroom before I start the section where you come onto the scene."

"Sure, do you remember where it is?" she asked.

"Yup, I'll be right back."

As I entered the kitchen, the men broke off their banter and stared at me questioningly. "It's fine, I'm halfway through my story. And you both suck for your little coordinated plan."

Max grinned and said he loved me. I flipped him off on my way to the bathroom, and they laughed.

When I returned to the sunroom, Ginny was still quiet. I felt a little bad for ruining her good spirits, but she smiled at me when I sat down. I grabbed the blanket and my wine glass and noticed she'd put a box of tissues on the table between us.

She said, "I know the part I don't want to hear is coming soon, but I deserve every bit of it. There will probably be a lot of tears, but don't let that stop you from telling it all."

I nodded and continued, summarizing our friendship and how close I felt to her during the time we worked at the restaurant. She and Alex getting along when they first met made me naively happy because they were both important people in my life.

I recounted the last time Alex and I were alone together on the way to his grandparents' house and how there might be something stronger between us. I was truthful about liking him more than I'd let on, but also not being sure we were fundamentally right for each other.

Then I got to the hard portion and took a healthy swallow of wine. I concentrated on looking at the blanket on her lap and not her face. I detailed my confusion when she no longer showed up to check on me while I was sick. I told her my fear that she was really ill because of me and suffering in isolation.

I went on to portray my irritation when I didn't hear anything at all. She heard about me sitting outside her apartment and all the phone calls and messages that went unanswered.

I described my absolute shock when our boss told me she quit and apologized for being the one to break the news to me.

I went through the following weeks of contemplating what I'd done or said to upset her. My descent into depression when I wondered why I was being ostracized again like in high school and spending my twenty-fourth birthday alone because I still couldn't bear to be with people. I heard her sob at that point, but I kept going until I got to the time of my date and showing up at the restaurant.

I took another drink of wine and went through all the thoughts that rushed through my mind when I saw them. That I didn't know what I was going to say when I turned around outside, I just let my anger do the talking.

I even shared how I wrapped abandonment, hurt, and sadness up into the rage because it was so much simpler to be irate than to face the other painful emotions.

The tears started for me when I confessed that I was more furious with her because she meant more to me, and I was already used to Alex not being around on a regular basis. His acting like a jerk to me was infinitely less surprising than her doing so.

I talked about closing my heart to both of them and burning the bridges of friendship to ashes in my mind.

I admitted that the D Score haunted me for years whenever I'd start dating someone, and how I wished multiple times for her to help me with makeup or to chat about something significant happening in my life.

I reached for another drink and wiped my cheeks. Then I went into the time of meeting Max but not allowing myself to fully trust him for a while so I didn't get so hurt again.

The feelings of abandonment and betrayal faded much faster after we got married, and I was able to lock those fears away and forget about them as I adjusted to life as a wife and mom.

I wasn't sure how to make the transition to the night of my mom's funeral, so I simply said, "Skipping forward to this past summer… When the two of you were suddenly standing in front of me again after twenty-seven years, I froze with panic. All the anger, and pain, and anguish came rushing out of that locked box with a vengeance, and I exploded.

I will say again that I'm glad I decided to meet with you the next day and hear your sides, because it feels better to know." I sighed, looked her in the eyes again and finished with, "And now we're caught up and you can speak."

She opened her mouth as if to say something, but instead she let out a long wail and started weeping hysterically. Alex and Max turned toward us, and I gave them a look of alarm, so they came out to check on us. I went over and hugged Ginny awkwardly in the chair, and she clung to me.

Alex whispered that she'd be all right, this needed to happen. Max asked if I was okay, and I said I didn't know.

I regretted spilling my guts and making a mess of a nice night.

They went back inside and Ginny's sobs gradually receded to the point of her being able to clean herself up and talk again.

"My God, Tabby. Thank you for sharing all that with me, even though it was so much more awful than I imagined. I know that 'I'm sorry' isn't nearly enough for everything I did, but I really, truly, sincerely am sorry from the bottom of my heart for how much pain I caused you.

It scared me to face you then, but waiting twenty-seven years to see your expressions now while re-living it all MUST be worse. I wish I could go back in time and kick my own twenty-two-year-old ass. What was WRONG with me?"

She started crying but quickly got it under control. "Is there ANYTHING I can do or say now that would make you feel any better?"

She peered at me with her sad, innocent eyes, and it was hard to imagine her ever hurting me again. Remembering what happened last time I thought that, I told myself to remain cautious.

"I don't know. Now that everything's out in the open and I've given a voice to all those memories, I just feel kind of empty… It's like a big heavy stone in my chest is suddenly gone, and it's freeing but weird. Disorienting. Does that even make sense?" I shook my head at my own discombobulated thoughts.

She smiled compassionately and said, "I'd like to think we've reached a different level. I would never ask for your forgiveness because I don't deserve it, but I hope this means we can move forward without you hating me."

I returned her smile. "I can honestly say that I no longer hate you."

"Hooray for that!" she said excitedly, and we clinked glasses to seal the deal. I had forgotten how instantaneously she recovered from strong emotions and went right back to her default sunny disposition. She jumped up and hugged me hard, and I sensed again that an old wound inside me was slowly but surely healing.

We realized it was quite chilly out there at this time of night, so we went back into the kitchen to warm up and tell our husbands that everything was fine. We did a four-way celebratory cheers, possibly louder than necessary since we were all well on our way to being drunk.

Topher and Arica emerged from the living room and said they were done with their movie. When they saw us getting along and laughing together, they smiled and quietly left us alone again.

An hour or so later, we were ready to head back to the hotel.

Ginny gave me one more big squeeze and thanked me for opening up and helping her understand where I was coming from. She said she loved me and had never stopped, and I teared up a little hearing that. I hugged her again but couldn't bring myself to say the same. It would have been a lie.

Topher dropped us off at the hotel, and the three of us got on the elevator. Arica said, "Mom, I can't tell you how happy I am right now. Not only can Toph and I relax that our parents aren't mortal enemies anymore, but I can tell this was good for you. You even look lighter!" I smiled tiredly and thanked her. Sleep came quickly for all of us.

We were slow-moving the next morning, but we got ready for our 11 a.m. apartment visit.

Kate had asked how things were going. I replied that I aired all my dirty laundry the night before and it was cathartic. She was glad for me and told me to have fun apartment hunting.

Arica informed us when Topher was downstairs, but I was still a few minutes from being ready, so she went down first. Max and I hurried to the elevator, and on the way down he expressed how extremely proud of me he was on my handling of everything. I thanked him, kissed him, and reminded him that he would pay for his collusion with Alex. He chuckled and pretended to be frightened as we stepped into the lobby.

Topher took us to the first place of the three for today, which was in a different Boston suburb and farther off the main highway. As soon as we pulled in, we were all impressed.

The building appeared to be fairly new and modern and there were woods in the back. Picnic tables lined one side of the parking lot on a large stretch of grass that sloped down to a pond and more trees. We held our praise until we saw the inside, but it was a charming start for sure.

The apartments were also higher quality, and our sales rep told us they had a few available with a wooded view for an extra $100 per month. She walked us through the gym area and down near the water to show us that residents could bring food to cook on the four charcoal grills spaced along the bank.

If Arica wanted to buy a kayak or canoe, they had a dedicated storage room and would provide her with a key. The thought of her paddling around the pond was comical, but I kept my opinion to myself.

The walk-through ended later than we'd figured, so we found a nearby café for a quick lunch and gushed about the place. We all loved it, and consensus on the score was an 8.5. It only got demerits for the extra drive from a major highway and that it did not allow pets at all. She didn't have plans for one, but the option of having a cat someday was ideal.

We then visited the second one for the day, which was also attractive and got a 7 on our scoring. It only had minimal outdoor appeal, though. The last one we saw at 3 p.m. was just okay. It still was better than the two from Sunday with a 6.5, but it did not beat the ones from earlier.

As we got back in the car, we were a pensive bunch. Arica mapped the route from the first apartment to Topher's, which was forty-nine minutes without much traffic. The second one was similar, only six minutes shorter.

We didn't have plans for dinner, and Topher asked if we wanted to meet his parents at one of their favorite restaurants. My husband looked over at me and our daughter turned around with pleading eyes, so I said yes. All three of them smiled, and Topher called Ginny.

Unsurprisingly, she was elated. Topher said he'd drop us off to freshen up and analyze the day, then he'd be back at 6:30 p.m. I told him we could drive ourselves there, but he insisted that we drove long enough to get here. The least he could do was be our local tour guide.

Max and I sat on our bed and talked to Arica about what she thought so far. She was sure about the third one being her favorite, and we concurred.

We asked if she wanted to keep looking, but she said no. The rent amounts between the five weren't incredibly different, although the one she liked was the second highest. She still couldn't see herself in any of the others, so we decided it was the one!

She called the sales manager back and told her we'd like to sign the lease tomorrow. She answered a few questions before hanging up and was happy with the conversation. Since the specials weren't applicable to our situation and the rep was excited we confirmed so rapidly, she was offering one of the woods-view apartments for the regular rate. Arica accepted, and we were one step closer to getting her established in her new life.

Topher took us to a hibachi restaurant about halfway between our hotel and Ginny and Alex's house. Business was slow for a Monday night, so they paid close attention to us and gave us extra flair during the cooking of our food. Ari and Arica sat next to each other and chatted the entire time. Topher was helping Max and me describe the places we'd seen. Alex and Ginny offered to help us move everything in when we figured out which day she could get the key, and we said we'd let them know.

It was a pleasant dinner. Alex and Max must have really hit it off the night before since they picked right back up and were laughing in no time.

I had a few bewildering moments trying to comprehend that this was all occurring in the present. It felt VERY surreal to be sitting here with my husband, my former nemeses, and our children having a delightful time.

~ *Chapter 11* ~

Back Again?

Topher decided to work the next day, so after a late breakfast we got in Arica's car and used navigation back to the apartment building. When Max pulled into the parking lot, we all smiled that this was her soon-to-be home.

We found the sales rep from the day before, who had the lease already prepared. She asked if we wanted to see which one she was suggesting for us, so we went there first. It was a corner unit on the fourth floor, with only one floor above it. Arica was fine with what she showed us, and the sales rep invited us into a conference room to go through the paperwork.

Since our daughter didn't have a lot of credit history, they requested a co-signer, which was Max. We went through all of the documents, with Arica signing where necessary and her dad adding his when required.

When we were finally done, the manager went to make a copy to send to us electronically, and the rep handed Arica the keys to her first solo apartment. I took a picture of her proudly holding them and the lease agreement and shared it with Dawson in our family chat. He replied right away with congratulations.

They requested a day to go back through the unit with their new tenant checklist. Arica was provided with a list of local utility companies to get everything hooked up. We set the time for 2 p.m. on Thursday for move-in and left for the hotel.

When we were back on Wi-Fi, Arica got on her laptop and started looking into the utilities options. She created accounts and was able to arrange for the electricity and water to be turned on Thursday afternoon. Internet wasn't available until Saturday morning. Max complained that they hardly had to do anything but flip a switch on their side, but he said we'd make sure the equipment was ready for them to connect.

We notified Topher and Ginny of the plans and by 4 p.m., we had everything arranged that could be. Arica asked if it was okay for her to have a date night with Topher. Max and I gave our blessing and thanked her for getting so much done today. She was giddy about finalizing the arrangements to be here full-time, and she understandably wanted to celebrate with her boyfriend.

She freshened up, changed into a cute outfit, and left. Max and I had been busy and accidentally skipped lunch, so we were both starving. We took Arica's car and had a Thai dinner just the two of us.

Back at the hotel, we watched TV for a little bit but turned in early. I heard Arica come in around midnight, and she was fast asleep soon after.

The next day, we decided to drive over and investigate the area her apartment was in to become familiar with the nearby stores, restaurants, gas stations, etc. We spent several hours in the neighborhoods around her new place and discovered she would live within fifteen minutes of nearly everything she could ask for. It was a great location!

We drove to her work, which was approximately twenty minutes away. The corporate office was in a gentrified zone surrounded by other business buildings and backed up to a lake. There wasn't a vast amount of eating places near there, so Arica reasoned that she should plan on taking her lunch most days.

The three of us also explored a section of downtown Boston we hadn't seen before. It was a pleasant evening of walking around, finding a festive Mexican place for dinner, and then heading back to the hotel.

We all woke up early, likely due to anticipation of a long and life-changing day ahead of us. Topher arrived at the hotel, and Arica and I followed him to the apartment. He got in with us, and we went shopping for groceries.

We were done earlier than anticipated, and Max showed up with the trailer. Arica went into the apartment office and asked if they minded if we started unloading. They were ready, so we all grabbed bags and her luggage and went up to the fourth floor.

When she opened the door, she was surprised to see a small vase of flowers sitting on the kitchen counter with a note from the staff welcoming her to Boston and her new home. It was very thoughtful of them!

Alex and Ginny arrived just before 2 p.m. and jumped right in. We spent the next hour and a half getting everything unloaded. Max returned the trailer to the rental place to avoid paying for an extra day.

Alex and Topher went back to the bedroom to unpack and assemble her bed. We had ordered a modular frame and headboard and left it in the box for easier transportation. Max went in to help when he got back. Unfortunately, it was apparently missing a few screws. After some debating, Max went back with Alex to their house and returned with a tool set.

The electrical company serviceman knocked on the door around 4:30 p.m. for Arica's signature on the paperwork and to let her know everything was now hooked up and in her name. He was distinctly interested in the attractive young woman he got to talk to, and he stood close to her while they were going over the details.

He took his time showing her the fuse box, the HVAC controls, and how to reset the kitchen and bathroom outlets if they got tripped. Topher noticed as well, and he was keeping an attentive eye on the situation.

When the electrician asked if Arica knew many people in the area, Topher took the opportunity to walk over next to her. She happily said her boyfriend and his family, who were kind enough to help her move in. The service guy was clearly disappointed, and he left soon after.

Ginny and I shared a knowing glance and smiled. Our husbands were still in the living room constructing furniture and oblivious of the entire interaction.

Ari showed up after she was done with classes and asked what she could do. We gave her the difficult task of ordering pizza and soft drinks because we were all massively hungry!

I didn't realize Alex provided his credit card for the food until after it was delivered. I chastised him for paying after a long and sweaty day unpacking and building **our** daughter's things. He said it was nothing, but I made a mental note to try and repay them before we left for home.

After we ate, we cleaned up the crazy mess of empty boxes, packing materials, paper plates and towels from the pizza, and other trash and stacked it in the dining room area. We were a tired and hot group of people. I was flabbergasted at how much everyone had done to help.

Alex was working the next day, but the rest of us would meet here at noon tomorrow to finish setting up and going back to the grocery store for the remainder of the essentials. Ari only had morning classes on Fridays, so she would be able to assist most of the day.

Topher was staying for a while *(I suspected all night but didn't ask)*, so we said our goodbyes and tromped down to the elevator. The cool January air felt fantastic as we left the building for the first time in several hours. Max and I bid the Yateses good night, went back to our hotel, showered, and were asleep in seconds.

The next day, Ginny and Ari pulled into the apartment's parking lot as we were getting out of our SUV. The four of us went in together and knocked on Arica's door. She let us all in and we quickly made a plan. After an hour, we women accomplished our tasks. Max and Topher were studying all the cords for the TV and other electronics, so we told them we were going grocery shopping and would be back. I'm not sure they heard us, but no matter.

We returned with enough food to feed the entire building and loaded up Arica's fridge and freezer. She was very grateful that she wouldn't have to do this all by herself and thanked us profusely. The men finished their projects, and we were able to sit at the completed dining room table and on the living room futon to rest. It was almost 3:30 p.m., we were ahead of schedule.

After a few minutes, Ginny turned to her son and asked, "Are you and Arica planning to go out for dinner tonight?"

He responded, "We'd like to if there aren't other plans. We're flexible for whatever, though."

Ginny then aimed a questioning look at Ari, who said, "I'm meeting up with friends. I'll probably just stay overnight at one of their places."

Lastly, Ginny set her gaze on Max and me on the futon. "If you're both okay with releasing our kids to do their own thing, you're welcome to come over and eat with me and Alex – just the four of us. We can either order takeout or have something simple like pasta."

Max nodded at me and I said, "We're fine with all of that as long as we don't have to move much!" I looked at my daughter. "What time is the internet provider supposed to be here tomorrow?"

"Between 9 a.m. and 1 p.m., but they said they'd call twenty minutes ahead of arriving."

Max assured her, "We'll be ready whenever to show them the router, modem, and so forth. What else would you like help with to make sure you're comfortable to start your job on Monday?"

"I think all that's left is cleaning up, but Topher and I can take care of that. You have all done a ton of work, I can't thank you enough."

Max and I got up to leave and gave our daughter a giant hug. "Get some sleep, sweetie, you earned it." I told her. She thanked me again, and we walked out with Ginny and Ari.

Ginny said tiredly, "How does 7:00 sound for dinner? You're welcome to come over any time after 6:30."

"How about we show up at 7 with food in hand? You guys got the pizza last night; we can bring a meal with us tonight. It will give us all a little more time to nap after we shower!"

She laughed and agreed, and we drove off in different directions.

Max and I both regained some stamina later, and we ordered takeout to be ready on our way to their house. That evening was light and breezy conversation full of laughter and witty repartee, and I had a thought that this is how it should have been all along. Ginny gently brought up after dinner that we were welcome to save our money and stay in their guest room if we wanted. I told her the offer was very generous and we'd talk about it.

Now that Arica was moved in, I felt kind of useless and like we might as well go home now. But we had promised our daughter we'd make sure she was set up for success on her first day at work, and we intended to keep it. That meant a minimum of three more nights here in the Boston area if we left Tuesday morning.

None of us were up for a late night, so Max and I were wrapping up our visit around 10 p.m.. Ginny suddenly smiled broadly.

"Oh, I almost forgot! Tomorrow is what we call "Guys and Dolls Night" in my family where all the men get together and we women do our thing one Saturday night a month. The guys go over to my dad's house and do manly stuff like drink Scotch, smoke cigars, grunt and spit a lot, pee in the bushes… Whatever it is they do when they don't have to impress us."

Max and I laughed hard!

Alex rolled his eyes and said to Max, "Don't listen to her. The cigars and alcohol part is accurate, but we usually either watch a college game of whichever sport is on or play cards. Sometimes Nick hires a party company to bring craps and blackjack tables and a few of his buddies join us for casino night.

It mostly depends on Nick's mood. Hot Rod, Topher and I just go along with it. Spitting is optional, but I'm pretty sure pissing on the landscaping is off-limits. Nick pays his gardeners way too much to have things dying. We can ask though, if that's a dealbreaker for you." His eyes were twinkling with good humor.

Max was cracking up at the two of them, "Hot Rod?" he asked, and he and I both laughed again.

"Yeah, we called him that once as a joke and it somehow stuck! Jade hates it, which makes it even better!" Alex chuckled.

Ginny said, "Tabby, us 'dolls' hang out here or at one of my sisters' houses with wine or margaritas and talk smack about our husbands, kids, celebrities, getting older, or whatever's on our minds. If there's some new facial or makeup product out, we might try it and see what we think. Or if anyone has a special event coming up, we vote on outfits to wear. Ari joins us if she isn't busy, and your daughter is invited if you think we won't scare her too badly! I believe we're supposed to be at Jade's tomorrow, but I need to double-check."

I smiled and said it sounded like fun. Max and I bade them good night and went back to crash into bed once again. It had been an exhausting trip so far!

Max set his alarm and texted Arica in the morning that he was ready to come over whenever the internet serviceperson called. Since we were up, we talked about our sleeping location for the next few nights.

He was fine staying wherever, but he deferred to me due to the potential awkwardness. I liked the idea of saving money on three hotel room charges, but I was also enjoying our quiet and freedom to come and go as we pleased.

I suggested telling the hotel we'd check out the following day and staying at Alex and Ginny's for two nights. He approved the plan, and I texted Ginny to make sure it worked for them. She responded with "YAY!!!!" and lots of celebratory emojis, of course.

Arica asked us to come over around 10 a.m., so we got ready and went to her apartment. She talked to us about getting some blackout curtains since her bedroom window faced east. The blinds were thin, which meant bright sunlight well before she was prepared to wake up. She also requested a power strip, some more hangers, and a couple of night lights.

With her and Max waiting for the installer, I volunteered to go pick up those few things. Topher said he'd join me if I wanted, there was a big home store nearby. We had some quality time together, and he was extremely efficient in locating the items we needed. He also thoughtfully recommended a cushioned mat for the kitchen floor in front of the sink.

When we returned, the internet rep had finished, and Max and Arica were arranging things. Everything was finished slightly before noon, and Arica said she wanted to make us lunch. As we ate at her new dining room table, I was amazed once again at how grown-up and capable she had become.

We talked about the evening's activities, with Topher giving us a couple of hilarious examples of past escapades at his grandpa's house. Arica was excited to come with me, and she'd convinced Ari to join as well.

As we drove back to our hotel, I told Max, "I can't believe you get to meet Nick before I do! I've been hearing about him for thirty years, and I've always wanted to see if my assumptions are correct. You have to take a few pictures tonight so I can see what he looks like now!"

He chuckled at me. "I'm sure you could stop by before your 'dolls night' shenanigans."

"No, that would seem weird!"

He shrugged, "Okay, fine. I'll try to take some stalker photos for you."

On the way to our room, I went to the desk in the lobby and talked to them about checking out tomorrow. They made changes in their system and we were all set.

When Topher picked us up, he informed us that in the interest of consolidating cars, he was going to drive to Nick's house and then Ginny would take us to Jade's from there.

So, I WAS getting my chance to meet the infamous Nick Beckett in person! Max gave me a big smile.

After half an hour or so, we pulled into a driveway with a gated entrance *(not surprising)*. Topher punched in a number with the well-practiced ease of something he'd done many times. We drove through the gates up to a large brick house with ivy growing up one corner and several cars already parked. Alex wasn't kidding about the landscaping — it was immaculate even in January.

The three of us followed Topher up the broad front steps to an oversized set of double wooden doors, which he opened and waved us all through. The foyer was gigantic and beautiful, as was the entire interior. Topher gave us a brief overview of the rooms while we walked toward the loudness of multiple people in the kitchen.

As we entered, everyone stilled and gawked, then greeted us with hugs and welcomes. Rod *(who I now couldn't think of as anyone but "Hot Rod")*, Jade, Lisey, and Ari all said hello.

There were some we didn't know, and they introduced themselves. We met Nick's sister Naomi Ross and her husband Trevor, Hot Rod's brother Preston Fletcher, his wife Jocelyn, and their daughter Kayleigh. And last but certainly not least, Nicholas "Nick" Beckett came over and shook hands with Max and me.

"It is so great to meet you both, and welcome to our little world here in Boston. We just love having your daughter in our lives, and it's marvelous that you're able to be here with her at last. Tabitha, I can't tell you how many times I've heard your name over the years, I'm glad you and Ginny were able to reconnect and put old grievances behind you. Max, I look forward to spending some time with you tonight. A little birdie informed me that you might like to relieve yourself in the wild outdoors, and I may have a solution for you."

He gave us a wink at the end. Max laughed heartily and looked accusingly across the room at Alex, who smirked at the inside joke. I couldn't help but feel like we were already part of the family.

We thanked him for having us over and inviting Max to join them for Guys Night, and he nodded courteously.

"Would either of you like a drink to start your evening?" I asked for a small glass of red wine before the dolls left. Max said he'd have whatever Alex was drinking, and Nick smiled and went over to one of the caterers I hadn't even noticed to tell them what to bring for us.

The boisterous voice, fast-talking, self-assured lawyer who dressed well but wasn't too ostentatious was everything I'd envisioned and more. His immaculately combed hair and manicured hands were above and beyond my expectations. His manners were impeccable, and he was at ease with everyone he met, yet I could tell he was analyzing us with a practiced skill of reading people.

Arica came over to me and asked, "He's really something, isn't he?"

"It's like my imagination come to life! You could have done a lot worse on families, sweetie." I put my arm around her and kissed her cheek. She blushed and mumbled thanks, and then Ginny was at my side.

"Tabby, you're finally here with EVERYBODY! All the people I love most in my life are in this one room, and I feel like I'm going to EXPLODE!" Her eyes were bright and she was almost dancing with exhilaration.

I had to laugh and put my other arm around her, hugging my beloved daughter and my former best friend. I never in my wildest dreams would have conceived of this scenario.

We spent about forty-five minutes in Nick's kitchen before Jade stridently announced that it was time for the dolls to depart. We began grabbing our purses and saying goodbye to the guys. I told Alex to behave and not corrupt my husband too much; he laughed and said no guarantees. I kissed Max and thanked Nick again for his hospitality, and we left.

I didn't register how long it took to get to Jade's place; we were all talking. When we pulled up to a gorgeous white two-story brick house with black shutters and roof in a gated community, it fit precisely into what I would predict.

Ginny's house was small in comparison to the two from tonight, but it was comfortably homey and none of them seemed to mind the size. It was the people inside that mattered. This family had the closeness and familiarity neither Max nor I grew up with, and I suddenly wanted something I never knew I was missing.

Welp, there was yet another disappointment I would need to confront later…

Dolls Night was comical, loud, and so much fun that my cheeks hurt from laughing when I went to bed. Jade ordered catering from a nearby Mexican restaurant, and she had large jugs of pre-made margaritas waiting for us in the fridge. When the food arrived, it was a free-for-all on all kinds of options, and the drinks were going down a little too easily.

Naomi turned out to be hilarious, and I discovered she'd been kind of a surrogate mom to the older sisters and later some to Ginny when she returned to Boston. I didn't know that Jade and Lisey's mother died in a bad car accident when they were quite young. With no hesitation, Naomi graciously stepped in to help her brother through both the grief and parenting of two little girls.

When Nick decided to marry Ginny's mom, none of them were too sure about it, but when "baby G" was born, they all became a closer family. From the sounds of it, I wondered if Ginny's impending arrival had influenced the timing of the wedding, but I didn't ask.

Naomi got married later and had three stepchildren from Trevor's first marriage but no biological children. She claimed that raising Lisey and Jade had been more than enough for her, and they all applauded her bravery!

Jocelyn Fletcher was quieter, but she was very nice and shared funny stories about when she first joined the extended Beckett clan.

When they got around to asking me questions about Ginny and my college age adventures, I recounted a few incidents, as did she. She described my "heroic" *(her word, not mine)* effort saving her from the creeper at the restaurant, and everyone gave a margarita cheers to me.

I told them when Ginny explained the D Score to me, it became our favorite topic. At the mention of it, the sisters burst into laughter and said they hadn't thought about it in decades! That led to an explanation of the Date Worthiness Scale, with more humorous stories of putting it to use. Both Ari and Kayleigh declared it would serve them well going forward!

At some point, I heard an unmistakable beat when Arica began loudly broadcasting the "Whoomp! (There It Is)" song into the room. Ginny laughed and looked at me, and we started yelling out the lyrics again, with Jocelyn and Jade joining in. Lisey and Naomi didn't remember it, but they grabbed their phones and recorded most of our performance.

It was phenomenal to re-live the memories of fun with Ginny with this group of women. I had blocked them out for so long, but there were too many wonderful, funny, loving, and carefree times to keep them locked up.

In this moment, it felt like the TAG Team was, in fact, back again – maybe in a slightly different, more mature form. I smiled at my daughter and saw tears in her eyes but a gigantic grin on her lovely face.

Things started winding down around 10:30 p.m., and we all headed back to Nick's. We found the men lounging in the den with drinks in hand and a haze of smoke in the room. We mingled for a few minutes but then said our goodbyes as the group dispersed just before midnight.

Everyone told Max and me that we had to come back soon, and it was rewarding to hear we'd been so accepted. Topher drove us back to our hotel. I realized on the way it would have been a lot easier to have stayed at Alex and Ginny's tonight, but oh well.

I woke up earlier than Max on Sunday morning and had a short time to myself to think about the past week.

Wow, I can't believe how much has happened in just eight days. We searched for and secured a great apartment for Arica to live in the city she wants to be in. We've moved her halfway across the country twice now, perhaps long-term.

After waiting twenty-seven years, I told Ginny everything and how deeply she hurt me. Afterward, it felt like a huge stone was no longer sitting in my chest. It feels like the stone is still nearby, but getting further and further away with each day. Am I seriously past it all? Is the stone actually gone forever?

Is that what forgiveness is?

This week with everyone here has been AMAZING. I didn't expect to fit in so quickly and easily. Would they embrace anyone whose daughter was dating Topher?

Ginny really did talk about me during all this time, every single family member we've met has confirmed it. I never gave her the credit she deserved because I didn't see that part. Now that I have, I guess it balances with her being too chickenshit to be honest back then.

She told me she loves me and always has, but I couldn't say it back. Do I still love her? Or love her again? I wholeheartedly used to, but I don't feel like I can trust her 100% now. As Max would ask me, what would it take for me to do that? Is it too soon, or even possible?

Was I in as much pain as I was then because of the girls who ditched me after my foreign exchange summer? I thought I was smart enough not to trust people fully, but I did with Ginny, and it burned me a thousand times worse than the first time.

I also knew not to count on my dad when he was in a good mood because it would change at a moment's notice. On the flipside, my best decision was to depend on Max — look how well that worked out!

Is there something wrong with me for holding these grudges too long?

We're all older and wiser now, I think Ginny deserves a second chance to earn my trust. We were young and stupid and she made terrible choices. She's compensated for it — she patiently let me air my bitterness, she's been loving and kind to Arica, and she now knows she can tell me things.

She and Alex have welcomed all of us with open arms, and she said she wished she had faced me then instead of letting it fester all those years. That means she wouldn't make the same mistake again, right?

Yeah, I forgive her. I don't know if I love her again, but I probably do and don't want to admit it.

Max was starting to wake up, so I left my train of thought and focused on breakfast and the plan for today.

We had been granted a noon checkout, so we didn't have to rush getting around and packed.

I texted Arica that we were available if there was anything for us to help with before she starts work tomorrow. She replied after 11 a.m. and said she was okay for now but would tell us if things changed. We weren't the only ones having a slow morning!

We got everything back into our SUV and went to a nearby restaurant for lunch. Max wanted to watch at least the beginning of football playoff games. I checked in with Arica again to see how she was doing, and she said she's nervous but good overall. She thanked us again for all our help and she looked forward to seeing us for dinner after her first day of work.

We hadn't given Alex and Ginny an exact time when we'd head their way, so I texted her to see if 2:30 p.m. was okay. She responded that any time was fine.

She was excited to welcome us when we arrived, and Max immediately gravitated toward the TV Alex had on in the living room. They started discussing NFL stats and players, and Ginny led me to the kitchen where she had something in the oven that smelled delicious. She was also slicing vegetables for salads, and I asked if I could help. She said no, she was just prepping now so she wouldn't have as much to do later.

We laughed about the previous night and some of the silliness that ensued. We talked about life things in general, and I admitted I was anxious about returning to an empty house soon.

Before I knew it, almost two hours had passed, and Alex and Max came into the kitchen between games. The four of us chatted for a bit, and then they took their drinks back into the living room. Ginny asked if I wanted to have a glass of wine out on the porch since the sun was out, and we curled back up in the familiar chairs.

She asked me about my friends back home, and I told her about Kate and the other women who were my support system. I said that a few of them had been huge helps when my mom died and I felt guilty, and then we talked about parents for a while.

After Ginny's grandparents passed, her mom stayed back in the Midwest because she had siblings and nieces and nephews close by. Ginny was fine with talking to her periodically nowadays. Their relationship suffered greatly when she got pregnant with Hudson, and they hadn't worked very hard to repair it.

She went back once when one of her uncles had a heart attack and perished suddenly. Her mom was devastated and angry and barely spoke to Ginny, so it was a wasted trip and effort for mending those fences.

Ginny was connected to a few of her maternal cousins on social media and had a vague idea of what they were up to. Their communication was limited to birthday wishes and erratic comments here and there. With such loving people out here in Boston, there wasn't much need for Ginny to visit too often.

We finished our glasses, went back in to warm up the stuffed shells and breadsticks, and I volunteered to put the salads together for everyone. Alex asked if we'd be willing to play euchre after dinner. He and Ginny were rusty but had missed the card game. No one out east was eager to learn it, so they wanted to take advantage of hosting some Midwesterners!

Once they got back into the rhythm of it, we played multiple raucous rounds, mixing it up between teams and yelling at each other when we didn't get to lay the cards we wanted. I had my best game with Alex as my partner; we were very in sync with coordinating our hands and won by several points.

I hadn't heard Ari come home, but when we finished, I noticed her standing in the kitchen drinking water and giggling at our bizarre behavior. It was a tremendously fun night! Alex was taking the next two days off work so we could all spend more time together until Max and I left. We stayed up later and watched some TV, but we were all worn out. As I mentioned, middle age sucks.

Before I went to sleep, I texted Kate that I was spending the night in the enemy's lair. If no one hears from me after a few days, send help. I added an LOL and told her things were going better than I expected, and I couldn't wait to tell her everything over drinks soon. She sent a funny meme in response, and I chuckled as I put down my phone.

Sometime in the night I woke up and needed to use the bathroom, so I shuffled down the hall. In my sleepy haze, I accidentally opened the door next to it first. It was temporarily confusing when I switched on the light and saw a bedroom half full of storage totes and boxes. The other half contained academic trophies and ribbons hanging from a shelf, band posters on the wall, and a large H above a twin-sized bed.

Then I understood this had been Hudson's room before he moved out. I quietly shut the door and went into the bathroom. It was an interesting revelation, but I was too tired to do anything with the information at that late hour.

An early text woke me up in the morning, and I saw Dawson was wishing his sister a great first day in our family chat. He was so sweet! I added my well-wishes, and she replied with several hearts.

Max was already out of bed, so I went to find him. He and Alex were sitting in the kitchen having coffee and laughing about something, and I told him about the texts. He promptly sent a message so Arica would know we were all thinking about her.

I inquired about coffee. Alex nodded and got up to grab me a cup. Ginny joined us shortly thereafter and asked if we had anything we wanted to do before we left. We didn't, so she smiled and said she thought we could go into downtown Boston and do some fun things and maybe a little shopping. We said it sounded great!

It was a fabulous day seeing more of Beantown and visiting some of their preferred spots. After lunch, we were walking, and Alex and I started talking about high school and the classmates I kept in touch with, predominantly through social media. He scoffed and said he couldn't care less about that stuff, but he did want to hear how some people were doing.

I gave him the highlights of the ones I thought would interest him and showed him pictures in the apps. We joked about some of them, shared a couple memories, and had a really good conversation. He and I hadn't had much time for just the two of us to talk before now. After a few more minutes, I suddenly noticed that our spouses were no longer with us.

We glanced around but didn't see them anywhere. We began back-tracking and they came out of an ice cream shop about a block behind us. I was irritated they hadn't notified us, but Ginny said we were so involved in catching up that we didn't hear them call out. She stopped anyway because she HAD to have their ice cream, no matter what season it was. She and Max held two cones each and handed us our treats.

Truth be told, it **was** quite tasty.

We decided to walk part of the Freedom Trail, which was historically fascinating. By the time we were done, it was almost 3 p.m., and Ginny said she had one last shop to take us to before we went back to the car.

We zigzagged several blocks to get to her favorite dessert place. The smell of melted chocolate and baked goods was divine when we walked in. She made a beeline to the case where her beloved goodies were. She advised us to look around and take something home, and maybe something to eat on the drive. She mentioned that there were free samples of a lot of the items, which Max was happily discovering already!

We spent more time and money than we should have, but she was right about it being too delicious not to indulge. We found our way back to our parking spot, and Alex navigated through the congested traffic to their house. We all dumped our purchases inside and freshened up before we met Arica and Topher for dinner. We couldn't wait to hear about day one at the new job!

Poor Topher was doing a lot of driving this week, but I figured after today they would likely work out a better schedule for weekly visits and trips back and forth.

During the meal, Arica said her day went well and she was immensely excited about this position and her supervisor. She couldn't stop gushing about all the beautiful fabrics and outfits they housed in their headquarters warehouse, and she'd barely seen anything yet!

Everyone she met was incredibly helpful and kind, and she could tell they all respected her boss. Vast corporate experience had taught me that office politics would come into play soon enough, but I wasn't about to burst her bubble this early. I would have to remember to talk with her at some point about being careful with gossip and alliances within the groups she dealt with on a regular basis.

Arica was clearly tired after a nerve-wracking first day, so we didn't stay too long after we ate. In the parking lot, Max and I gave her prolonged hugs, mine with tears included. We told her how proud we were, how much we loved her, and how she should call us if she needs anything at all. She was crying too as she thanked us again for everything and we all said goodbye. She got in with Topher and waved as they drove away.

My sniffling continued as we got back in Alex's car to go back to their house. Alex and Ginny were quiet as Max comforted me and reminded me what a strong daughter we had. I was intellectually cognizant of all that, but my momma heart was having a hard time. It couldn't comprehend that she was on her own now and I didn't know when I'd see her again. Why did she choose to live so far away?

I was marginally better by the time we got back to their house, but we were still a morose foursome. I apologized for bringing down the mood, but Ginny assured me that what I was feeling was totally normal and they could empathize.

She recounted what she went through when Hudson and then Topher moved out. Alex nodded along with her description of random crying and worrying that she'd never see them again, even though each of them was less than half an hour away. He added that he was already dreading the time when Ari leaves, and Ginny sighed with sadness at it becoming a reality.

Then she perked up. "We have nowhere to be in the morning, so who wants to get drunk? Let's party the blues away just like old times!"

We laughed and said we'd give it a shot *(pun intended)*, and the four of us had a few hours of alcohol-infused euchre and merriment to end the night.

~ *Chapter 12* ~

NEW NORMAL

Max and I were feeling rather rough the next morning, so we weren't "up and at 'em" as early as we'd originally planned. After coffee, breakfast, and some slow packing, we got our luggage back out to the truck and started to say our goodbyes. Ginny was already tearful, but she was also quite happy.

"Tabby, this has been a primo week for me. I love that we got to spend so much time together! Our kids are mad for each other, Max and Alex get along great, and you met the majority of my family. It's so exciting!

And best of all, you got everything off your chest so we can go forward with nothing bad between us. Thank you for letting that happen, and I'm so glad you accepted us back in your life. You're still the best friend I've ever had, and I've loved every single minute over the past nine days!" She squeezed me tight for a few moments.

It was hard to follow that, but I said, "Thank you for all you've done for Arica, for us, and for allowing me to spill my guts to you even though I'm sure it was tough to hear. I've had a lot more fun this week than I expected, and I appreciate you letting us stay with you. This trip has been awesome despite leaving part of my heart here in Boston."

"Alex and I think the world of your daughter, and we'll be here for her if she needs anything. And if you want me to ever run over to her apartment and check on her, or whatever, please don't hesitate to ask." We hugged again, and I heard the men grumble and chuckle.

Both of them received a 'wife look' and I said, "Cut it out, you're lucky we're friends again and aren't trying to pull each other's hair out."

Alex smiled. "Actually, I was hoping more for a mud wrestling event on the front lawn. I could sell tickets to the neighbors and make a little cash." Max encouraged him by laughing, and Ginny and I rolled our eyes in unison.

"On that note, I suppose we should get on the road," I said to Max.

I hugged Alex and told him, "I'm glad you're part of my life again. I guess you and I are stuck together whether we like it or not. Class Caboose forever!" We smiled, and I finished with, "Thanks for helping so much this week and for entertaining my husband."

He gave me a smirk-smile and replied, "Can I send my wife with you and keep Max?" We all laughed and Ginny smacked his shoulder in indignation.

With that, Max and I got in the truck and turned on navigation to home. We backed out and waved goodbye, Ginny was already crying as Alex put his arm around her. It was reminiscent of me leaving them standing outside the restaurant so many years ago, but this time it was an upbeat departure instead of a furious one.

As Max drove us toward the highway, I silently watched out the window and briefly wondered what it would be like to live here. It was a weird thought, and I pushed it aside knowing we had too much of a life where we are and didn't need to start over.

We didn't rush our trip, but we made decent time due to the dry and fairly clear weather and traffic being lighter on weekdays. There was plenty of time to talk, and I went through many of my encounters from our time in Boston.

Quite a bit was around our daughter, and he expressed some of his thoughts and feelings as well. Most of our conversations were in regard to Alex and Ginny and putting the pain behind me.

He started by asking me, "So, do you feel any different after talking with Ginny?"

"Yes. It was the right thing to do. I told her that it felt like a huge stone was no longer in my chest, which I'm guessing was the balled-up emotions you and I talked about. It's hard to describe, but I'm pretty sure I am getting closer to either forgiving them or just accepting them as regular people."

"Wow, babe – that's amazing! I know you weren't happy that Alex and I conspired to give you two the time together, but we thought it was best. If it ended in a huge fight, he said I could blame it on him!" We both chuckled at Alex's nonsense.

"Well, I do feel better about things, it was good to get it all out. That was the only time I'd vocalized everything since it happened. It was strange to think about my twenty-three-year-old self from where I am now. The whole thing was both fresh in my memory and like a million years ago.

Ginny's family is a riot. I thought yours was wild and loud, but they've got to be close!"

He laughed, "Yeah, I was reminded several times of Ganter gatherings from my childhood when I could hardly hear myself think!"

I sighed. "Despite it all, she's still one of the few people in my life I've ever felt so comfortable with. Alex, too. It's like trying on a sweater you haven't worn in decades and finding out it still fits and is just as soft and snuggly as you remember."

I smiled at comparing them to clothing, but I knew Max understood.

"I'm really proud of you for letting go and telling her your part. I believe you'll be much stronger for it."

"Thanks, I'm proud of myself as well. I appreciate you listening through all the drama and helping me work past it. I wouldn't be this far along without you."

"Glad I could be of assistance. I'll send the invoice to your email." I laughed and shook my head. Alex was rubbing off on him!

He told me later that he and Alex had a lot of excellent chats, and he was grateful for becoming acquainted with him. As we got closer to home, I said I was having a hard time thinking about the empty house.

With my mom dying and both children leaving less than seven months later, I wasn't sure what I'd do with myself. If I didn't have someone to take care of, then who was I? He didn't know how to answer and reminded me that he was still there every day. I clarified by explaining he was fine on his own and didn't NEED me the way my mom and the kids had. I cried during our discussion and presumed it would be popping up again in the near future.

We arrived back in our town at dinnertime on Wednesday, and we just grabbed fast food to eat at home. Perhaps I was hypersensitive, but our footsteps seemed extra loud and the rooms especially empty.

There was a lot of cleaning and reorganizing to do after the rush of moving Dawson, my brother and family leaving, and then Arica taking so many things with her. At least that would keep me busy and distracted for a couple of weeks.

After we ate, I let everyone know we made it back safely and took a shower. Max and I were exhausted from the drive, so we crashed early. It was incredible to sleep in our own comfortable king-sized bed after so many nights in unfamiliar queen-sized ones. We had nothing on our agenda for the next morning, so it was a relief not to set any alarms and get the rest we desperately needed.

Dawson came to see us that weekend, and we shared the details of our trip, showed him pictures of Arica's apartment, and depicted the members of the Beckett family. We video chatted with Arica so she could tell us about her first week. She said it went even better than she'd hoped. Topher arrived while we were talking, so he said a quick hello. They were leaving soon to meet a couple of his friends. She looked happy and seemed to be adjusting perfectly well.

It was so good to have Dawson in the house with us and then converse with her as well. I valiantly tried not to cry when he left and succeeded for the most part, but Max handed me a tissue when he saw a few tears leaking out. He asked if I wanted to talk, but I said no and focused on watching something on TV instead.

We went back to work the following Monday and began figuring out what our schedule was going to be now. I started making plans with friends again, and we met up with other couples sporadically. Kate and I hung out more often, which was outstanding.

Max, however, didn't do much outside the house. He wasn't interested when I tried to persuade him to reach out to some of his friends or ask his favorite co-workers to go out after work. He said he was content with simply coming home, making dinner, and doing his own thing until bedtime. I didn't understand it, but I quit bugging him about going out.

I joined a monthly book club at our local library; it was good to read again. In addition, I started attending a beginner's yoga class once a week. It surprisingly helped my back feel better than it had in years, plus I met a couple of nice ladies there. One of them already knew Kate as well, so the four of us hung out when we could.

Max and I talked about planning a trip to the West Coast to visit Micah and his family sometime soon; we hadn't been out there in a long time. I threw out the idea of visiting Stacey and her husband for a weekend getaway, but he suggested maybe I go see her myself.

We also began going to see Max's dad and relatives more often, usually about once a month. Dawson sometimes joined us and was happy to help his grandpa around the house again.

All in all, we got into a comfortable rhythm. I found ways to stay busy, and I wasn't as lonely or aimless as I'd feared. Max and I were sitting on the couch one night, and he was busily texting during a show we were watching. I asked who he was talking to, and he showed me a long string of text messages with Alex – they kept in contact regularly. Ginny and I texted one or two times a week, but I think the men had us beat! She and I had also become Facebook friends and followed each other on Instagram now, so we did have those connection points advantages over our husbands.

As summer approached, I began to question when we'd be able to see Arica again. We talked to her every other weekend or so, and she was thriving in Boston. There wasn't much reason for her to come home until the holidays, but that was too far away for me to wait.

One night I asked Max's opinion on taking a holiday weekend, maybe Memorial Day or Fourth of July, to go out to Boston. He smiled and said he'd been wondering how long I would last! I planned to bring it up next time we talked to Arica and see what she thought about timing.

When we told her we'd like to visit, she was delighted to hear it. She asked if we would consider Labor Day weekend so we could be part of the Beckett boating tradition, but she understood if September was too late in the year for us. Max and I said we'd talk it over.

She requested that whenever we ultimately decide to come out there, she'd like us to convince Dawson to join us. We agreed to ask him about it and see if one of the time frames was better for him.

I was quiet after we hung up. Max reminded me that summer would go fast and Labor Day would be here before we knew it. It still seemed like forever. Memorial Day weekend was coming soon, which had snuck up on me and meant it had been a year since my mom's surgery. That realization hit hard. Max went to do something else, and I kept the sad thoughts inside.

After talking to our son, he said Labor Day would be perfect for him. He could arrange to take final exams for his program in late August and be done right before the trip. It would then be easier for him to take off that Friday and enjoy a carefree vacation. He said the other two holidays would be harder for him to get away. I had to resign myself to waiting until September, but it would be extra special to have all four of us together again.

We told Arica the news, she was thrilled. An overly gleeful text came from Ginny the next day telling us she CANNOT WAIT to have us all out there for a fun family holiday on the water!

The following few weeks went by normally, then May arrived. The weekend of Mother's Day was horrible for me. Both of my kids were gone, and I couldn't honor my own mom or Max's.

Dawson came over Sunday. He and Max tried to cheer me up, but I didn't feel like going anywhere or doing much. Arica called, but she ended up talking to her dad more than anyone. I appreciated everyone's efforts, but I felt like it didn't deserve recognition.

Memorial Day was right after that, so for half the month I was grouchy and jittery. In addition, I couldn't sit still at home – I was constantly cleaning things, re-organizing drawers and shelves, and generally an anxious mess. Max kept gently nudging me to talk to him about what I was thinking and feeling, but I resisted.

On the Sunday before Memorial Day, we were watching the Indianapolis 500 race, and I had a flashback to doing the same thing right here with Mom the previous year after her surgery. That was apparently the "straw that broke the camel's back" as the floodgates opened and my sobbing seemed endless.

I mourned the absences of my mom and mother-in-law as well as the loss of having our kids in the house.

Max handed me the tissue box and sat wordlessly next to me with his hand on my leg and the TV volume muted until I was ready to talk or be done with it. I didn't have much to say. I guess acknowledging the grief was what I needed most.

When my weeping began to subside, I was able to tell him, "Sorry for the breakdown, it all hit at once that both of our moms are gone, and I feel like less of a mother because our children aren't in this house with us anymore. I know it's dumb, but that's where my state of mind has been lately."

"No worries, babe. The way you've been acting the past few weeks, I kind of figured it would all come to a head soon. I'm not sure why the race was the catalyst, but we don't have to watch it if you don't want to. And you're still a great mom no matter where our kids live."

"The race is fine, I just remembered seeing it last year with Mom after her surgery, and I had no idea it was one of the final things we'd do together." The tears started again on a moderate scale.

He looked surprised. "Oh, I hadn't thought about that. I'm so sorry it brought up all those feelings at once. Do you want to do something else?"

"No, I feel a lot better after getting those thoughts out of my system. This week is probably going to be rough for me, but I'll get through it."

He told me he loved me, and we resumed watching TV. There were more small bouts of tears, but most of the sadness seemed to be over.

Over the next few weeks, I did struggle against my emotions, but I got past it like I said I would. Summer arrived; the sunshine and warm weather was good for my soul. I spent time in our gardens, with friends on outdoor patios, and with Max seeing new movies and visiting his family.

We video chatted with Arica on her birthday and Ginny held the phone so we could sing along as our daughter blew out twenty-three candles on a beautiful cake. It was touching to see her surrounded by lots of loving Beckett family members.

Dawson somehow turned twenty-one in July *(my baby!)*, which was conveniently on a Saturday. We invited him to come over for lunch that day since we assumed he'd want to go out with his friends to celebrate at night. We made him his first (legal) alcoholic drink and took a sip together before he opened his gifts. We had a marvelous afternoon and called Arica so she could add her birthday wishes. She'd sent him money virtually to buy him some drinks, which he was happy about, and she said she'd take him out in Boston over Labor Day weekend.

Max and I also gave him some funds to use however he wanted, and we had him blow out the candles on his cake. He was excited to finally reach this milestone, especially since he was the youngest in his friend group. We didn't ask many questions, but he told us later he'd had fun and remembered most of it, and we left it at that.

As we entered August, the texts from Ginny increased regarding the plans for the upcoming holiday weekend. Max and I were going to stay at their house again, and they were contemplating what the best plan for Dawson was. We said he'd be fine sleeping on their couch for a few nights, but they insisted they would find something better for him. I had a brief thought about Hudson's bed, but there was no way I was going to bring that up…

Ginny later said Arica wanted him to sleep at her place; it was resolved. Our daughter missed her brother, so I certainly had no complaints about the arrangements.

Max and I got ourselves packed throughout the week, although I was conflicted about the level of formality on the boat. I asked Arica if we should dress up for that night. She said it was casual, but some of the women wore sundresses if it wasn't super windy. Shorts and comfortable shoes were fine; I was glad I asked. Max didn't know why I was fretting about it, but straight men just don't understand these kinds of things.

Dawson came over after finals and work on Thursday. We were all going to the airport together Friday morning. The three of us got up and saw that our flight was delayed thirty-five minutes, so we had an unhurried breakfast at home and then headed out.

At the gate, they announced that it would be an additional twenty minutes later, which was frustrating but not terrible. We watched an angry couple argue with the desk agent about missing their connection and sympathized with everyone involved. Having the option of direct routes to Boston was invaluable. I sent Arica and Ginny the updated arrival time. They said it was no big deal, and Ginny would pick us up whenever we got our bags.

We landed a little after noon, and Ginny pulled up to the curb at baggage claim and cheerily greeted us. We loaded our luggage and chatted all the way back to Alex and Ginny's house. She said she had some sandwiches ready if we were okay with a homemade lunch, which sounded delicious.

We unloaded and showed D around, then ate out in the sunroom *(it was perfect weather at this time of year)*. Arica insisted on hosting dinner at her apartment, so Alex, Ginny, Max and I would drive together. Topher would swing by to pick up Ari and Dawson so we could all be there at 7 p.m.

I was concerned about eight of us fitting in Arica's place to eat but didn't voice it. If our daughter was excited to have everyone here and wanted to be the "hostess with the mostest" for a night, we would make that happen.

Ginny asked Dawson some questions about himself since she hadn't talked to him much yet, and they had a cordial conversation when we finished eating. He seemed somewhat awkward in these new surroundings, but that wouldn't last. You couldn't be around the Beckett family very long without feeling like one of them. Even Max had been sucked in!

The front flower gardens were full of life this time, so I told Ginny I'd like to go outside and look at what she had. She gleefully said she'd give me the "grand floral tour" and snatched her sunglasses off the counter. We leisurely strolled through the yard talking about gardening, comparing flowers and vegetables we each grew, and enjoying the sunshine. When we re-entered the house, both Max and Dawson were asleep on the couch with the TV on some sportscast show.

She and I shook our heads and went back to the kitchen. She grabbed a bottle of wine and nodded toward the sunroom, and I took two glasses out of the cabinet as we went out there. It was way too easy to lean into this friendship again, it felt like this was my second home already.

Sitting on her porch again gave me a small sense of déjà vu, and I decided to take advantage of us being alone.

"Ginny, I have something to tell you." She looked at me inquisitively, but not cautiously.

"First, thank you once again for everything you've done for my family. You and Alex have been nothing but gracious and kind to us, and it's appreciated. Not to mention including us in your lives as fully as you have.

When we talked last time out here, you said you didn't deserve my forgiveness. You were right, but a lot has changed since then. Both of you have shown me that you've matured and grown into more conscientious people than you were in our younger days. I feel like my anger is finally water under the bridge and I can trust you again, which is a monumental step for me.

What I'm trying to say is… I do forgive you and your knucklehead husband. I'm glad we've put the past where it belongs."

She gasped, and her eyes were as big as saucers. She simultaneously jumped up and shrieked with joy, then nearly knocked over my chair as she wrapped me in a bear hug. She eventually stood up and faced me, beaming.

"TABBY! That is the best thing you could ever say to me, THANK YOU from the bottom of my heart!"

My smile was just as wide. "You're welcome. Cheers!"

We clinked our wine glasses, and it felt like the world was a tad brighter than it had been when we arrived.

We caught up until Alex walked in the door just after 4:00, and he teased the other men about passing out in the middle of the day. He and Max bantered back-and-forth a bit, and Dawson was looking at them curiously. He wasn't used to his dad being this way, and I smiled that Alex brought out the witty and fun side of my husband.

Alex came out to greet me and kiss Ginny, which didn't irk me like it would have before. *(Hooray for progress!)* She and I went inside to mingle with everyone.

Alex asked the age-old question of what they'd like to drink, and Max got a kick out of talking about whiskey with our now legal-aged son. Dawson took small sips of some of them until he found one he kind of liked and said it "didn't burn as badly as the others," which brought a laugh from the dads.

Ari got home about half an hour later, and she hugged Max and me and introduced herself to Dawson. He was clearly distracted by how attractive she was and a little tongue-tied when he was chatting with her. Ginny and I shared a look and smiled; it was endearing to watch them trying to politely get to know each other.

Topher arrived just before 6 p.m. and told us there'd been an accident on one of the highways and he was grateful he knew the backroads.

The word 'backroads' caused me to immediately think of Alex, and he apparently had the same reaction as we made eye contact. My cheeks burned as I blushed. Mercifully, no one else was paying attention to us while Topher was describing the traffic issues and advising we take a different route to Arica's than we normally would.

Not long after that, we loaded into the two vehicles and wound our way through many suburban streets and an industrial area to arrive at the apartment. Topher had a couple of shopping bags to bring in, and Dawson got his luggage out of the trunk and gazed around appreciatively.

He said he understood why we all liked it right away; it was much nicer than his place back home. We led him up to the fourth floor and knocked on Arica's door, which she opened with a flourish and squealed joyfully to see us all standing in her hallway.

The delicious aroma of barbeque sauce emanated from the kitchen, and I was instantly hungry. She hugged Max and me hard, said hello to the Yateses, and grabbed Dawson's arm to show him around. She asked Topher to put the alcohol on the counter and stir the sauce, which he promptly did. I recalled the first time we had dinner at Ginny's house when she asked him to do the same thing, and it made me giggle internally.

I examined the changes since we moved her in. There were now multiple art pieces on the walls, a fluffy blanket and throw pillows on the futon, a centerpiece on the dining room table, and a bicycle tucked into the far corner of the living room. That one was unexpected; Arica had not always been the most athletic person!

She'd added a few more decorative items in the kitchen, as well as some canisters for flour and sugar. It was becoming her own space to match her personality, and I loved to see it. There was steam rising from a new Crock

Pot on the counter and cornbread muffins cooling on the stove.

After she gave her brother the tour, she invited us all to have a seat since dinner was almost ready to serve. Topher got our drink requests and began working on those. Ari offered to sit on one of the barstools at the island, and Dawson did as well.

Arica got everything on the table and thanked us all for coming. She had tears in her eyes as she exclaimed how happy she was we made it out there so our families could share this food together in her home. We all dug into slow-cooked BBQ chicken, cornbread with butter, fresh green beans, and salad. We were tightly packed around the table, but the proximity didn't bother us, we all had a fantastic meal.

Afterward, we helped clean up and store the leftovers in the fridge. There weren't a ton of seating options, but we spread out as much as possible. Ginny gave us a rundown of what the rest of the weekend would entail and when everyone needed to be at different locations.

Since tomorrow's weather was forecasted to be better, we would spend most of the day on the boat with the family. Breakfast would be available at Nick's starting at 8 a.m. if we were up, but we should arrive no later than 10 a.m. to go to the dock. We were encouraged to wear our swimsuits if we wanted to enjoy the water and/or do some sunbathing, and the festivities would last until after the sun went down. She recommended we bring an extra change of clothes just in case.

Sunday would be at Nick's house for lunch at noon, afternoon swimming in the pool if desired, and maybe some yard games. Dinner would be on the back lawn if the weather permitted, or in his dining room if necessary. There were fireworks planned when it got dark.

After she finished explaining, I asked Arica to see the balcony now that the weather was warmer. She took me out there to admire the summer view and nighttime peacefulness. She'd added a bistro table and two chairs with cute cushions, as well as a few small pots of flowers.

It was adorable, and I held her and complimented all the improvements she'd made. She put her head on my shoulder and said she was the happiest she'd ever been and thanked me for the part I'd played in getting her to this point. It was a tender mother-daughter moment I'll cherish to the end of my days.

We went back inside and I used the bathroom, where I saw more improvements and decorative additions. She'd been productive in the seven months of living here!

After a bit, we parents decided to let our kids finish out the night by themselves. Following goodbye hugs, the four of us left to go back to Alex and Ginny's. None of us asked what our kids planned to do tonight; it was probably better we didn't know!

We agreed on the way to be ready to leave by 7:30 a.m. so we could have breakfast and bug our offspring to wake up if necessary. Alex drove us back to their house, and we went straight to bed. Between the week of work, travel, and an overall busy day, Max and I were done.

~ *Chapter 13* ~

YATES & YACHTS

The next morning was bright and sunny and shaping up to be a gorgeous day. Max and I got our things ready but had to borrow some beach towels and a bag from Ginny.

On the way to Nick's, I texted both our children but didn't receive a response right away, which was fine for now. Breakfast was a giant spread across the kitchen island with hot foods galore plus fruit, oatmeal fixings, and even a charcuterie board. Caterers were serving coffee and mimosas at the table, and I opted for one of each!

At 8:30 a.m. I called Dawson, and he answered the phone with a bleary voice. I reminded him that they all needed to be at Nick's soon, and he said he understood. Ginny finally received a reply from Topher at 8:50 a.m. saying they were up, so we relaxed.

As people we knew arrived, hugs and greetings were exchanged. We met Kayleigh's boyfriend and two of Rod and Jade's kids: their daughter Piper Fletcher and their son Winston Fletcher with his wife Ruby, who was noticeably pregnant. It looked like Gigi was going to have one local grandchild soon!

Lisey said hello but seemed grumpy, and she told us she was exasperated by her son's laziness in getting his ass in gear this morning. She'd left him at home, and if he didn't make it on time, he could spend the day with his worthless father for all she cared.

After she walked away, Ginny whispered to us that Lisey's son Liam was a talented musician, but undoubtedly the least ambitious of all the cousins in his generation. His dad, Sam Klein, was a deadbeat and Lisey's biggest regret had been marrying him. As a younger woman, she'd been infatuated with his singing aspirations and rock star attitude.

Once they got married, his motivation faded and he was content with sitting around the house playing instruments and pretending to try to write music while his wife worked long hours as an attorney even when pregnant with their son.

Lisey had enough when Liam was eight. She divorced Sam, reverted to her maiden name, and had primary custody. Regrettably, Liam *(they named him by combining their names, which I thought was clever)* took after Sam in too many ways. He had dropped out of college twice and was now twenty-eight, with a dead-end job and living at home with her, which was driving her crazy.

Preston and Jocelyn Fletcher sat next to us and caught up with us and Alex and Ginny. They lived closer to Providence, so they weren't up here for all the family gatherings, primarily the major ones. Naomi also came over to give us a hug, and Trevor waved enthusiastically from the end of the long dining table.

Nick was surrounded by a loud group of older men and women. Ginny leaned over to fill us in that those were his golfing buddies, retired former colleagues, and a few lifelong friends from his childhood.

She and her sisters play a game each year to guess how many of the "old folks" would be passed out on the boat at the same time in the afternoon. Max and I laughed, and she informed us that Jade had the longest winning streak. It was broken last year by Lisey, and Ginny desperately wanted the title today.

We had long since finished our breakfast when our four children entered the house. A new round of greetings ensued. Poor Dawson was in the spotlight when the Beckett family descended upon him as the unknown person in the group. Arica introduced him all around and stayed with him until he got acclimated to who everyone was. I was proud of them both for the way they handled the social situation.

Ari and Dawson had several quick chats and seemed more comfortable with each other than last night. Kayleigh and her boyfriend went over to the young crowd and met Dawson, then they all got some coffee together.

With only a few minutes to spare, another young man walked in, and I knew at once he was Liam. His hair and smile were exactly like his mom's, and Lisey's shoulders loosened when she saw him. Liam sauntered over to the island to grab food, saying hi to people along the way. He wasted no time filling up a plate and eating quickly before we had to leave.

In total, I believe the group was close to thirty people. Nick did a loud whistle at 10 a.m. and proclaimed that the bus was outside to take us to the marina. His booming voice caused everyone to stop and pay attention.

"If you have larger bags, please put them in the luggage storage underneath the bus. The seats will be quite full. If any of you are driving yourselves, park in the large lot to the right of the main building at the pier. The bus will be using the loading dock area to let us off.

I'd like to thank you all for coming. It's a beautiful day to be on the boat! I'd now like to have a moment of silence for those who are no longer with us."

There were a couple of names I didn't recognize, but then he mentioned his first wife (Lisey and Jade's mom) and his beloved grandson Hudson, both of whom had been taken from them way too early. We were all quiet and bowed our heads, and he finished his speech on an upbeat note.

"I'm very glad that this weekend has become a yearly tradition for those closest to me. Let's have a fun and safe day, and I look forward to catching up with all of you out on the water!"

It was a bit of chaos as everyone began moving toward the front doors at the same time. It was going to be an interesting day!

The bus took us about twenty minutes along scenic winding roads. When we turned into the marina, I gasped at the sight of so many vessels. There were sailboats of all sizes and colors and motorized boats for fishing and water sports. Jet skis bobbed alongside some of them. Fancier pontoons had their own section off to the far left. Then there were a few smaller yachts on the right side of the piers and several medium-sized ones toward the back, I assume where the water was getting deeper.

Max was fixated on them as well; it was mesmerizing. We had never witnessed this part of "how the other half lives" before, except on TV and in movies. Alex pointed out which boat was Nick's, a handsome maroon and silver beast at the back of the docks. It appeared so much bigger in person than what I'd seen in Arica's photo from last year.

The bus parked and we unloaded. A handful of people who drove separately met us at the edge of the parking lot. Max and I instinctively hung back to follow the ones who knew what they were doing. That way we could mimic their actions and not look like the newbies we were.

Our group spread out and walked all the way back to "Beckett's Bona Mobilia," where a ramp took us on board with staff at the ready in case anyone needed help. As we came onto the deck, caterers greeted us and told us where the bathroom and seating areas were, followed by taking our drink orders. It was luxurious on a level I hadn't imagined!

Alex must have seen us gawking, because he came over and gave us a brief overview of what was shipboard.

"The upper deck is where they drive the boat and there's only a small area for other people, so I'd suggest not going up there unless you're invited. On the sundeck above this one are some comfortable couches and pool chairs, but the majority of it's open, so be careful not to spend too much time and get burnt. This level has most of the social areas and will be where lunch and dinner are served. They told you where the bathroom is already, right?" We nodded.

"Downstairs are the sleeping cabins and crew areas, but there are also two additional bathrooms down there if urgency is an issue. If you feel sick at all, talk to one of the caterers. They will bring you something to help with it. It's hard to believe that some people have this all their lives, isn't it?"

We emphatically nodded, and he continued. "I admire Nick for building his firm from a small group of young lawyers into what it is today, and that he's able to afford extravagant things like this monstrosity. When I first met him, I thought he'd be a pompous silver-spoon type who was clueless about real life. But that's the opposite of the truth, he didn't have anything handed to him. He shares his wealth with the people he loves, which means a lot to me. He's still kind of pretentious," he smirk-smiled "but he's also a really good guy and a superb father and grandfather."

Alex's praise was genuine, and it made me happy to see he'd gained a loving father-figure he could look up to and have mutual respect with. A strange thought came to me that marrying Ginny was so much better for Alex than being with me would have been. My dad would never have provided him with the same missing piece.

Alex excused himself to go do something. Max and I walked slowly around this level, mingling and commending the high-quality furnishings and decorations. We started joking about, "On our future yacht, we would keep those, but move the chairs over there, have the dining room table angled that way," and so on.

In reality, it was a masterpiece. Dawson joined us near the back of the boat as it began pulling away from the dock, and he was also fascinated.

"Holy moly, I didn't know you guys were bringing me into the lap of luxury out here! I'm never going to want to go home to my boring apartment in our land-locked state!"

I smiled, "Well, it seems like there are plenty of rooms on this thing, maybe we should hide out and hope they won't notice we're missing!"

He came with us up to the sundeck. I noticed his gaze lingering on the cousins Ari, Piper, and Kayleigh already sunbathing and chatting. At least he had prime taste in the fairer sex, but I felt a moment of fear about him trying to pursue one of the single ladies in the Beckett family. That would complicate everything even more.

I brushed away my crazy thought, surely it wouldn't happen. Besides, Piper was several years older and Kayleigh had a boyfriend who was literally on this boat with us. I was being irrationally paranoid.

We went back down to the main deck and asked a caterer for our drinks to be refreshed. Ginny came over to me and said she wanted to introduce me to one of her dad's friends who is a master gardener and expert on plants. I told her I'd join her as soon as the caterer returned. Topher approached Max at the same time as our beverages arrived, and he asked to show Max something as I was leaving to find Ginny.

She and I had an hour-long, very informative discussion about our outdoor gardens with Nick's friend Veronica, who asked us to call her "Ronnie." She generously offered for us to reach out any time for advice. She met Nick when he hired her to come out and evaluate what he should do with his home landscaping. She had provided her suggestions for the overall plan and which gardening crew would do it best.

From what I'd seen of his place so far, Ronnie really knew her stuff. She and Nick got along well and stayed friends after she finished her work. My curiosity wondered if there had been more to their relationship based on how she talked about him, but I wasn't sure how Ginny would react if I asked her about it later.

Caterers were starting to bring lunch out, and my stomach growled in anticipation. Jade came over and we started talking while we waited for the food to be ready. Max and Alex were immersed in conversation off to one side.

Dawson and Liam each had a beer in hand and were laughing about something on their phones. It was still strange for me that my son was able to drink now. I didn't see Arica right away, but then she came downstairs with the three other young women who'd been catching some rays.

I told Jade I envied their youth and vigor and twenty-something bodies that I'd long outgrown, and she concurred. She also reminded me how dumb we were at their age, as well as broke and naïve. I retorted that I'd trade my wisdom and paycheck for my previous flat stomach and energy level any day of the week and twice on Sunday. She and I laughed as we finished filling our plates.

Jade and I found an area to sit, Ginny joined us, and Lisey came over as well. I listened to them debating the "old folks' game" and smiled as I ate. The goal was to count the most at one time, which commonly occurred between 2–3 p.m. They asked if I wanted to join and I politely declined, saying it wouldn't be fair at this point. After much deliberation, Jade took five, Ginny took six. and Lisey took four.

They enlisted me as the impartial judge, to which I agreed. We moved on to other topics, and I had a blast with the Beckett sisters for over an hour. As it approached the prime time of two o'clock, I spotted Max to tell him I'd be preoccupied with the contest for a while. He seemed edgy and perturbed, and I asked him if everything was all right.

"Yes, I'm fine," he replied curtly. "Have fun with your judging, I'll catch up with you around dinner time."

He was acting strangely, but I decided not to push it further and left him to go count sleeping old people. *(That didn't feel weird at all…)*

After investigating all decks of the boat and taking inventory several times, the highest number was four. Lisey had now won two years in a row. She was pumped about her victory and taunted Jade that her previous streak of five years was now in jeopardy. Jade scoffed and said it would be a long time before she'd worry about her title. Ginny lamented her continued losses and swore retaliation for next year.

We all grabbed a snack and a drink after the contest, and Alex came over to ask who this year's champion was. We told him, and he kissed his wife prior to heading back to whatever he'd been doing. I couldn't help but be happy for them lasting this long as a loving couple.

I checked in with Arica and Dawson, who were both reveling in the elegant setting. I located Max again and put my arm in his as I led him to the side of the boat.

"You okay, babe?" I asked. He nodded and gazed out at the distant shoreline. "If you don't feel well, I'll ask someone for assistance. Or if you're not enjoying today, we can find an excuse to stay in tomorrow," I added in case he was miserable.

"No, it's fine. Sorry I was short with you earlier, I guess I just needed to eat something. I didn't realize I was heading toward hangry status."

"All right. I'm glad that's all it was. Love you." He kissed me, and we watched the water slide by for a few minutes.

Some downtime sounded good, so I curled up on a couch in a little nook and closed my eyes for a while. If this meant I was part of the old crowd, then so be it. After a busy half day of sunshine and socialization, I was tired.

Being shaken gently by my daughter woke me up. She asked if I'd seen Topher recently with a hint of either irritation or concern in her voice. I told her not since lunch. She frowned and apologized for waking me, and she headed off to continue her search.

I rested for a trifle longer, texted Kate about our lavish experience and sent her a couple of pictures, then got up to stretch languidly and see what was going on.

It appeared that we were docked in a quiet area not far from shore, and an inflatable slide had been set up on one side of the sundeck. I went upstairs to view it firsthand. After watching multiple people go careening into the river and having a marvelous time, I wanted to try it as well. I took off my outer layer, stepped up to the edge in my comfortable two-piece bathing suit, and let 'er rip! Laughing all the way down, I splashed noisily into the invigorating cold water!

I swam over to the back of the boat, got up on the deck, and was smiling as I went to retrieve my clothes. Ginny came bouncing over and said I'd done great, and I thanked her as I headed to our bag for my towel. Max saw me dripping wet and asked if I was all right, and I told him I was jazzed after a refreshing slide!

I sat in one of the plush lounge chairs on the sundeck to dry off while Ginny told me about these parties. They started out small quite a few years ago and gradually continued getting bigger. The weather sometimes kept people home, but usually it was warm enough to get a healthy crowd out there. Naomi and Jocelyn came and sat down, then Ronnie as well. They all added commentary about the evolution of the holiday tradition and some of the wild things that had occurred out on the water.

Nick and Max stopped by later. Nick said he hadn't been able to greet us before and he was very glad we made the trip out to be with them. He told us he talked to Dawson earlier and thought he was a wonderful young man. Nick congratulated us on our two intelligent and compassionate children. We smiled and thanked him and complimented the yacht.

I praised his creative naming of it now that I knew the meaning of "Bona Mobilia." He laughed and said he and Lisey had a ball coming up with the right one.

Dinnertime came not long after. The catering crew set up stations for us to choose from hamburgers, hot dogs, bratwurst, chicken breasts, and pulled pork with multiple fixings and side dishes. There was an entire section dedicated to desserts, which all looked delectable.

At this point, two bars also opened with bartenders ready to mix drinks or serve wine in addition to the beer we'd had available all day. It was quite a holiday feast! Everyone ate, mingled, and enjoyed the ambiance.

As people finished eating, the sun started to sink closer to the horizon. We were now headed in the opposite direction we'd been going most of the day, back toward the marina. I was sad that the glamorous boat adventure was nearing its end.

Soft music began drifting out of the yacht's speakers, and many of us were admiring the beautiful sunset over the water. Topher and Arica passed me – he was holding her hand and leading her toward the bow of the ship. I heard him saying they should take a couple's photo with the sunset in the background. He was right, it was a picture-perfect opportunity. I started looking around for my husband so we could take one of ourselves as well.

As they neared the front, Topher paused and handed Max his phone. I thought that was rather strange but dismissed it. I smiled when I saw them posing for the picture; they were such a cute pair. Max took several shots, and then suddenly, Topher reached into his pocket and got down on one knee in a single swift motion.

Ginny and I both gasped loudly, and our reaction caused everyone else to look at the young couple. Arica turned toward him to see what was happening, and she whimpered, covering her mouth in awe.

Everything seemed to start moving at double-speed as I stood there stunned and utterly overwhelmed.

I have no idea what Topher said during the actual proposal; I'm sure it was flawless and eloquent. My mind was racing with thoughts of our little girl through the years, what this meant for her future, if I had prepared her at all to be a wife, and so forth.

Max was calmly recording the whole thing, and I wondered if he had known about this and not told me. Maybe that would explain his odd behavior earlier today…

My precious daughter was crying and nodding her head yes. Topher put the ring on her finger, and they kissed.

Everyone was celebrating, and Ginny was squeezing me saying we were officially going to be sisters after all. Joyful tears were streaming down my face. Then Max was hugging me and choking up.

The rest of the way back to the dock was full of congratulations, champagne cheers, and hugs. Arica and I seemed to be the only dazed individuals. I was in absolute shock that it had transpired right in front of me. I was grateful Topher chose to include our family in the special moment, and I admired his bravery in case she hadn't accepted.

Max, Dawson, and I found our way through the crowd to Arica and embraced her in a group hug. We congratulated the two of them and welcomed Topher to becoming part of our family.

He put his arm around Dawson and said, "I'll finally have a little brother to pick on. Just what I always wished for!" to which we laughed merrily.

When Max and I had a moment to talk alone, he sighed and said, "I felt terrible knowing and not being able to tell you, but Topher wanted it to be a surprise. He pulled me aside earlier to make sure he had our blessing to marry Arica. He understood the whole 'asking for her hand' was old-fashioned and she could make her own decisions. However, he also thought it was appropriate to see if you and I would support their marriage so they didn't start out with contention. Of course I told him we'd be thrilled to have him in our family, and we knew our daughter was madly in love with him."

He waited to see if I had any questions or comments, but when I stayed quiet, he continued. "Alex and Nick were the only other people who were in the loop because Alex helped him pick out the ring and figure out when to propose, and Nick made sure the boat was in an optimal place for a beautiful sunset backdrop.

Topher asked if I would mind being the photographer and videographer, and I couldn't say no. I was snappy with you before because it was a heavy burden of foreknowledge and I'm not comfortable with keeping things a secret from my amazing wife." He kissed me, and I silently accepted his apology with a smile.

"You've had quite a day!" I told him, and he nodded tiredly. "It's great Topher trusted you with that, and I'm VERY glad it was hard for you not to tell me! Max, our baby girl is getting MARRIED soon!"

My voice cracked as tears started falling and I grasped the enormity of the near future. He pulled me in close and held me for a few minutes as the yacht slowed to dock in the twilight.

As everyone prepared to leave the boat, we were all fairly quiet. It had been a **long** day! When it was securely fastened, we filed down the ramp, along the piers, and up the small hill to the bus. It took us back to Nick's house, and most people went straight to their cars and left.

Ginny said she needed to run inside for one minute, but we could go to the car with Alex if we wanted.

We put our bags in the trunk, and Max and I plopped down in the back seat. Alex groaned as he got in behind the wheel. He said every year his brain took a while to get back to land and not feel like he was still swaying on the boat. There was a joke in there somewhere, but I was too exhausted to come up with anything even remotely witty.

Ginny came back out, and the four of us headed to their house. Even she was subdued and yawning on the trip. I suspected she wouldn't be able to keep everything inside the whole way though, and I was correct. After a few minutes, she turned around to us and grinned.

"I know we're all dead tired right now, but I still have to share how freaking excited I am that we're going to officially be related soon! Our kids are getting married — this is just the best day EVER!" We both smiled back at her, and I responded with as much enthusiasm as I could muster in the moment.

"It was a huge surprise for sure, and that proposal was gorgeous. Well done on the advice, Alex!" He gave me a thumbs up. "I don't think it's fully sunk in for me yet, but I guess the four of us are going to spend a LOT more time together."

She clapped her hands with joy and turned back around to the front. I'd appeased her for now.

Ginny told us there was no set time frame for tomorrow's activities; people showed up whenever they chose. My body was begging for many hours of rest, so I was immensely glad we didn't have to get up early.

I took a shower and crawled under the sheets while Max finished his. He came in and asked if I was okay and wanted to talk about anything.

"There's a lot to consider, but even MY mind is too damn worn out to deal with it now. Thanks for asking, but let's just crash." We kissed good night and were out in no time.

We both slept until almost 9:30 the next morning, which felt fantastic. I had been so deeply asleep that it took me several seconds to remember where I was when I woke up. A bathroom trip was needed, so I went there first and then wandered out to the kitchen. Alex was sitting in the sunroom with a coffee and talking on the phone, and he waved to me and finished his conversation.

"Grab some java if you want any, I can make more if we run low." I thanked him and got myself and Max a cup, and we joined Alex.

He told us that Hot Rod called to say Jade wasn't feeling the best and they wouldn't be over to the house until well after lunch. Ginny was still asleep, as was Ari. None of us heard her come home last night, but Alex said her door was shut and her car was outside.

He also mentioned Dawson being sacked out on the couch. We were surprised, but Alex commented that our young lovebirds probably wanted to spend the first night of their engagement alone. I blushed at the implications, and Max thankfully changed the subject to talk about Nick's yacht.

Alex gave us the backstory that Nick bought the boat for pennies from a guy who was getting an ugly divorce. He didn't want the ex-wife to end up with much, so he sold a bunch of stuff for next to nothing out of spite. The yacht was in decent shape but was due for some upgrades and a few repairs because it hadn't been used for several years.

Nick didn't know a lot about boats, but he learned in a hurry and began renovating it slowly but surely until it reached its present state. Alex said the transformation was almost unbelievable from where it started, and the Labor Day weekend parties had become a highlight of everyone's year. We could see why.

We talked about other low-key topics over our coffee up to when Ginny joined us. She was predictably focused on the main subject and was bursting to talk about bridal showers and wedding plans ad infinitum. She hit me with a barrage of questions, most of which I had no answer for because they involved what Arica would want to do.

Either Max saw me tiring of the interrogation or he was simply over it, because he intervened. He told her that we were excited for their future, but we'd wait for them to tell us what they planned.

Alex smirked and turned so Ginny wouldn't see, but I caught it. He was clearly amused by the whole scene playing out in front of him. His wife could be relentless when she had her sights set on something, and it was imaginably a welcome change for someone else to be in her scope.

Before she came up with more wedding talk, Dawson groggily joined us. Alex asked if he wanted coffee, and D said he could go for a gallon of it. Alex chuckled and walked out to make more.

We asked what time they came in last night, and he said he thought around 2 a.m. but he wasn't sure. The youngsters had apparently visited a popular bar to continue the celebrations and partied until they were too tired to move. Ari kept her drinking to a minimum to drive home, and Arica had politely asked Dawson if he'd mind staying here just for tonight.

He shared that Kayleigh caught her boyfriend flirting with another girl, and they had a massive fight and broke up. The now-ex wouldn't leave, so the rest of them walked down the street to another nightclub. It had a cover band playing lots of great tunes and was more fun than the first place anyway.

Liam knew a few of the band members, and they invited him on stage to play and sing a couple of songs. Dawson was impressed by Liam being so talented. We told him he was talking loudly. He apologized and said they'd been close to the speakers, and his ears were still ringing.

He finished his cup and excused himself to go take a shower, but then he halted and grinned at us sheepishly. His clothes were at Arica's apartment, and he had nothing to change into. We laughed and Ginny said she would take him over there. He thanked her but said he could easily arrange for an Uber or Lyft. She scoffed and said that was nonsense and she'd go grab some sandals and her keys. They left not long after, and I glared at Alex.

"Were you enjoying seeing me in the hot seat earlier?"

He smirk-smiled and said, "I pitied you, but I wanted to see how it played out. You're one of the only people who has told her off in her lifetime, so I was curious if you'd get fed up and tell her to leave you alone."

I sighed and said to Max, "Thanks for changing the subject before I did get too irritated. At least ONE of you was on my side." Turning back to Alex, I asked, "Is she going to be like this the ENTIRE time until the wedding?"

He shrugged, "More than likely, yes. She has a bad habit of trying to do everything at once. All the thoughts that are in her head come tumbling out of her mouth and it's like a verbal tidal wave." I nodded at his accurate depiction.

"But it's best if we rein her in sooner rather than later so she doesn't drive everyone else nuts as well. I don't want your daughter to be annoyed with her future mother-in-law before the kids are even hitched.

If possible, you can turn Ginny loose with her sisters and let them get all in a tizzy together. That's what I usually do. Nick and Rod and I call it 'The Sister Twister' and try to stay away when the tornado of emotions is in full swing. Eventually they tire themselves out and things can return to normal."

Admittedly, it wasn't a terrible plan.

We heard Ari rustling around in the kitchen, and she waved and said good morning to us as she prepared herself some breakfast. She was showered and in a fetching summer dress and didn't seem the least bit tired or sore.

Oh, to be young again.

When Ginny returned, it was after 11:30 a.m. already. She humorously said Topher and Arica were not very motivated to do anything. She and Dawson had to keep calling to wake them up.

She said, "Tabby, I'm sorry about the endless list of questions earlier, I'm just SO ready for the planning. I know not everyone is on the same track yet, so I'll try to control myself as much as possible. When I told your daughter I couldn't wait to talk about all the decorations and showers and deciding dates and venues, she looked at me like a deer in headlights."

She sighed. "I will do my best to be patient until the rest of you reach my level, but it's going to be SO HARD!"

We all laughed at her dramatic speech, and I gave her a hug and assured her we'd get there.

With that resolved (for now), Max and I said we would be ready in twenty minutes or so, and Alex and Ginny were the same. We agreed to leave for Nick's house around 12:30 p.m. to still catch lunch. We shared our plan with Ari, and she decided to come with us. The five of us arrived to a somewhat small group of people but plenty of food left. We said hello to those in the kitchen area and helped ourselves to another delicious buffet.

We took our plates and drinks outside to the back patio, where relaxing music was playing lightly through hidden speakers and more people were gathered and talking. Nick, Naomi, and Lisey greeted us and came over to chat. There were a few swimmers (including Liam) in the gorgeous in-ground pool and some younger children running around the backyard. New visitors I didn't recognize were predominantly neighbors and Nick's current co-workers and their families.

Extended Beckett and Fletcher family members periodically came by as they were passing through during the holiday weekend. It sounded like Rod and Preston also grew up nearby and had a lot of relatives still in the area. Both large families had integrated over the years and went to each other's reunions when they could. Nick's bountiful hospitality was renowned, so his parties were routinely well attended.

As Ginny stated, people came and went as they pleased. It was a slightly overcast day, but there were intermittent stretches of radiant sunlight that warmly caressed my skin. Nick had made the right call to have us go out yesterday on the boat when it was bright and sunny.

Our children showed up in the afternoon, looking refreshed and back to their normal selves. Everyone congratulated Topher and Arica again, they were inundated with loving support.

Hot Rod and Jade also joined us later, and Jade said she was feeling much better than she had in the morning. We teased her about a late night of partying and a bad hangover. She laughed with us and said she wished it had been the result of a fun night and not just a nasty migraine.

Piper had chosen to do something with her friends during the day, but she might join us for fireworks. Preston, Jocelyn, and Kayleigh arrived closer to dinnertime, as did Rod and Jade's son, Winston, and his wife. Ruby was glad to be on land today. She said being pregnant had apparently made her seasick on the boat, which she'd never suffered from before.

It was such an easygoing, restful occasion, I thoroughly enjoyed it. The yacht ride had been a luxurious, high-energy day, and this was the perfect antithesis to round out the weekend. There had been a slight chance of rain in the forecast for the afternoon, but so far it had not made an appearance.

Ronnie came over and offered to take us for a walk around the grounds and show us her visions for the various areas, so Ginny, Lisey, Jade, Jocelyn, Naomi, and I followed her. We gained a lot of great tips about landscaping and native plants that went well together. I took notes on my phone of things I now wanted to change at home to improve my own gardens.

The engagement topic came up several times in conversations with separate people, but no one was as dogged in their inquisition as Ginny had been. It was more compliments about how impeccably timed the proposal had been with the beautiful sunset, how they were such a sensational couple, how it would be a spectacular wedding, etc.

Just before 6 p.m., Nick declared that dinner would be served at 6:30, and I heard Topher, Ari, Kayleigh, and Liam whoop jubilantly. Lisey was sitting next to me and groaned. I gave her a questioning look, and she explained that the kids struck a deal with their grandfather years ago.

After dinner they got to take control of the music selection until the fireworks started. They looked forward to it every year and created playlists throughout the summer in preparation. Oh boy, I was not expecting a dance party!

Everyone began filing into the house for a seafood extravaganza, and it got loud in the kitchen. A small bar was also now set up and serving drinks. After getting my food, I went back outside to return to quiet and comfortable on the patio.

I sat facing the door and watched the group as they flowed in and out and fraternized. No one had been disrespectful or upset this entire weekend. Not a single person had even been standoffish or unsocial. It was pleasantly surprising to see so many people spending this amount of time together without disagreements.

While I was contemplating these observations, Dawson and Max joined me at the outdoor table. We chatted about the food selection and some of the things we were unfamiliar with but were willing to try. As we were finishing our meals, D asked if we could have brunch tomorrow around 10:30 a.m. – the four of us and the four Yateses. Our flight was scheduled to leave at 1:25 p.m., so it sounded like a fabulous plan.

Dinner was winding down overall, and I saw the young crowd excitedly enter the house and head back to wherever the music was being played. After a minute or two, the jazz and acoustic shut off, and Liam's voice came over the speakers.

"Good evening, ladies and gentlemen. This station is now changing to modern dance and party music curated by your favorite group of disc jockeys: Topher Tunes, Ari the Artist, Kickin' Kayleigh, and your handsome host, Luscious Liam. The beats are hard to resist, so anyone who's inspired to boogie your behinds off is welcome to do so. Enjoy, and make sure to tip your DJs."

Lisey shook her head as people laughed and a popular K-pop song I'd heard on the radio earlier this summer played. The volume had increased dramatically, but it wasn't so loud that we couldn't still talk.

Max asked me if I wanted anything from the bar and went in to grab us drinks. Ginny came and sat next to me, and I saw Alex laughing with Max inside.

"Did anyone mention brunch tomorrow?" she asked.

"Yes, D told us the plan was for 10:30. Do you know where?"

"Yup, it's a great place we've been going to for years. It's on the way to the airport too, so it works out perfectly."

"Awesome. I can't believe this weekend's almost over, it's gone so fast. You know what's crazy? That our husbands have quite a text string going, maybe even more than we do!" I waved my hand toward them.

She laughed, "I KNOW! I said the same thing to Alex not long ago, and he replied that they got along well and Max was easy to talk to. He then said something about you having the best taste in men, but I ignored his self-indulgent compliment."

It was my turn to laugh, "He really hasn't changed after all this time. Still a weirdo!" We smiled at each other as the topics of our conversation approached with beverages for all four of us. Raising my glass, I toasted, "To the future!" and we clinked and sat back to enjoy our beverages.

The music was quite an eclectic collection of different artists, beats, and genres, but it was intriguing to hear what they'd chosen. I had to admire Nick again. Not only did he throw these elaborate parties, but he also still let his grandchildren be involved and have their way with certain things.

My phone kept dinging multiple times with notifications, which was rare for me, so I picked it up to see what was going on. It was texts from several friends and family members congratulating us on Arica's betrothal. She presumably posted something on Instagram.

I checked online to see a stunning photo of them from yesterday – Topher kneeling down with the ring and her looking amazed and happy. She said she was overwhelmed by the love and support during the first twenty-four hours of their engagement, and she couldn't wait to be Mrs. Yates soon.

That was a gut punch, I had not yet thought about her married name… I must have had a strange look on my face, because Max asked if everything was all right. I showed him the post and smiled so I wouldn't have to explain the bewildered feeling I got when I saw our daughter's comment.

Max's phone was also beeping at him, as well as Ginny's and Alex's, so we took some time to answer the well-wishers in our lives. The instantaneous nature of social media is most certainly both a blessing and a curse.

The sky darkened steadily, and the people who had been inside the house made their way out to find a seat for the fireworks. I had assumed they were Nick's private display, but in reality, it was the town he lives in firing them off. Fortunately, they weren't far away, and the yard faced the perfect direction for viewing. Of course it did!

Moments before they were supposed to start, the music faded down to nothing and the indoor lights dimmed. Liam thanked us for being a splendid crowd, and all the DJs cheered into the microphone.

One of Nick's neighbors had brought over a basket of glow bracelets and necklaces, and many of us donned the festive plastic jewelry while we waited. Right on time, we heard and saw a golden rocket shoot into the sky and explode in bright red, white, and blue. The show lasted less than ten minutes, but they were entertaining, loud, and directly over our heads. What fun!

The party began winding down then, with everyone saying goodbye one last time. We made sure to thank Nick for an extraordinary weekend, and he invited us any time we were able to come. I spent some time hugging the sisters, Naomi, and all the Fletchers. We told our kids we'd see them in the morning and followed Alex and Ginny out to their car. There was a sense of sadness as we drove back to their house; we were all thinking about the fact that Max, Dawson, and I were leaving the next day.

Before bed, Ginny thanked us profusely for making the trip out and joining their traditional family outing. We expressed how much we appreciated the whole experience

– the food, the fancy boat, the rides everywhere, and letting us stay so we didn't have to pay for a hotel. She was tearful as we said good night, but I knew she'd be fine.

The morning was rather hectic as we showered, packed, made sure the kids were awake, got everything into the car, and went to breakfast. It was a great ending meal together for the eight of us. Alex and Ginny were taking the three of us on to the airport, so we said our last goodbyes to Arica, Topher, and Ari outside the restaurant.

I embraced our daughter extra hard and said we'd talk soon. I congratulated her one more time on the engagement and her gorgeous ring. She had tears leaking as she told us all she was so happy we came and she'd miss us. The ride to the airport was mostly silent. We unloaded at the drop-off point and hugged Alex and Ginny the final time.

I thought I'd be sad on the flight, but I was tired and slept almost the entire way. On the drive home, Dawson informed us that the six of them (Topher, Arica, Kayleigh, Ari, Liam, and he) went out again the night before with much less drama. They had a lot of fun singing karaoke at a place Liam suggested.

He was glad he got to spend time with his sister and see where she's living now, and he had nothing but compliments about all the family members he met. Liam had told him about some new bands and music he was excited to check out. Ari felt like a little sister right away; he'd even been feeling kind of protective at the bars when he saw guys trying to flirt with her. He was pleased that Topher had started calling him "little bro" already. He said he'd had an awesome weekend and thanked us for taking him along.

We walked into our house at dinner time and dragged our bags inside. Dawson yawned and said he should go home and do some laundry before he had to work the next day. We hugged him goodbye and then it was the two of us.

Max asked how I felt about getting pizza delivered; I told him it sounded heavenly. We took our suitcases upstairs to change into comfy clothes and unpacked some of our travel stuff. I wasn't ready to be back to "real life" again, but there we were.

Max and I got back into the routine we'd created, and late summer faded into fall. Early in October we attended Dawson's graduation ceremony for his program. It was a smaller affair, but they did a great job in acknowledging each graduate for their individual path and what they planned to do going forward.

Kate, Louis, Max's brothers, and two of our nephews came with us, and we celebrated afterward. Arica was busy at work and couldn't make it back home at that time, but she sent a lovely card. She'd asked us to record everything for her to watch later.

We were extraordinarily proud of D, and he told us he was feeling optimistic about finding a new job soon. In the meantime, he would stay where he was and keep learning from the people he was currently working for.

When we began talking about the holidays, Arica and Topher asked if we were okay with them staying out east for Thanksgiving. They would come here for Christmas, which was fine with us. We said we'd happily host and have several of Max's family members attend so they could officially meet Topher.

Once that was finalized, Max and I decided to go out to California for Thanksgiving to visit Micah and his family. We convinced Leo and Dawson to join us as well, so we would all fly out together and spend some time on the other side of the country!

A few days after we solidified our West Coast plans, Max asked me during dinner what I thought about inviting Alex, Ginny, and Ari to Christmas if they wanted to come. I pondered it and then said it was a good idea. Secretly, I highly doubted that Ginny would want to leave her family for a Midwest winter, so I didn't expect them to accept.

I messaged her about it on Friday night. She said it was really kind of us to invite them and she'd discuss it with

Alex and Ari over the weekend. She replied the next afternoon that she and Alex were in for sure. They asked Ari to figure out her answer by the following day because there were still some seats available on the flight Topher and Arica were taking.

Well, talk about surprising! I wasted a trip upstairs to tell Max, he already knew. Alex must have been texting him at the same time, because he said we're going to have a full house for Christmas. I rolled my eyes at the husbands in general and went back to what I'd been doing.

He later told me he was going to check out some liquor stores soon to see if they had a couple of the whiskeys that weren't sold near Boston but were popular here. Goodness, those two were absurd!

Ginny messaged on Sunday that Ari was coming with them and they'd booked the seats they wanted. Arica also texted our family chat how she couldn't wait to show the Yates our area and introduce them around.

Dawson replied with a big question mark, so we filled him in. I asked him to reach out to his cousins and tell them the plans for Christmas lunch, and he humorously sent me a salute emoji. No turning back now, it was going to be a rowdy holiday for sure!

~ *Chapter 14* ~

Best Intentions

In early November, Ginny asked to call me about something. We arranged a time, and I could tell she was anxious when I answered because she started with awkward small talk to avoid what she actually wanted to say.

"Ginny, you're making me nervous. Just spit it out!" I told her in a half-joking laugh.

"Fine. I feel bad for asking a favor, and Alex doesn't know yet that I'm working on this, and you have every right to say no if you want to. Okay?"

"Sure, hit me with it," I replied, now even more curious.

She went into a fast ramble in true Ginny style, "Alex's parents are only two hours away from you, and I thought maybe we could spend some of the holiday with them. But it would be rough to go back and forth, and worse if the weather isn't cooperative.

So, I wondered if they could possibly come to lunch too. As far as we know, they're still driving well and comfortable with making the trip, and I kind of figured it would be nice for them to meet you all since you'll be extended family soon. But I also know they're basically strangers to you guys, and it's rude to invite more people to a meal we're not hosting, so I completely understand if you don't want to do that."

She finally inhaled to take a breath, and I had my chance to speak.

"That's fine, they're more than welcome. At this point, two more people aren't going to make much of a difference at all! As a matter of fact, you can invite your mom as well if you're open to her coming. You just might want to warn all of them that it's going to be a lot of us, and Max's family is as loud as yours, but more on the male side than female. Feel free to send them our address, and they can call us if they have any questions about getting here."

I held the phone away from my ear for a moment as she shrieked with happiness. "Thank you SO MUCH, Tabby! It's so generous of you and Max to open your home to all of us so we can celebrate Christmas as one big FAMILY!"

Her vivacity never ceased to amaze me. She'd said nothing about her own mom, but I believed I did the right thing by offering.

"Of course, we're happy to do it. Please give the kids an extra hug for us at Thanksgiving, we will miss them!"

"We will, and have a good time in the balmy weather on that other coast we don't acknowledge out here!" I laughed and we hung up.

A week later, I decided to test the waters and asked Ginny if she reached out to her mom yet about Christmas. She read the message but didn't answer right away, which was pretty much what I expected. She wrote back that she didn't want to deal with it this holiday season, we should enjoy the time with the people we'd already invited. I talked to Max about it.

"She's avoiding her mom and that entire side of her family. I know they don't get along well, but if Ginny's going to be here and her mom isn't very far from us, I think we ought to include her."

"Babe, have you considered that maybe you're interfering with things you don't thoroughly understand?"

Slightly aggravated at his attitude, I said, "I think I'm trying to help a friend of mine deal with something she's been putting off for too long. Of all people, I can be trusted on the fact that she needs to face it instead of continuing to ignore her feelings! Hey, you have a direct line to an expert on this. Text Alex and see what he says. I bet he'll back me up."

He picked up his phone but hesitated. "Guys don't really do that kind of thing; I don't know what to say…"

"Give it here and I'll do it then. I'll tell him it's coming from me so he doesn't take away any of your man points." I smirked as I said the last part, and Max gave me an annoyed look. He thought about it momentarily and handed me the phone. My message was short but asked what Alex thought was best.

Returning his device, I told him to let me know when there was an answer. About an hour later, I sat down on the couch with him, and he said I was mostly right. I smiled triumphantly and asked about the "mostly" part.

"Alex said they should talk, but maybe not during the big meal with everyone. He said it would be easier for Ginny to avoid one-on-one interactions, so it might be better to schedule something separately in addition to meeting all of us."

I nodded. "Got it, smart idea. I need to think about how to make it happen." Max sent a quick text and held my hand.

"You're a thoughtful person and a caring friend. I hope this goes the way you want it to." His voice was skeptical, but I smiled confidently that this was the right thing to do for both Ginny and her mom. Alex replied with the contact information just before we went to bed, and I resolved to reach out the next day.

I called Violet during my lunch break, but she didn't answer, so I left a brief message asking her to text or call me back. She didn't respond that day, and I was wondering if Alex had the correct details since her voicemail greeting only had her number and not her name. I heard from her the following afternoon, and it was a strange conversation.

"Hi, this is Violet calling you back about Guinevere," was how she started with a light Southern drawl in her voice. It took me a second to register Ginny's full name, I hadn't heard it in a long time! I thanked her for returning my call, and she continued.

"I don't do much of that texting stuff, it takes too long. I find it easier to talk. How do you know my daughter again?"

"We were friends in college, and we've re-connected lately because my daughter Arica is engaged to your grandson Topher."

"Arica my granddaughter?"

"No, my daughter is also named Arica. She met Topher when she was in college out in Providence, Rhode Island."

"Well Christopher and Arica live in Boston. Guinevere and her husband moved back out there many years ago when they first found out they were having a baby too young and out of wedlock. Guinevere's father takes care of them. She always preferred him over me anyway."

This was heading in an uncomfortable direction. I was unsure how to steer it back gently, so I just dove into the reason for my call. "Well, Alex, Ginny, Christopher, and Arica are coming to my house for Christmas this year, and I thought maybe you'd like to come visit with everyone while they're in the area. I don't live too far from you if you're willing to drive an hour and a half or so. We'd love to meet you and have you over!"

"Honey, I'm not sure I can drive that far, my eyesight isn't what it used to be. Perhaps I can talk to my sister Hazel and see if she could bring me. I haven't seen my grandkids in way too long. None of them visit anymore."

I decided to go with a chipper approach, "It's great that they'll be back here for the first time in quite a while! *(Leaving out the part about three of them being here for my mom's funeral.)* I hope you can make the trip. Your sister is welcome to call me for directions. Would you like my address?"

"Not right now, but I'll talk to her and see what she says. When would we need to be there?"

"Well, they'll be landing early on Friday the twenty-second. So, I thought either Saturday the twenty-third or Christmas Eve on Sunday would be better. Whatever works best for you!"

She took a moment. "All right. Let me see what Hazel says. We'll call you back. What's your name again?" I told her and answered her question about which town we lived in and then we said goodbye. That had certainly not been the talk I expected, and I didn't know what to think about it.

As I briefed Max about it over dinner, he had a concerned look on his face. "I'm not sure about this. When Alex and I talked about Ginny's family, he said she and her mom had a strained relationship. I don't necessarily want to spend Christmas Eve in the middle of a family feud right here in our living room."

His reaction didn't make me happy, but I was at a loss for defending my actions. My decision was made with the best intentions, but I was starting to second-guess myself.

A week later was our trip to California, and wondering about Violet's attendance was not on my mind in the least. We had a fantastic Thanksgiving vacation! It was wonderful to be in a warm climate in November and see Micah and his family in their native habitat.

Elise and I went shopping on Black Friday and had a grand time together. She and my nieces took me to their favorite salon for mani-pedis, which involved lots of laughs and consultation over which color I should pick for mine. I let them choose, so one niece decided my toes and the other my fingers.

All the men did the proper ooo-ing and aaah-ing when we got back to the house and told us we looked glamorous.

Dawson is eight years older than my nephew, but they bonded over online video games while we were there and became better acquainted. We video chatted with Arica and Topher on Thanksgiving Day, the three-hour time difference meant it was already evening in Boston. They said it had been a big, loud feast at Rod and Jade's house. I wished she was with us, but at least she was in good company and felt loved where she was.

On our flights back to the frosty Midwest, I told Max we needed to immediately focus on preparing the house for Christmas. We had a multitude of people coming and several staying with us. He agreed, and we asked Dawson to come over one or two weekends to assist with decorations and getting beds set up for guests. He said he would, but he wanted better gifts than Arica. We laughed and promised him he'd get his due!

Max and I went back to work, and it was again a busy end-of-year time for me. I was working longer hours, so Max took it upon himself to move some things around in the bedrooms like we'd discussed. He and Dawson brought all the holiday stuff up from the basement, and by the first weekend back they'd accomplished quite a bit. We tackled cleaning and the outdoor lights and yard ornaments together.

On Sunday afternoon, I was resting for a few minutes when I suddenly remembered that I'd never heard back from Violet. I should face the issue at hand, so I texted Ginny to see if she was able to talk. She replied yes shortly after, and I called her.

Unlike her, I jumped right in. "Don't get upset, but I reached out to your mom to see if she wanted to join us for Christmas, maybe a day or two before the lunch with the larger group. She was going to talk to your aunt, but I never heard back. Do you want me to drop it, or do you want to see them while you're here? We can go to her if we need to, she said she didn't feel comfortable driving that far."

Ginny exhaled slowly. "Is this your way of punishing me and getting me back for being a terrible friend?"

I was too shocked to answer at first! "WHAT? NO! I thought I was helping you see the other side of your family so your mom could meet her grandson's fiancée!"

Her voice was hard and icy; I'd never heard her like this before. "I told you nicely that I didn't want to deal with her. Just because I'll be geographically closer for a few days doesn't mean I want to hear her passive-aggressive digs at me and snide comments about how I've chosen to live my life.

There's a reason she doesn't see her grandchildren, she is a CRANKY, MEAN OLD WOMAN WHO DOESN'T DESERVE THEIR TIME!

So no, I don't want you to arrange anything, I have NO DESIRE to be around her at all. I can't believe you went behind my back and called her! I have to go, I'm too mad to talk right now." And she hung up.

I held my phone in my hand and stared at it in disbelief. In all the time I'd been friends with Ginny, we'd never had as much as a small argument, let alone a fight where she was angry with me. For her to yell at me and think I was punishing her was beyond my comprehension at that moment. Max came in and saw me and asked what was wrong.

Looking up at him through the tears forming in my eyes, I said, "I guess you were right after all. Ginny's super pissed at me for reaching out to her mom. Seems like she kind of hates the woman."

He pursed his lips and thankfully chose not to say anything. He began taking some items out of the pantry for dinner. It may have been my imagination, but he was setting things on the counters a little more aggressively than usual.

After a few minutes, his phone dinged a couple of times, and he picked it up. He typed a response and then told me, "Alex said the storm will blow over soon, don't worry about it. He's sorry he led you into the lion's den, but he keeps hoping they can reconcile before it's too late. He thought maybe if you suggested it instead of him, it might go over better."

Nodding my acknowledgement, I got up to help him with the food. We fixed it wordlessly, and as we sat down to eat, I saw that Ginny was calling. I let it go; I wasn't ready to talk to her yet. She sent me a text when I didn't answer saying she was sorry she overreacted and yelled at me and wanted to discuss it calmly when I could. I put my phone on the island and continued eating with my husband. It was a quiet meal until he finally broke the silence about halfway through.

"Tab, I know you had charitable motives, but I told you I was worried this wouldn't go the way you thought. I really like being friends with Alex and Ginny, but this isn't about us. It's about our daughter and her relationship with her soon-to-be in-laws. It already feels like we're treading on thin ice given the messy history between you and them."

"I get that you didn't want me to do this, you made that clear. Maybe I should have kept my mouth shut, but I honestly was trying to help. Violet doesn't seem interested in seeing anyone anyway, so hopefully we can just forget about it. Ginny will realize I didn't do it with malicious intent – no harm, no foul kind of thing." I shrugged.

He gave me a doubtful look, and we finished our dinner. Making waves with Ginny wasn't my goal, but I couldn't quite bring myself to feel guilty. Her contentious feelings toward her mother were going to haunt her, and she may not have a ton of time left to rectify it.

When the dishes were done, I took my phone to the couch and sat down to call her back. She answered on the first ring. I started with, "I'm sorry I went against your wishes and called your mom. I should have respected how you felt."

She was back to her usual self when she said, "No, I'm the one who needs to apologize. I have a lot of baggage when it comes to her, and my first thought was that you were doing it to get revenge. I shouldn't have assumed, you're a much better person than that. I understand you wanted to make it easier on everyone since we'll all be close, I just dread being around her unless I have to."

She sighed. "She makes me feel so shitty about myself, and I don't know why. And I'm still crazy mad and hurt that when I called her and told her about Hudson's passing, she basically said it sucks, but that's how life goes. She was never sympathetic, or loving, or cried about how she'd lost her oldest grandchild. She abruptly changed the subject, and we never talked about it again."

I heard her voice catch with sadness, and I felt worse.

"Oh geez, I'm so sorry she was that heartless about it. I had no idea that's how she treated you. It's no wonder you don't want to be around her. I wish I hadn't tried to convince her to visit!"

"You didn't know the extent of our problems because I didn't tell you. I try not to think about it, and I definitely don't enjoy telling people I still can't get along with my own mother."

I took a beat to organize my thoughts on what I wanted to tell her.

"Ginny, I'm going to say this with love, so don't take it any other way. In the past, I wasn't just frustrated with you and Alex, in my mind you were two of the most wretched people on the planet. Before Arica and Topher, I would have gone out of my way to make your lives miserable if I knew how.

Then I did a lot of internal reflection, talked to Max, cried a ton of tears, and drank a decent amount of wine. Thanks to all that, I discovered I COULD get over it and accept you both as regular people and not my worst enemies.

After I spilled my guts to you at your house, I felt lighter. I mentioned the heavy stone in my chest. Well, I never realized how much the anger had been weighing me down.

You know how rough my relationship was with my dad. I wish I had sat down and told him how I'd felt all those years. Maybe I could have lightened that load as well, but I didn't make the effort I should have.

I don't want you to carry around that residual guilt if you don't have to. Your mom might not be a forgiving person, but it doesn't matter. You have to do what is right for YOU. If continuing to avoid it until she passes away is what you believe is necessary, then so be it, but I don't think you truly want those feelings to haunt you.

If you tell her how upset you were after Hudson's death and how much her comments hurt you, it will at least make YOU feel better about getting everything out in the open. Who knows, it could even improve your relationship. I mean, look how far you and I have come since my mom's funeral."

She was quiet long enough to make me wonder if she had hung up on me in the middle of my speech, but after a prolonged pause, she replied in a soft voice. "Well, shit. I wasn't expecting a lesson in humility using my own actions against me, but well done."

I had to laugh! "I do have a weird question for you. Do you think your mom could have dementia or something?"

"Oh! I don't know. Why do you ask?"

"It was just strange when I talked to her, and it reminded me a lot of when my dad started being confused. He had a hard time keeping up with conversations when his mental acuity problems were becoming more noticeable."

"Huh. I remember my cousin telling me a year or so ago that my mom got lost going somewhere she was more than familiar with. We joked about her ditziness and that was the last I heard of it. I guess I haven't paid much attention since then because our talks are as short as I can make them."

She heaved another sigh. "Maybe I should call her. If she can't drive to your house, I'll think about renting a car and going to see her."

"She said your Aunt Hazel might be able to bring her, she was going to ask her about it."

"What?" Ginny sounded startled, and I didn't understand why. "Are you sure she didn't say she'd talk to Lily?"

"Um, no. Your mom definitely said Hazel. I didn't know any of their names, and I thought it was interesting that one was a flower name and one was a different kind of plant. I would have noticed if they were BOTH flowers."

Her voice was strange when she replied, "Aunt Hazel has been in a nursing home for a few years now after she had a major stroke and couldn't take care of herself anymore. Shit."

"Oh, hell! I'm sorry to be the bearer of bad news. And don't even think about renting a car. I'll either drive you or loan you mine while you're here. Whatever you need to do."

She thanked me quietly and said she needed to process all of this. I told her I was here if she wanted to talk, and we said our goodbyes.

Max was fiddling with Christmas lights upstairs, and he raised his eyebrows at me questioningly as I approached.

"I just jumped from the frying pan right into the fire! I might have revealed to Ginny that her mom has cognitive issues." I sat down heavily on Arica's old bed, which was now in Dawson's room, and put my head in my hands.

"Well, that's certainly not what I was expecting you to say. How on earth did that come up?" I recounted the exchange, and he looked as surprised as I felt.

He huffed and said what we were both thinking, "Wow. Next month sure is going to be interesting!"

The days seemed to fly by after that, there was so much to do. We got all the bedrooms arranged, and Kate came over a couple of times to help me clean and bake some cookies. I caught her up on all the latest happenings, and she was invited to Christmas lunch with us. She said she wouldn't miss it for the world, she HAD to meet these people. It was like having her favorite soap opera play out live in front of her, which was the opportunity of a lifetime!

Amid our weeks of preparations and decorating, Ginny texted that she'd called her mom and suspected I was correct about the memory problems.

Ginny wanted to visit her on Saturday and hoped Alex and I would go with her. She said she could use both our strength and support to help her through it, especially if she was going to confront her mom with some of the painful emotions she'd been keeping to herself. She didn't want her kids to come along in case Violet had a poor reaction. I discussed it with Max and told her it was a plan.

Let the Christmas chaos commence!

The next morning, we had breakfast, made sure all the holiday lights were turned on and the house was extra festive, and we left for the airport. We wouldn't be able to fit the five of them plus their luggage and us in our SUV, so Max and I took both cars.

We parked in the cell phone lot until Arica texted us from baggage claim. We found them easily, gave quick hugs and got everything loaded. Unplanned, it ended up with us four women in my car and the men and most of the bags in the SUV.

Back at the house, we unloaded and showed our guests to their respective sleeping rooms with a very brief tour on the way. Once they were settled, everyone came downstairs. Max and I made sandwiches for lunch while we talked about their flight, what had been going on recently, etc.

We had a low-key afternoon and watched one of our favorite holiday movies together, then ordered pizza for dinner. That evening we got two euchre games going so Ari and Topher could learn how to play. It was fun and bizarre teaching them and concurrently trying to win!

Dawson and the young ones left around 8 p.m. to see his apartment and meet some of his friends. Max and Alex were chummily reviewing which whiskey he'd been able to acquire locally. Ginny was uneasy about the next day. She said a few of her cousins were going to stop by after she had some time with her mom, so at least she had that to look forward to.

I asked her if she wanted Alex and me to be part of the conversation or to preoccupy ourselves elsewhere, but she wasn't sure. I reminded her that it was difficult for me to open up to her about my past feelings, but our friendship needed it to survive. I assured her she'd feel better about being honest even if her mom didn't accept it well at first.

The next morning, the three of us prepared ourselves for whatever the day might hold. My husband was kind enough to back my car out and let it run for a few minutes so it would be warm for us when we left. Ginny had already sent me the address, so I plugged it into my GPS and waved goodbye to Max.

This was the first time I'd been alone with the two of them since we'd re-entered each other's lives; it was strange. I mentioned it to them, and they were surprised at the realization.

Alex asked if I'd been waiting to enact an evil plan to leave them stranded in the snow in the middle of nowhere. I replied that it completely depended on how nice he was to me. He chuckled and said that was fair. Ginny told him she wasn't coming back for him if he misbehaved. He scowled at us for ganging up on him, and I grinned at the banter I'd missed for so long.

Somehow, I almost felt young again being with two of my favorite college friends.

The last thirty minutes of the trip were several turns on side roads, so I concentrated on following the map's voice prompts. Ginny was uncharacteristically quiet, and I heard her take some calming breaths as we turned onto the final street.

She sniffled as I pulled into the driveway, and Alex asked what was worrying her the most. She said she hadn't been back here in so many years; it was sad to see how much of the house was in disrepair. But she cleaned up her face and reapplied her lipstick. After taking one more deep breath, she said, "Let's do this" as she exited the car.

Alex and I followed her up the front steps, and the large lady who opened the door smiled hugely and said, "Oh Gwinny, it's so damn good to see you, baby girl!" She had a slightly stronger Southern accent than her sister's, and I made a mental note to ask Ginny about that later.

Ginny's voice was muffled from a loving hug, but she happily exclaimed, "Hi Aunt Lily, I've missed you!"

We were introduced, Lily hugged us as well, and we entered the house. There was an odor of furniture that had been sitting unused for a long time. The living room carpet and furnishings were what could be considered "vintage," and I wondered how much of it was the same as when Ginny lived here. The contrast between this and Nick's house was light years apart, and I hoped Ginny wasn't too disappointed that I'd essentially forced her into this.

Mercifully, the kitchen was better. The cabinets, flooring, and appliances were all well-used and older, but the smell of coffee and pastries was more prevalent. The sunlight streaming through the sliding glass doors made the room seem more cheerful. Lily invited us to have a seat at the table.

She told Ginny, "Your mom is finishing getting ready, she's a bit slower in her actions these days. We have a service that comes in to do some cleaning and laundry for her once a week because it's tough for Vi to get around and to carry things. Is anybody thirsty or hungry? There are donuts if you want one, and I can put on another pot of coffee."

We all politely declined, and she said she'd go check on her sister's progress. Ginny walked into the living room, reviewing the pictures on the walls and on top of the TV cabinet. She picked one up and smiled as she brought it over to us.

She explained this was her and all her cousins when she was about fifteen. They were suntanned and grinning widely in front of a beach somewhere, with their arms slung around each other. A couple of bunny ears were showing behind heads wet from swimming. A few of them had the same curly hair that matched Ginny's, and she pulled out her phone to take a photo of the photo. She wiped the dust off and frowned, but she carefully put the picture back where it had been.

I whispered to Alex, "Have you ever been here?"

"Nope. The last time we all came back together, we met up with the family at someone else's house. I sort of recall meeting Lily, but it's been so long. I don't even think Ari was born yet when we were here. Did you meet her mom during college?"

"Oh no, she and Ginny weren't talking much then either. If I remember correctly, they had an argument over Ginny's car, and suddenly she didn't have one anymore and needed rides."

He nodded. "She told me about that when we first started…" he considered his words, "…getting to know each other." I smirked at his avoidance of the word 'dating' in my presence, and he blushed.

Ginny came back over as we heard her mom and aunt coming down the hall. As Violet entered the room, I picked up on several undeniable similarities, including the tiny spiral curls of her white hair. She was walking slowly and keeping her hand on her sister, the walls, or the countertops as she went. I wondered if she had balance problems or a physical issue. She smiled at all of us and went directly to her daughter to give her a long hug.

"It's good to lay eyes on you again, Guinevere. Thank you for coming to visit. Alvin, it's nice to see you again, too," as she nodded toward Alex across the table.

"It's Alex, Mom. Not Alvin." Ginny corrected her gently.

"Oh, sorry. Alex, that's right." Violet said, "And you must be the friend who called me," and she looked at me.

"Yes, ma'am, I'm Tabitha. I'm glad to meet you," I reached out my hand, and she put her frail one in mine. Her skin felt paper thin, and I was afraid to squeeze at all, so I just applied a slight amount of pressure and smiled at her. Lily helped her down into the kitchen chair without falling, and we all sat back down as well.

We made small talk for a while, with Violet speaking slowly and sometimes losing track of the conversation. She told us about her town and some of the recent changes, and she and Lily caught Ginny up on family news. We clarified how I fit into the picture and how Alex and I had known each other forever, and then there was a lull.

Lily again offered drinks, and I was thirsty this time. She poured us all a glass of lemonade, and she whispered something in Violet's ear. Ginny's mom nodded and had a somewhat sad look on her face. She looked at her daughter.

"Darling, I have a couple of things to show you while you're here. Can you come back to your old room with me for a few minutes?" She turned to us and said, "Please excuse us, it shouldn't take long."

"Sure, Mom." Ginny replied, and she got up to steady Violet as she stood and headed back toward the bedroom. Lily followed them as well, and the three of them shuffled out of the kitchen. Alex and I faced each other and didn't know what to do or say…

I started, "I'm convinced now that Violet has dementia. I can tell a lot of this is hurting Ginny to see it, I hope she doesn't hate me for this."

He shook his head at me, "Stop it. She knew this was long overdue, and I think you might have to murder one of our children for my wife to actually dislike you. This is a strong wake-up call for sure, but it needed to happen."

"She really needs to take this opportunity and have a heart-to-heart with Violet. There might not be much time left before something like that will be useless. I never had the nerve to do it with my dad, and I wish I had. It was horrible when he started to forget people's names, beginning with my cousins. That's when I knew there was no prospect of us having the kind of reconciliation that would have benefited me."

Lily came back out after several minutes and rejoined us at the table. She apologized for leaving us alone while they talked, but Violet wanted to take advantage of Gwinny being here. We told her we understood, and I asked Lily what Ginny had been like as a teenager. She laughed and shared some stories that sounded exactly like what I would have envisioned.

"With Gwinny growing up far away, she was pretty different from her cousins, but after a long while they all got closer and became a normal group of relation. A few of them were plain feral, Gwinny included. She had quite a fiery temper, but her fuse burned fast and then turned into tearful apologies. She'd be sad for a bit and then back to normal in no time. We sure had our hands full!" She paused and smiled at the memories. Alex and I had been chuckling and nodding along as she talked.

"I will say that Vi wasn't the most loving mom. Our own mother treated us more like workers than daughters, so that's what Vi knew and did herself. Not that our upbringing is any excuse, just an explanation. Hazel and I tried to change things with our own kids. We also did our best to make Gwinny feel loved when she lived here, but I guess we didn't do enough. Maybe if we'd tried harder, she would have come to visit us more over the years."

She looked remorseful about their family dynamics.

Alex reassured her that it wasn't personal or deliberate. So much had been happening with them in their struggles with Hudson's health, coming back here had barely entered their minds for a long time. He gave her an overview of their time raising kids, and Lily teared up about poor baby Hudson enduring all those procedures. She said she'd only heard tiny bits of that, so Alex continued with more of their Boston life.

He strategically left Nick and the sisters out of the narrative. The Becketts deserved a ton of credit for how much they helped, but it was smart not to dwell on it given the little I knew about the tension between Violet and Nick.

We were interrupted by a loud knock on the door, and Lily smiled and went to answer it. A couple entered and were chatting with her as they walked back toward us. We all introduced ourselves, and Lily and her daughter began talking about things that didn't concern Alex and me.

He seemed fidgety, and I asked him what was wrong. He was perturbed that his wife didn't tell them much over the years. It wasn't fair for Ginny to be mad if Violet hadn't even known what they went through. He said that for a woman who talks non-stop almost every day of her life, she sure clammed up with the maternal side of her family. I couldn't disagree.

Two more visitors showed up not long after, one of Hazel's daughters with her husband and Lily's son with his teenage son. All three of Ginny's cousins had naturally curly hair, just not as tight as her curls.

Listening to them all talk, I could sense some of Ginny's characteristics and facial expressions. I mentioned my observations to Alex, and he nodded emphatically in agreement.

"It's like someone badly cloned my wife!" I laughed out loud.

That made them notice us again, and the group of them swarmed us to ask questions about Alex and Ginny's kids, how I fit into everything, where I lived, etc. Hazel's son had shown up recently with his wife, so there were more introductions.

The small house was quite full at this point, and I was starting to feel a little overwhelmed. I excused myself to the bathroom after asking Lily where it was. Walking out of the loud common areas and around a corner, I heard Ginny crying from one of the bedrooms. Her mom's voice was too soft to tell what was being said before I shut the bathroom door.

When I stepped out, Ginny was talking. Her voice seemed reasonably even-keeled, so I hoped they were having the discussion they needed as I returned to the mêlée.

Violet and Ginny eventually emerged from the back of the house and came out to greet everyone who had arrived. There were many hugs and teasing and laughing as they all reunited.

When it receded into normal conversation, I glanced at my phone to see it was almost 1:30 p.m. My stomach grumbled at me, and I told Alex maybe we should volunteer to go pick up some lunch. He was very on board.

We walked into the living room, and I asked the group if that was okay with them. They all loved the idea and suggested a fast-food place nearby. We said we'd get burgers and fries for everybody to share. Lily said there should be enough drinks to go around, so Alex and I left.

In the car as I was carefully backing out and through all the other vehicles, he said, "Thanks for devising a brilliant escape plan." I laughed.

"My pleasure, I was feeling a mite claustrophobic in there." He nodded.

"Please drive as slowly as possible so I can enjoy the quiet and fresh air. I'm beyond grateful you came with us so I don't have to be alone in this." I smiled and said I felt the same.

We cruised through the small downtown area for a minute, then Alex said, "Oh hey, there's her high school! Pull up in front of it, please." I parked in a spot so he was facing it. He put the window down and took a photo of the building.

"She's told me some stories about high school life. I don't know why I'm this fascinated by seeing it in person.

I'm so used to her Boston life and family that it's almost disorienting to be here with her mom's side.

The same could be said about my life back here, I suppose. Part of what drew us together was our feelings of failure due to our parents' disappointment and how we tried not to address it too much. Over time, the memories start to fade, and you just don't think about them anymore. Maybe that's not healthy, but it's what I did regardless."

I replied, "I can understand that. Now that I know what I do, I'm glad the two of you found each other. You both overcame your childhood unhappiness and broke the generational cycles. Now you're a rock-solid couple, you each make the other better and stronger and built a beautiful family. Instead of thinking about what I lost in my friendships with the two of you, I'm trying to change my perspective to be proud of being a factor in connecting you."

"Thanks, Tabby. You mean the world to both of us, and thank you for doing this for Ginny. Today hasn't been fun for you and me, but it's going to make a humongous difference for her.

I can't even tell you how much closure and peace you've brought her by forgiving us, and this will hopefully bring her closer to reconciling with her mom. She's been broken since we lost Hudson, and every time something positive like this happens, it heals a part of her."

"That is far and away one of the nicest things you or anyone else has ever said to me," I told him with tears falling down my cheeks. "I've spent a lot of time in cars with you over the years, but this might now be my favorite!" He laughed loudly, and I joined him.

I adamantly believed the three of us were destined to be linked in some way for the rest of our lives. That thought now brought me comfort instead of terror or anger.

Before getting lunch, I filled up on gas. *(Yes, we were procrastinating!)* We went through the drive-thru lane and ordered more food than they were probably used to. We navigated back to the house and delivered the goods to everyone's appreciation. There was hardly a break in the discourse while they ate, and I realized that maybe Ginny got her talkativeness from both sides of her genealogy. Lord help us all!

Violet sat in her ancient recliner chair and smiled at everyone enjoying each other's company in her house, but she didn't contribute much to the dialogue. She chimed in every now and then, but more than anything she watched who was talking and tried to keep up. I was sad for her, I knew all too well how debilitating and awful dementia and Alzheimer's were.

Alex and I patiently listened to them catching up, had our own chats, spent time on our phones, and waited for Ginny to be done. The cousins eventually started winding down and saying they needed to get going, and they filtered out over the course of an hour or so.

Ginny talked to her Aunt Lily for a short while longer, then she said we should head out so I didn't have to drive in the dark. She sat next to her mom and said she loved her and she was glad she came. Violet smiled and said she loved her too and missed her, which seemed to be an improvement.

Alex and I finished cleaning up the remnants of lunch and thanked the sisters for their hospitality. Everyone hugged before we walked out the door. The three of us didn't speak as we got in, set the navigation for home, and waved as we backed down the driveway.

Ginny wanted to drive through town for a minute, so I retraced our route from earlier and took her past the area where she spent her junior and high school years. She mentioned a few things that had changed, laughed at a couple of spots with fond memories, and pointed out her high school. When we reached the end of the main drag, she said she was finished and we could leave now. I reset my GPS and aimed us toward home.

Alex looked back at her and asked how she felt. She quietly said it was worth the trip. She was exhausted and wanted to take a small snooze if that was okay. She hadn't slept well the night before, and Alex said he'd wake her up when we were close to my house.

He asked me if he could connect to my Spotify or something, so I guided him to which app had the music on my phone. He smirked as he went through my selection and said I was still stuck in the '90s. I told him if he didn't like the options, he was welcome to walk home, and he laughingly played something.

Ginny woke up about halfway back and claimed she was more clear-headed. We asked if she wanted to talk about any of it, and she said maybe tomorrow.

It was a relief to pull into my own driveway, and the three of us went inside to freshen up before leaving again for dinner. I put on different clothes because I would otherwise smell like Violet's house all night. Both Alex and Ginny also changed, and I wondered if it was for the same reason.

We had a laid-back meal with our offspring and even talked about wedding plans, which cheered Ginny up immensely. She was quieter than usual, but she didn't appear to be too overcome with emotion.

With it being Saturday night, the kids wanted to go out again. Arica said a few of her high school friends were around and she'd like them to meet Topher. When it was just the four of us on the couch, Max asked how the trip went, and Alex and I turned to Ginny expectantly. She sighed and said she'd give us the highlights.

"My mom took me back to my old bedroom to show me where all her important papers are. She said she's been having some trouble remembering things lately, and she wanted me to know in case I need them.

She reminded me that as her only child, I am the primary beneficiary in her will and the Power of Attorney if anything happens to her. My Aunt Lily is next in line, but Mom hopes I'll handle it if I can since Aunt Lily also takes care of my Aunt Hazel. My Uncle Oliver was the one who died years ago from the heart attack, so he's obviously out of the picture.

After we got through the legal stuff, I said I wanted to tell her some things. I went into the major ones about her criticisms of my life choices and not being sad about

Hudson. She admitted that she used to be pretty mad because she felt like I wasted my potential to go to college and make something of my life. She didn't want me to follow in her footsteps.

She was sure that Alex and I would divorce and I'd end up like her but with a rich daddy to take care of me. She wanted more for me on all of it, and her frustration came out in her comments. She sees that I'm happy now and everything worked out well for me.

She confessed that she should have been easier on me, which may be as close to an apology as I'm ever going to get. She also said that when I told her about Hudson, she didn't realize his health was still a risk and it didn't sink in until after we hung up. She couldn't think of what to say to me in the moment, and she regrets not calling back to tell me how devastated she was.

Aunt Lily backed that up when we talked later, and she said Alex explained more of the details to her about our early days and how rough we had it.

She laid her hand on her husband's leg. "Thanks for that, hon, I guess I never shared much with them back then. My mom and I have had such a rollercoaster of a relationship, we've both been at fault for not treating each other very well. As a mother and a more mature woman now, I can appreciate how some of my actions were more hurtful than I realized at the time."

Alex put his arm around her, and she laid her head on his shoulder as the tears began to fall. "I can see that she's failing physically and mentally, and she's let the house get to a terrible state. I don't know how much longer she'll be able to stay there by herself. I had no idea everything was falling apart; I feel like the worst daughter in the world."

She started crying harder now, and Max's face showed that he had a lot of questions forming.

Alex comforted her by saying their relationship was a two-way street, and she nodded. "I agree, but I could have done better. I should have swallowed my pride years ago and checked in on her. Until we came back here for Tabby's mom's funeral, I hadn't even considered making the trip in at least a decade. That's not right!

She was a homebody and didn't like to travel much, I'm still surprised she came out for our wedding. I could have made more of an effort once the kids were old enough to take care of themselves. I have a feeling I may be back here several more times in the near future. I also want her to spend time with her grandkids before it's too late."

After a few moments, I changed the subject to lighten the mood, "It seems like you had a good time catching up with your cousins! It was fun to see your family resemblances from your mom's side, and they are a hoot!"

She brightened back to normal Ginny status and talked about that for a bit. She said it was fabulous to see them again, and the photo she showed us was one of her happiest memories from growing up there.

Alex got up to use the bathroom, and on his return, he pointed at my husband and simply said, "Shots needed, STAT." Max smiled and got up to accommodate the request.

I asked if Ginny wanted some wine, and she replied, "More than ever." Max said he'd bring it to us, and she and I began talking about the wedding things Arica had mentioned at dinner. I let her go on for a while, she'd had an arduous day and deserved to focus on a lighthearted topic.

The four of us stayed up late drinking, playing two rounds of cutthroat euchre, and singing along to yet another '90s playlist that Alex ridiculed. Max pointed out he still recited every word despite his complaints, and I laughed heartily that Alex was outnumbered. The kids were surprised to see us still awake when they got home, and we all had a couple of drinks together before going to bed.

~ *Chapter 15* ~

Future Days

Sunday was a lazy morning for everyone. Dawson brought lunch over, and he teased us about what a slow-moving group we were. After we ate, he started organizing the tasks and who would work on which ones. His leadership was admirable, and I let him take over.

By the time Leo arrived in the afternoon, we had the tables in place and folding chairs ready, tray tables in the living room, and Ginny and I were constructing the cooking plan for the following day.

Leo introduced himself to the Yates family. He joked about how different the place looked from the previous year when we had piles of packed items all over the house and bragged to Dawson about having the big downstairs bed. He was once again in charge of our traditional Christmas Eve lasagna, so he began prepping.

I asked Kate if she wanted to join us for dinner, but she was at her mom's and wouldn't be back until late.

At one point I asked Ginny about her mom's and Aunt Lily's Southern accent, and she laughed.

"It used to be stronger, but it's faded for both of them over the years. My grandpa grew up somewhere near Savannah, Georgia and moved to the Midwest for work on a big farm. He met grandma there, and they bought their own farm nearby after they got married.

I remember grandpa's thick accent from a few holidays when I was a kid, and then when I first moved back. He sounded even more Southern when he was drinking!"

I also inquired how Violet ended up in Boston when she was so attached to her family and didn't like to travel much.

Ginny explained that, "A friend of hers was starting a job in Boston after college, and Mom helped her move. The friend was going to pay for her to take a bus back home, but Mom loved the city life and having the ocean nearby.

She stayed longer than she'd originally planned, and then she got a job and met my dad. They fell in love right away, and they learned about me fairly early in their relationship." *(So my suspicions about the timing had been justified.)*

"They decided to get hitched despite Dad's plan to never marry again after Jade and Lisey's mom died so unexpectedly. Mom and Dad's 'honeymoon phase' lasted for a few years, but then Mom found out my grandpa's health was failing and grandma was struggling to keep up with the farm.

She wanted to move back and help, and she thought Dad would come with her due to his love for her and me. In reality, he had no interest in leaving Boston. He'd worked so hard to build his law firm from the ground up and didn't want to start over. He had no problem flying her back and forth several times, but the travel got old quickly. That led to them arguing more often and threatening each other with divorce."

We walked back into the living room, where Alex was on a call with his parents. He then handed Max the phone to give them detailed directions to our house. When they hung up, Alex was irritated they couldn't use navigation, but we assured him it was an easy drive, and they were just unfamiliar with the technology. We knew from our own parents that it wasn't worth getting upset about. Alex and Ginny were used to Nick, who was more tech-savvy than most people his age.

We had a delicious Christmas Eve dinner and crowded into the living room to watch another holiday movie together. A feeling of incredible gratitude swept over me for the people sitting here with us. I was looking forward to seeing a lot of Max's family the next day, but right now was cozy and quiet.

Christmas Day was cold but sunny, which was a pleasant change from the normal gray dreariness of Midwest winter. Everybody wished each other Merry Christmas, we got the coffee going, and we all got to work. Dawson and Kate showed up later in the morning, she was ecstatic to meet the Yateses. She gave Arica and Topher a quick congratulations, then made a beeline toward Ginny. The two of them chatted up a storm as they were putting chairs in place and setting the table for the entire crowd.

Max's dad, brothers, sisters-in-law, nephews, and nieces descended upon our house around 11:15 a.m., and the decibel level immediately rose!

Alex's parents arrived last at 11:30, and the party was complete. Max and I were at the door when they entered and welcomed them to our home. They were very polite and potentially intimidated by the noise, but they walked right in.

Ginny and the kids came over to hug and love on them. Topher was proud to introduce Arica as his fiancée, and they were happy to finally meet her. They commented on the girls' names, and Ginny said she'd explain later.

More presents were piled up around the tree; it was going to take us a while to open everything!

People introduced themselves and wished each other Merry Christmas.

Snacks and drinks were consumed.

Family members admired Arica's engagement ring and congratulated both of them.

The Ganters met the Yateses.

There were more people than we'd ever had in our house at one time, and I was thrown off by the fact that I had to squirm between loved ones just to move from one room to another. What had we gotten ourselves into?

But when everyone started settling down and finding places to sit, it was much more manageable. Max, Leo, Kate, and I began pulling food out of the oven and fridge, putting things into serving dishes, and setting it all on the island and a side counter.

When it was done, Max whistled to get everyone's attention.

"I'd like to thank you for being here, this is a very special holiday for us. Both of our children are building successful careers and made us empty nesters this year. Our lovely daughter is now engaged to our future son-in-law, Topher, and we're honored that his parents and sister came all the way from Boston to celebrate with us today. We're also glad Isaac and Elaine Yates have joined our crazy Christmas gathering, plus Tabby's brother Leo, her best friend Kate, and of course the Ganter group. Tabby and I love you all, please enjoy this delicious meal she's prepared!"

Everyone cheered and grabbed a plate to fill. There were several minutes of semi-organized chaos as people chose their meals and went to sit down. The younger folks instinctively gravitated to the couch and tray tables, while most of us claimed an empty seat at the dining table and began digging in.

I made sure our guests had drinks or brought them one, then I put a few things on my own plate. The hardest part was achieved. Kate put her arm around me and commented that I'd outdone myself. I smiled and thanked her as tears threatened to leak out.

When everybody seemed to be finished eating, one of Max's sisters-in-law told us not to worry, they were taking care of cleanup. My nieces and nephews groaned and said that meant them. We giggled as they started hauling plates, silverware, and glasses to the kitchen. With several of them cleaning in tandem, they made quick work of it, and we were able to visit more.

The next few hours were filled with conversations between so many different combinations of people; I lost track of who had gotten to know who. I observed Dawson, Louis, and Isaac sitting and talking for a good deal of time. Leo and Max's brothers were in deliberations about football stats, and there was some yelling at the TV during the NFL games.

Kate was floating around the perimeter and observing the scene, and I went over to her.

"Is it everything you dreamed and more?" I asked teasingly.

"Oh man, it's great. My favorite part is imagining you standing outside in the cold telling Alex and Ginny to go fuck themselves, and then all this happened." She waved her hand at the Yates family members. "You were like their angry little sherpa, leading them up the mountain of love!"

I laughed and elbowed her. "You're preposterous! But I'm glad you're here so you can understand better when I tell you things and ask for your expert advice."

Micah was calling. I answered and video chatted with all of them, sharing the phone around. Ginny followed my lead after we hung up and connected with her sisters to send everyone in Boston our holiday best. We all waved hello, and we could see they were gathered in Nick's kitchen. I wondered what it would be like to have the Ganter family, my brothers, and the Beckett crew all in the same space. It was too much to visualize!

One of my nieces came over and shyly asked when we would be opening the gifts, and I smiled and promised her soon. It was cute that even as a teenager, she was still excited to see what she'd gotten!

After a few more minutes, I clapped my hands and announced that we would be opening presents shortly. I requested two volunteers to pass out gifts. My niece who asked me about it immediately raised her hand, and Ari put hers up as well. I told everyone to find a spot to gather their presents so our helpful elves could deliver them. Nobody was to open anything until everything had been distributed.

I stayed near the tree in case either of them had questions about who someone was, but they did a perfect job handing them out correctly. Once the space was cleared, I said "Go," and instantly heard the sound of ripping paper, then a lot of happiness and surprise. I waited a minute to watch people and enjoy the moment.

Quite a bit of time was spent thanking others for presents, cleaning up the wrapping paper and empty boxes, and people putting their things in the bedroom for later. A couple of the kids received board games, so they were trying those out and arguing about the rules as they went.

Ginny and her mother-in-law were absorbed in discussion, and Alex had taken his dad into the kitchen with Max to show him some of the whiskey choices. Louis joined them, and the four of them did an impromptu tasting. Then Leo and Max's brothers wanted in on the action, and that started a whole new conversation about tastes, smoothness, bang for the buck, and on and on.

Dinner time snuck up on us, and a couple of my nephews asked if they could partake in the leftovers. I told them to help themselves, and whoever else was hungry was welcome to eat any time. It was already dark, and Max's brothers started talking about heading home. They didn't realize how much time had gone by either, so it wasn't just me!

The Ganter families began packing up their belongings, and many hugs and farewells ensued. The house seemed almost empty after they left, although there were still a dozen of us remaining!

Kate helped me clean up and put away some of the folding chairs and tray tables, then she said she was ready to be home as well. She was grateful for me including her in a great Christmas and said goodbye to everyone.

Topher and Arica were talking to his grandparents on the couch, and Ginny came over to tell me that seeing them spending time together was priceless. She squeezed me and thanked me for allowing them this opportunity. I hugged her back and told her I was glad to do it, and I loved her and her family. She gasped and sniffed with tears. It was the first time I said it back to her, and she was euphoric.

Dawson came over and asked if we minded if he went home, and I said he was free to go. He had been substantially helpful with everything leading up to and including today, and I thanked him for all his work.

I walked over and asked Alex if he thought his parents would be okay with a late drive in the dark. He said they'd been talking it over, and he was nervous about them.

I suggested they spend the night – Leo could move to the couch, and they could sleep in the downstairs guest bed. He nodded and said he'd ask if they prefer that once they were done talking to the kids.

Unfortunately, both of them had some medications they needed to take before bed, so they didn't feel comfortable staying and skipping that responsibility. I offered for Alex and Ginny to borrow my car – one of them could drive his parents' vehicle with the other following and come back either tonight or tomorrow morning. Everyone seemed to like the idea, so I handed Alex my keys.

There was a little more visiting between grandparents and Ari and Topher while Alex and Ginny packed some things for overnight. Then the four of them got ready to leave.

Mr. and Mrs. Yates expressed their appreciation for us hosting Christmas in our home and letting them join the festivities. We told them they're family now and always welcome any time.

After they left, Max and I looked at each other tiredly, we were spent. Leo stated he would be passed out pretty soon, too. Arica, Topher, and Ari said they were going to watch a movie before bed.

It had been another amazing Christmas; I was so glad we'd done this!

The next morning, I awoke to a text from Ginny saying that Alex's parents wanted to take them out to breakfast as a thank you for helping drive them home. I assured her there was no hurry at all, they could come back whenever they were ready. She thanked me and said she'd let me know when they were leaving. I sent her a string of emojis with pancakes, coffee, a car, street sign, and stoplight to amuse her.

Dawson texted to ask what the plans for today were. I responded that there wasn't much going on, but we should at least have dinner together since Arica and the others were flying out the next day. He said to give him a shout when we wanted him to come over.

Max had already gotten the coffee brewing, so I didn't have to wait long for a warm drink when I came downstairs. Leo was packed up and had started his car. He told us he said goodbye to the kids the night before because he (accurately) figured they might not be up this early. He took some leftovers and a travel mug of coffee and headed out.

Max and I sat on the couch and enjoyed our beverages as we talked about some of the conversations we'd had. Between showers and breakfast, the girls and Topher wandered downstairs and floated in and out of the living room.

Topher sat with us and talked about his law degree pursuit and how he hopes to graduate in two years and pass the bar exam. He was passionate about using his skills to benefit people someday. He said he's gained a lot from his grandpa and Aunt Lisey, but he was contemplating going into a different legal realm. I didn't know what kind of lawyers either of them were, but I wasn't intrigued enough to get into those details right then.

When Arica joined us, I took advantage of Ginny's absence to ask what wedding plans they've made so far. We touched on it, although they weren't in a hurry to nail everything down just yet. That was surely driving Ginny nuts, but of course I didn't bring it up.

Topher went upstairs, and we talked to our daughter about how she was doing overall and if she was happy in Boston. She had the biggest grin when she told us she felt like she was right where she belonged, and we knew our efforts had been worth it.

Ari came back down and the two girls were joking about bridesmaids' dresses and colors. Apparently, there was an ongoing debate. Arica was obsessed with a certain style (no surprise), but it was more revealing than her bridesmaids were comfortable with. Ari showed me a picture, and I had to admit there was a lot of bare skin. The bride-to-be sighed and said she was considering a matching shawl or a slightly different look due to a nearly unanimous consensus.

I inquired about her dress, and she perked up. She said she was narrowing down which stores she thought would be the best, and she planned to schedule a weekend to visit a few of them. She absolutely wanted me to be part of the shopping trip if I was willing to come out, and I told her I'd make it happen!

Poor Max was sitting in between the three of us and probably tired of hearing dress talk. He eventually excused himself to refill his coffee, although he cleaned up the kitchen counters instead and then meandered upstairs.

We all got a message at about the same time from Ginny telling us they were about halfway back, so an hour away or so. I asked the girls if they wanted to do a little after-Christmas shopping when Alex and Ginny returned, and they were excited. Ari said she'd text Ginny, and I went up to take a shower after Max finished. I was a bit tired but was looking forward to girl time.

We ate a few leftovers for lunch before we left, and it was a fun afternoon at the mall. The two Arica's wandered off into some of the stores geared toward their generation.

Ginny said Alex enjoyed being with his parents for the first time in forever. He and his dad were laughing together about a few things, which she'd never seen! She also told me Isaac and Dawson had a fantastic conversation about construction management. That explained their prolonged talking, and I was glad they had built a connection *(no pun intended)*.

She said Isaac and Elaine were impressed with our house, family closeness, and our kids, and somehow it helped loosen them up with Alex and Ginny. She didn't know what our magical secret was, but we seemed to have a way with parents! I laughed pretty hard at that sentiment, and we talked about the other partygoers.

She also gushed about how awesome and hilarious Kate is and approved my choice of replacing her. I smiled but felt awkward, so I changed the subject and told her my thoughts during the party of how crazy it will be with all the Ganters and the Becketts together at the wedding. She agreed it will be utter pandemonium!

We'd just been walking and talking aimlessly for a while, and I suggested we grab something to drink at one of the food court places. I was extremely thirsty! We sat and chatted some more, and the girls met up with us there and enjoyed ice cream treats. None of us had any more shopping goals, so we took our time.

While walking to the car, I texted Dawson to see if he could come over in an hour or so. He replied that he was already at the house taste-testing whiskeys with the dads and Topher. I showed the message to Ginny, and she rolled her eyes and said we'd better go back and get things under control before they were all too wasted to go to dinner.

The eight of us went to our favorite Mexican restaurant and had a blast. Sadly, I was quite tired by the time we returned home, so I hugged everybody and went to bed. Max wasn't too far behind me, and I heard the kids laughing downstairs as I fell asleep. It was the best sound.

The Yates family and Arica were up early to pack for their 11:15 a.m. flight. Max and I loaded both cars and drove them to the airport. It was sad to bid them adieu, but we'd had a wonderful holiday together.

Ginny hugged me tightly and said she was glad I forced her to see her mother, it changed her perspective and she planned to come back more often. I told her she was welcome to stay with us any time she was here, and we'd be more than happy to be her chauffeur.

Alex greatly appreciated having his parents around for Christmas and that he got to spend a little more time with them than they expected. Topher and Ari thanked us for a fun holiday.

Arica cried and said she missed seeing us all the time, and I was tearful as well. We finally sent them on their way, and Max and I got back in our cars.

It was strange to once again walk into our quiet and empty house, but I was also relieved to simply relax. We curled up on the couch and watched a movie; I napped, and we cleaned up some. There was plenty of time to put everything back to normal, I wasn't concerned about it one bit.

It was best that they left when they did, because a winter storm hit us the next day. With a decent amount of snow and dangerously low temperatures, many flights were delayed or canceled. Max and I both worked from home the rest of the week. I checked in on Dawson, and he said his company was very conscientious about them not being outside for any length of time.

Max and I took it easy that weekend, putting some of the party items away and packing up about half of the Christmas decorations. New Year's Eve was Sunday night, and we spent it alone on the couch snuggling under a blanket. As usual, I reflected on the year we were finishing and was astounded at how much had happened.

This time last year, we had just moved Dawson into his apartment. We were stressed about moving Arica out to Boston and finding her a place to live. I was still trying to get over my mom's death and figure out how to deal with Alex and Ginny.

It's hard to believe how far I've come on accepting them back into my life. I guess Max was right about us working through my mess of emotions on our own. I'm extra glad that Max and Alex have each other, they are both lacking in the friend department.

If Topher and Arica have kids someday, my grandchildren will also be part Alex and Ginny. The three of us will literally have blood relatives linking us. How absurd is that? Ginny and Tabby from the TAG Team days would have been over the moon about our children getting married, although we probably would have assumed it would be me and Alex together. Life is such a wild ride!

Man, that stone in my chest made of grief and anger was really something, I'm SO glad it's gone. The time we spent with them in Boston moving Arica in was incredibly healing, I don't know if I understood it then.

Now that I think about it, it's kind of a miracle that Ginny was so patient with me. I'll have to tell her she's done a terrific job of waiting for me to trust her again on my own time!

I'm shocked that she thinks Max and I are the "parent whisperers" considering neither of us have truly come to terms with how we were treated when we were growing up.

Is that why I try to help others with theirs? I've talked Kate out of shutting her mom out of her life a couple of times, I thought it was specific to her situation.

I just don't want people I love to hurt if there's something I think I can do to fix it. I'm glad I had some time alone with Alex. Even without the physical element, there's still a camaraderie I've never had with another man besides Max.

It was rough to adjust to the kids being out on their own, but I think Max and I did all right. I discovered some hobbies, saw my friends more, felt more like ME than I have in a long time. All good things.

And I got to spend a day on the fanciest boat I could have imagined, that was badass! I can't fathom having the money Nick does, I wonder what that's like…

I caught myself dozing off, and I jerked back awake and sat up. Max asked if I was okay, and I said yes, but apparently too old to hang until the ball drops! We did remain conscious to welcome 2024, but we were in bed within minutes. Another year in the books, and by the end of this new one our daughter might be married!

And now we've reached the part I didn't want to write, so forgive me if I gloss over a lot of the details.

In summary, I started feeling miserable after the first of the year and was losing a considerable amount of weight. Getting rid of some was healthy, but too much became worrisome. After not being able to remedy it myself, I went to my doctor thinking I might need hormones, or supplements, or something mundane like that.

Ater many appointments, blood tests, scans, and discussions, the doctors determined and confirmed that I have late-stage pancreatic cancer. It had already spread to several parts of my body by the time we found it, and there wasn't much they could do. By the end of April, we had eliminated all possibilities of finding something that would help.

My remaining lifespan was now reduced to a relatively small number of weeks. Time was like water – running through my fingers and impossible to hold onto.

I moved to the Murphy bed on the ground level so I wouldn't have to wear myself out going up and down the stairs. I was grateful when I thought about all the love and hard work that went into creating this room for my mom. It was comforting to recall Dawson and Max building it with their own hands and Arica providing her decorative touches on the place where I would also spend my final days.

As soon as we learned the diagnosis, Max and I began putting our affairs in order, so to speak. We updated our wills and medical wishes and validated that Max's name was on everything. I made sure my life insurance was current, and we did the onerous task of planning our funerals.

As a way of coping, I began writing down some things I wanted my children to know about me. Adding to what I'd already transcribed about my past with Alex and Ginny, it turned into this memoir. Who knew I had so much to say?

Telling family and friends was more devastating than I could have conceived. I am NOT going to describe the abundance of despair and weeping it involved. It broke my heart piece by piece to hurt the people I love most. I picked a Saturday to start breaking the news so it would all be done and over within two days.

Dawson moved back into his old room the day after we told him to help Max and be near me as much as possible. Telling Arica over video was the hardest. She collapsed on her futon wailing and said she was resigning from her job to come home. I threatened to haunt her forever if she put her life on hold for me, and I demanded that she not jeopardize her career.

We then discussed reasonably when she should come and what she might want to tell her boss. I relaxed knowing she wasn't going to do anything rash. It would be strenuous for Arica and Topher to keep this to themselves very long, but I asked them to wait until the next day. I wanted to inform more family members before calling Ginny and Alex.

Max and I talked to my brothers and his dad and brothers that afternoon. It was horrible and exhausting, and I had to rest afterward.

Part of me wondered if it would have been easier for everyone if I'd just gone quickly instead of knowing it was coming, but deep down I realized how lucky I was to be able to say goodbye and tell people what they meant to me one last time.

The next morning, I told Stacey, Kate, and a few of my other local friends. Those exchanges took a large emotional toll.

After lunch, I summoned all the bravery I had for the call to Boston and pushed send. I asked Ginny to include Alex on the video chat as well, so I could talk to them together. She did, and I gave them the information.

Before I even finished speaking, she was shaking her head "No," and had an angry look on her face. She dropped the phone on the table and walked away, but Alex picked it back up. Tears were running down his face, which was a total shock to me. He was choked up and could barely speak, and he said maybe it was better if they called me back later. I nodded, and Max took the phone to talk to him for a few minutes. That one definitely did not go the way I expected.

When my health started making it difficult for me to get through an entire day at work, I told my boss in a very emotional meeting, and he hugged me and cried some, too. He advised me to work with our Human Resources Director to arrange everything to my advantage regarding disability benefits and what not.

My co-workers were unbelievably kind and compassionate and helped me box up my personal belongings on my last day. It was hard to leave a place where I'd spent such a large amount of time over many years.

To make a long story shorter, the next month involved a lot of people wanting to come and show me how much they cared about me. It wore me out to have visitors, but Max and Dawson did a great job of communicating with people and managing my time so I had opportunities to rest in between visits.

Stacey flew in to hang out with me for a weekend, and I regretted that we hadn't gotten together more over the years. She still couldn't believe that Alex Yates was back in my life and had caused so much trouble when we were younger. We video chatted with him and laughingly reminisced about some of our drama club stories from high school. I had always loved being with Stacey and was melancholy when she left.

My father-in-law stayed for several days to assist around the house, which was generous of him. He promised to be back in a few weeks as well.

The early summer weather was beautiful, so I asked Max and D to help me sit outside on the patio as much as I could handle. Many of my last conversations were out there in the sunshine, and I'm convinced the soothing powers of nature helped prolong my life by at least a short amount.

Max told me one night that the following day was going to be busy and overwhelming for me, so I should get some extra rest. I was intrigued when I woke up the next morning, but he wanted it to be a surprise. After lunch, he and Dawson voluntarily took me outdoors to enjoy the warmth of early June.

To my absolute astonishment, a contingency of Beckett and Fletcher family members streamed through our house to come see me on the patio. I laughed and embraced each one, it was wonderful!

When Ginny told him about my condition, Nick called in a favor and borrowed a friend's private jet. He offered for anyone to come with him if they wanted to, and almost everybody accepted! I required a break after a couple of hours, so Max helped me back to bed. It was perfect, and I thanked him for arranging this. I saw him smile as I instantly fell asleep.

When I was able to go back outside, I had a lovely time catching up with everyone. I took another short respite in the late afternoon. Lisey and Jade nicely arranged for a catering company to bring us all dinner. Although I couldn't eat much, it was delicious food. They also made sure Max and Dawson had plenty of leftovers so they wouldn't have to worry about meals for a few days.

I noticed that Nick, Naomi, Alex, and Ginny were missing, and Jocelyn told me they were on a quick trip to see Ginny's mom. I hoped it was going well.

After eating, I could tell people were getting uncomfortable as they struggled to decide how to say good night and the harder goodbye before heading to a nearby hotel for the night. Liam broke the tension and came over to give me a big hug, and the rest of them followed suit.

I requested Ari and Kayleigh to be there for Arica when she needed a shoulder to cry on, and they agreed through their tears.

Lisey and Jade were last, and they were both crying hysterically by the time they approached me. It was a sentimental few minutes, and I asked them to take care of their sister as she dealt with another hard loss. They nodded and smiled sadly at my sympathy.

As they walked back through the house, the sobs came harder for me. Max came out and informed me that Nick, Naomi, Alex, and Ginny would see me again tomorrow morning, but the rest of them would not be back at the house. I acknowledged that and let him know I was ready for bed.

Such a taxing day caused me to sleep late. When I woke up, I heard multiple voices coming from the kitchen, so I made my way out there and said hello. Dawson chastised me for not calling for help. I smiled and told him I could still walk, just not a 5K anymore.

I ate part of a bagel and chatted with Nick and Naomi for a bit since I hadn't had a lot of time with them the previous day. I thanked Nick for his generosity in bringing the family to see me, and he said it was his honor to be able to give everyone this forum to tell me how loved I am. Naomi kept wiping away tears, and I thought how fortunate they all were to have each other to lean on in the hardest times.

Alex and Ginny were quiet; I was going to require rest and I hadn't visited with them much. When I asked how long they'd be staying, Ginny smiled and said I wasn't getting rid of her any time soon. She had already put her stuff in the guest room and planned to stay indefinitely. Alex said he was here for this week and would be back whenever Arica and Topher decided to come.

What? I was stunned and told them they didn't need to take such a large amount of time away from their normal lives to sit around me and be bored. Ginny glared at me and said the last time I was sick, she abandoned me, and she was NOT letting it happen again. I laughed and thanked them for making the sacrifices they were. As I tired out, Nick and Naomi said their goodbyes, and there were more tears from all of us.

The afternoon and evening were low-key with Dawson getting home from work and catching up with Ginny and Alex. Max and Alex did their thing, and I observed the interactions with a full but heavy heart. I sure would miss this.

As I was closing my eyes to sleep, it occurred to me that tomorrow was two years since my mom passed. Suddenly I was very glad she transitioned when she did so she didn't have to endure this.

Not long after Alex left, Micah and family came to stay for a week during the kids' summer break. Elise and Ginny tackled a lot of laundry and shopping for necessities, and it cheered me up to have the energy of teens in the house. Leo came while they were here, and I had some heart-to-hearts with my brothers on topics we'd never addressed before.

Leo admitted that his "eternal bachelor" status likely stemmed from not wanting to end up acting like our father if he had kids. He also didn't trust himself to marry because he hadn't had a worthy role model for a successful relationship. He praised us for being able to do so, and he sometimes wished he'd been brave enough to take the leap.

Micah told us that moving to the other side of the country was his solution to get as physically far away from our dad as he could so it didn't affect his own marriage.

My confession was that I spoiled my children more than I should have because I never wanted them to feel "less than" or unimportant like I had, and Micah nodded in complicity.

We had all left Catholicism in the past because we felt it contributed mightily to the strict and often subjective rules in our house. It was sad but cathartic to talk about our upbringing and how it affected us later. We all had more in common as adults than I'd known. All three of us had our shortcomings, but we also had our strengths and positive characteristics because of what we'd been through. I expressed how proud I am of both of them and would miss them dearly.

After Micah and family left, I took a turn for the worse. The pain became more constant than it had been, and I tired out much faster. Strong meds helped but made me feel foggy and confused. I tried to go as long as possible without them each day, but it was difficult.

Max and Dawson must have told Arica it was time for her to be here, because she and Topher showed up and set up camp in her old room. I didn't ask questions about the length of time they'd be here or worry what her company would say if she was gone too long. I was just happy she was with me.

Alex came with them as promised, and at one point I had a revelation of how he is so much more reliable as an adult than he had been growing up.

As often as I could tolerate it, I left my bedroom, but the intervals kept getting shorter. Although I had been mentally preparing myself for this for months, my brain still fought against the reality of my failing body. I was now on borrowed time, and I made sure to share my final wishes and heartfelt thoughts with my beloved family and closest friends.

I was determined to have a little fun even as I knew the end was near. I asked Kate and Ginny and Arica to bring bottles of wine into my room one night and help me get drunk with them while we blasted some '90s rock music. In my emaciated state, it didn't take much for the alcohol to affect me. We yelled along to the songs until my voice was hoarse. I don't remember falling asleep, but I was smiling and happy when I woke up the next day and recalled our mini-party.

Max, Dawson, and Arica hung out with me one evening, and I asked the three of them to tell me their favorite memories of something we did together as a family. We all surprised each other with what we recalled and which adventures we treasure. It was amazing!

Another morning, I had Arica and Topher sit down and I gave them all of my best advice about life. I shared what I'd ascertained about marriage, love, parenthood, and making a relationship last and thrive. Arica recorded it on her phone so she won't forget anything I said. It was hard for them to think about some of those things now, but hopefully my words will resonate when they approach the later stages in life.

Dawson listened with tears streaming down his face while I told him how proud I am of him and how much I want him to be happy no matter where his path leads him. I sternly asserted that I don't want my loss to slow him down in his goals. I urged him to keep following his heart and not get bogged down by what other people expected of him.

If he finds a life partner, they should be as exceptional as he deserves. He could ask his sister about my advice for being in a loving relationship and children if he reaches that point. He is not overly-emotional by nature, but he sobbed in my arms for quite a while after I finished talking. It destroys me that I don't get to see where life will take my baby boy.

When Max's dad came back for several days, I shared how grateful I am to be part of the Ganter family. They have always treated me like one of their own with so much love, and it's a bond I cherish. I asked Louis to take good care of Max since he can empathize with losing a wife to cancer. My unspoken wish is that perhaps the two of them will reconcile their differences and find a way to bond that has eluded them for many years.

One evening I called Kate and Ginny in to tell them my men will need support when I'm gone even if they don't want to admit it or ask for help. Max will try to be the big strong male who hides his feelings when really a sympathetic listener is best for him. I am concerned about him being in our empty house alone.

I also asked them to be surrogate moms to my children. Dawson could use Ginny's organized mind to create the occasional checklist for challenges he doesn't know how to tackle. Arica would benefit from Kate channeling her "inner Tabitha" and firmly guiding my daughter to stay focused on what she should be doing vs. where her emotions compel her.

With Alex and Ginny, I told them how significant it is to me that we resurrected our friendships. It comforts me to know they are now as important to my family as they'd been to me. I thanked them for allowing me the time to adjust to them being back in my life and letting me process the years of anger and sorrow I'd been carrying around.

Due to their patience, I'm now able to have a much clearer conscience. I am so grateful that they've been here with me when I needed them most, and I encouraged them to keep doing exactly what they have been as a couple. They are perfect partners and set an excellent example for all our children to see what a solid, long-term marriage looks like.

And then there's Max.

Words are inadequate to appropriately convey what he means to me. There were many nights I tried to say things that instead ended in crying and clinging to him. He's taught me some of the paramount lessons in my life, and I have relished every day we've spent together. How do you articulate all those beautiful sentiments?

We've been through some hard times, but because of him and our relationship, I am a better person. From being his wife, I learned how to communicate effectively and be more patient, understanding, and kinder. With him I've known true happiness.

My hope is that he knows how profoundly I love him and how horribly I regret putting him through this. He doesn't deserve the heartbreak, and I would do anything to save him from the pain of watching me die. We've had a fantastic run.

That brings me to today, when I have decided to finish writing. It's difficult to sit up and type for any length of time anymore, and frankly, I'm just too weary to try as often.

I believe I have said what I wanted to and have given this world my all. The regrets I have are vastly outweighed by the love, kindness, generosity, and magnificence I've experienced in my lifetime.

I wish those same wonderful blessings for everyone. I love you all.

THE *(and my)* END